UNREASONABLE DOUBT

A C.T. FERGUSON CRIME NOVEL

THE C.T. FERGUSON MYSTERIES
BOOK 17

TOM FOWLER

For Lisa and Isabel, two very reasonable women

CHAPTER 1

THINGS DON'T BLOW up in Baltimore very often.

People die within the city limits, certainly. The city averaged close to a murder a day for several years running before finally dropping well under 300. It's remained around the same level since, though pundits, politicians, and professional assholes paid to shout on TV will often give the impression one can find a freshly slain corpse on every street corner.

Explosions, however, have always been pretty rare outside the occasional gas leak.

I was out for a run in the Federal Hill neighborhood of Baltimore. I'd finished my laps around the park and walked up Riverside Avenue toward my house. While it technically wasn't yet summer on the lunar calendar, high temperatures and humidity first descended on the region a few weeks ago and rarely took a day off. My Under Armour shirt found plenty of moisture to wick during my thirty-odd minutes of exercise this muggy morning.

About a block from my house, the sound of a blast

stunned me, and the force of it made me wobble on my feet. I leaned on a nearby signpost to steady myself. Brake lights flashed to life all around me. Not many people walked the streets, but plenty of cars already rolled along them. Something about this didn't feel like a gas leak. I spotted a telltale plume of black smoke rising above the rowhouses at my two-o'clock, and I set off at a brisk run.

A couple blocks away, I found the source. A car blazed at the curb. Windows in the two SUVs nearby and the house the burning vehicle sat in front of had already been blown in. Discerning its color was a challenge. Body panels came off in the explosion, and I guessed the sedan to be blue until a minute or so ago.

The unfortunate individual within was already a goner. Intense flames left little meat on the bones, and I looked away before the sight made me sick. The smell of roasting tissue, however, did not care about me averting my gaze. I backed away a step and covered my nose and mouth with my sweaty workout shirt. My own ripe aroma was far preferable to the stench of burning flesh. A woman lay on her back nearby on the sidewalk. She rose to her elbows, grimaced, and shook her head.

"Don't get up," I told her. "You might have a concussion." Even though I figured at least one person had dialed 9-1-1 by now, I still did.

"Is there any chance of rescuing the person in the car?" the operator asked me.

"No," I told her. I didn't need to look at the grisly scene again to confirm this. "Whoever it was died. For their sake, I hope it was quick." She said police and fire crews would be on the scene soon. Other than the woozy woman and me, no one else remained in the area, and people made sure to avoid it if they were walking. Not a single soul emerged from any of the nearby houses or businesses to lend a hand. It was a good thing no one was seriously injured apart from the person in the car.

Sirens approached. The cops would probably want to talk to me—never something I enjoyed—so I walked to the other side of the woman and sat on the curb.

———

"I think you might have a concussion."

The woman looked at me with a glassy-eyed stare confirming my suspicions. While I'd been a couple blocks away when the sedan blew up, where she lay on the sidewalk indicated she was in much closer proximity. A few scorch marks dotted the outside of her jeans' left leg. She remained on her elbows without trying to sit up. "Maybe you're right," she said. The lady touched the back of her scalp and pulled away red fingers.

She turned her head as if to let me check it out. Through her graying black hair, I saw a cut leaking blood. It didn't look too bad to my untrained eyes. "I don't think it's much to worry about. Probably a few stitches."

"How did you learn so much about injuries?"

"Reckless youth," I said. "If there's a record for falling off bikes and skateboards before you turn twelve, I must be in the conversation."

"It's bleeding a lot," she said, frowning.

"Head injuries tend to."

"Come on." The lady offered a weak chuckle. "You must have some sort of training. How do you know all this?"

"*Chicago Med.*"

"The hospital?"

"The TV show," I said. Sirens grew louder and closer. "Dreamy lady doctors and medical emergencies. What's not to love?"

She smiled despite the situation. "Well . . . thank you for keeping me in good spirits if nothing else."

Two police cruisers screeched to a stop ahead of the burning car. An ambulance and fire engine soon followed. More flashing red and blues heralded the arrival of additional emergency vehicles, though none of them could maneuver past the fire truck. Men in heavy coats and helmets quickly got to work on connecting the hose to a nearby hydrant. To my surprise, no one had parked in front of it. I waved the paramedics to our position and told them I thought the woman was close to the blast when it happened. She smiled up and squeezed my hand as the police waited for me.

Two officers who'd had the distinct pleasure of questioning me several times over the years waited with their arms crossed. Jennings was smaller than his partner Brennan, who looked a little older and like a recent immigrant from Ireland. "What a surprise to see you at the scene of a shitshow," Jennings said.

"I was as stunned as you," I said. "I even gave up shitshows for Lent."

"Looks like everyone else we might've found decided to be somewhere else. You might be our only witness. Take us through it." Jennings stood poised with his pen held over a small spiral notebook. Brennan's left hand fit inside a strap on the back of a tablet, and his right held a gunmetal gray stylus.

"Why's he more high-tech than you?" I asked.

"Sergeant asked for a volunteer," Brennan said.

Jennings snorted. "Yeah, and this dummy was fool enough to go along with it." He moved his pen in a circular motion a few times. "Wanna get on with what happened?"

"I was out for a run. Headed back home from the park."

"You live on this street?"

I shook my head. "Riverside. I'd gotten a block or two from my house when I heard the explosion. It shook the ground."

"You didn't think it was a gas leak?" Brennan wanted to know.

"Didn't seem like one. Besides, the black smoke was a pretty big giveaway. I ran here. The car was on fire, whoever sat behind the wheel was already dead, and the woman on the sidewalk there had been knocked from her feet."

"Pretty big blast," Jennings said. "You see anyone speeding away?"

"No," I said. "Looked like normal morning traffic. Not many people on foot." It occurred to me someone might want to drive away at a regular pace and blend into traffic after setting off an explosion. The same thought would probably cross the cops' minds, too.

"You know who's in the car?"

"No idea." I looked at the ruined husk of the sedan. Most of the identifying features got blown up or burned, so its make and model were hard to place. The front license plate was missing—along with the grill and headlights. "I'm sure you can figure it out." Faces appeared in nearby windows as cops farther along the block pointed at houses. With me as the only person answering questions, they would need to start canvassing soon.

Water sloshed near my feet as the fire department

sprayed the smoldering car. It took a moment, but the flames ebbed and went out altogether. They continued dousing the car—probably to bring the heat down and allow investigators to access the sedan and the unfortunate victim trapped inside.

"What time do you think the explosion happened?" Brennan asked.

I frowned. I didn't look at my watch or phone when I heard and felt the blast, and now I felt I should have. "Not sure exactly." I took my cell out of my pocket and checked the call log. "Looks like I dialed nine-one-one at eight-eighteen. It didn't take me long to run over here . . . maybe three minutes." A text notification popped up. My wife Gloria wondered where I was.

Thought I heard a bang and now I see smoke. You all right?

I tapped out a quick reply. *Yes. Definitely a bang. Talking to the cops. Back soon.*

"Anything else you want to tell us?" Jennings asked.

"Yeah," I said. "I thought you were retiring. Last time I saw you, you mentioned something about it."

He let out a rueful chuckle. "Shit. I was being optimistic. Got at least ten years to go before I can even think about it. Hell, my wife might want me to stay even longer."

"Speaking of wives, I should get back to mine. She saw the smoke and is worried. We good?"

Jennings slipped his notebook away. His higher-tech partner kept the tablet at hand. "We're good. Thanks."

"Sure," I said, and I headed for home.

———

"An explosion?"

Whatever weariness remained in my wife fled her body at the news of what happened. She sat at my small kitchen table nursing a mug of coffee, caught somewhere in the space between being asleep and fully waking up. Coffee normally eased this transition. This morning, news of an explosion a couple blocks from my house served the same purpose.

"It shook the ground when I was walking back up Riverside," I said.

"What did you think it was?"

I shrugged as I poured myself an overdue cup of coffee and joined her. "Not sure. It didn't seem like a gas leak. Those tend to take out entire buildings." Thanks to the interconnected nature of rowhouses, a blast in one could actually level a few—and even trigger secondary explosions to take a bad event all the way to terrible in a matter of seconds. "It didn't seem big enough. Then, I saw the smoke."

Gloria squeezed my hand. "I love you for who you are . . . but I'm not sure I'm thrilled about you running toward danger."

"I needed to check it out at least," I said. "If it had been some massive blaze, I would have called for the fire department and come home. It wasn't, so I stayed and helped. The poor person in the car was a goner even by the time I got there, but a woman nearby got knocked down in the explosion. Pretty sure she has a concussion."

"You run toward bad situations *and* you can diagnose people," Gloria said. "The total package."

I flexed my bicep. The gesture did not impress my wife as much as I'd hoped. Maybe I needed to add an extra day of strength training. "I also cook a mean breakfast, but it might be a little late to whip something together for this morning."

Gloria glanced at her watch. "I'm going to work from my house today. You have something you need to be in for by nine?"

"Other than avoiding the side-eye from my secretary, no," I said. "The new intern she convinced me to hire starts at ten. She probably shouldn't see the boss rolling in late on day one."

"Sure. Save that for the second day." Gloria grinned.

"I was considering the third, but I like the way you think. Gotta manage her expectations early."

"You've certainly been busy enough to take on an intern," Gloria said.

I nodded. "We have. I probably can't give her much to do at first, but every little bit helps." Thanks to some positive press coverage of a serial killer case last winter, my agency had been busier than normal even six months later. I remembered hearing about the long tails of advertising in college. Maybe this was just such a situation. While the extra income was nice, my work-life balance had taken a hit so far this year. Gloria hadn't raised the vacation topic in a while, but I knew it would be coming.

"T.J.'s been really good for you."

"I wasn't sure I needed a secretary at first. Now, I can't imagine getting things done without her."

"You like to surround yourself with smart women," Gloria said. "It shows a lack of ego."

"Don't tell anyone," I said. "You'll ruin my rep."

She smiled and chuckled. "Listen to the smart women you surround yourself with. The intern might end up being a good decision, too."

"Here's hoping." Considering who our new hire's father

was—and my overall opinion of the man—the arrangement would require a significant amount of hope. Still, T.J. offered a strong recommendation, and she'd proven herself to be smart and incisive over the last two-plus years.

"I'm just going to pick something up on the way to my house," Gloria said.

"I'll also get breakfast for the office. Might as well make things look good on our new girl's first day."

"What happened to managing her expectations?"

"She'll be working for a detective agency," I pointed out. "At some point soon, she'll have to get used to disappointment."

———

My goal every day is to get to the office by nine.

Thankfully, I've always seen goals as flexible. My secretary T.J. latched onto my nine-o'clock proclamation as if I'd carried it down on a stone tablet from Mount Sinai. Whenever I rolled in even a few minutes late, she made a point of looking at her watch. Some of my college professors did the same. This morning, I walked up the metal steps to our office door at nine-twenty.

We worked on the second floor of a car repair shop in Fells Point. The owner, Manny, rented the space out a couple years ago once he stopped using it. We sometimes needed to deal with banging and clanging from the body shop below, but it was a good arrangement. Manny even proved patient with some of the more interesting aspects of having a PI as a tenant. I dropped a bag of bagels on the table. "You're late even for you," T.J. said.

"There was an explosion this morning," I said. "Two blocks from my house. I was headed home after my run when it happened."

"Wow." She picked up her phone. "I saw something about that. A car blew up?"

"Yes."

"On purpose?"

"The cops will need to figure it out," I said. "It looked like a pretty new sedan. I can't imagine something like faulty wiring made it blow up."

"You checked it out?" she asked.

I nodded. "Didn't seem like a gas leak. We get shootings in Baltimore . . . even in Federal Hill . . . but things don't go boom very often."

"I guess I'll give you a pass this morning, then." T.J. pushed her blonde ponytail off her shoulder and stood. She was five-nine, athletic, reasonably pretty, and soon to turn twenty-two. One of these days, I might lose her to a better job or see her thoughts monopolized by a boyfriend. The latter seemed more likely. I'd given T.J. enough bonuses and pay raises to make her very happy. She plucked a sesame bagel from the bag and carried it to the toaster.

I made a cup of coffee. My late arrival left it less fresh than normal, but I'll drink just about anything which hasn't turned to sludge yet. Once T.J. finished heating her bagel, I grabbed a multigrain everything model and toasted it. "Gloria happy about you sprinting toward an explosion?" my assistant asked once we both munched on our breakfasts.

"Not especially. She understands, though."

"Good day to bring bagels."

I bobbed my head. "I figured we should wait until tomorrow before we start disappointing our intern."

"Lexi."

"Right," I said.

"You told me you'd give her a chance," T.J. said.

"And I will. If people start getting shot around us, however, all bets are off."

"You've had to shoot people before."

"And I hope I don't need to again." I paused for a deep breath. "I don't like her father much. You know this, and you know why. I still listened while you pled the case for your new BFF."

"She's not her father," T.J. said.

"I hope not," I said. "The apple needs to do more than fall far from the tree. It needs to roll down a goddamn hill into a different forest."

"I think she'll do well." Despite my protests, T.J. didn't look away or back down. She kept her gaze on me. I appreciated her willingness to stand up to me. On occasion, even I needed it.

"Trouble better not follow her here."

"She's not her father," my secretary said again.

"Thank goodness."

"I hope we can get her up to speed quickly."

I leaned back in my chair. T.J. was smart and eager to learn. At times, she made a better student than I did a teacher. She wanted to know how I did things, particularly my often illicit computer skills. "Let me guess . . . you want to hand some of your work to her so I can teach you more about what I do."

She grinned. "Wow. Your name really is on the door for a reason."

"Two reasons," I said. "My keen insights and timely rent checks."

After checking messages and emails and lamenting the number of cases we'd accepted, it was nearly ten. Footsteps came up the metal stairs a moment later. "I think she's here," T.J. said.

The witching hour was at hand.

CHAPTER 2

"WHERE WERE you on the evening of the tenth?"

I'd brought a desk lamp out of the closet, put a new bulb in it, and set it on the edge of T.J.'s desk. It shone into the face of new intern Lexi Tyler. She came dressed for work in a blue polo and khaki capris with her auburn hair tied into a ponytail. Maybe an inch of height separated her and T.J., and the winner of the longer ponytail contest would require a tape measure and keen eye. Lexi was pretty, meaning she didn't get most of her looks from her father, and at the moment, she squinted against the light.

"Was that a Friday?" she wondered.

"I'll ask the questions here," I said. I turned to T.J. in time to catch her rolling her eyes. "I'm not sure . . . was it a Friday?"

"You interrogate all your interns?" Lexi asked.

"You're the first one. Patterns need to start somewhere."

"I hope you don't ask me to write this in an SOP."

T.J. snorted. "Those have to start somewhere, too," I said. "Make sure you get the wattage on this bulb."

"Are we done?"

"I told you . . . I'll ask the questions here." The new hire smirked and folded her hands in her lap. "I only have a few more. Are you your father's daughter?"

"Like most people, I take after both my parents," she said. "My dad and I share certain personality traits."

"What's your opinion on shooting someone from a rooftop five hundred yards away when they're not a threat anymore?"

Lexi scooted forward a little, reached up, and turned the light off. "He told me this might come up."

"It almost kept you from starting at all," I said.

"He puts a little more . . . finality into his thoughts than I do. We talked about the situation. Your friend wasn't going to let it go."

Nearly two years ago, I'd corralled my former friend Vinnie Serrano in Herring Run Park. After a short fight, I'd gotten him to surrender. He spat a bunch of curses and promises, vowing to get out of jail early again and get his revenge on me, Gloria, and any future children we might have. John Tyler—Lexi's father—had helped me deal with Vinnie's remaining goons. Without my knowledge, he lingered on a rooftop and plugged Vinnie from about five hundred yards away. "I don't see the point in shooting someone over threats."

"My dad mentioned his former commander, right?" Lexi said. I nodded. "He made a lot of threats, too, and that's all they were . . . until he got into a position to act on them. As someone who got abducted by his cronies and groped at every opportunity, I can tell you how real some threats become."

"I guess we'll see how different you are," I said. I pointed to a small desk we'd set up near the right-hand wall. It was smaller than T.J.'s or mine, and with three desks, a table, fridge, and a coffee station, we were starting to strain the square footage of the second-story space.

"My very own work space," she said. It held a laptop I'd configured for her plus a keyboard, mouse, and twenty-three inch monitor. The desk itself came as a freebie from someone in T.J.'s apartment building who was unloading it in favor of a larger model. Despite a couple chips, it remained in good shape.

"T.J. will show you around and get you going." I opened my desk drawer and took out my trusty .45, clipping the holster onto my belt. "The publicity we got a few months ago is still showing up in our caseload, so I'm heading out."

"Do I get to come with you at some point?" Lexi wanted to know.

"Let's see how things go in the office first."

"I have a gun and a concealed carry permit."

"You do?" She bobbed her head. "What are you, twenty?"

"Yeah."

"How the hell did you get a permit?" I said.

She shrugged. "My dad was in the Army for twenty-four years. He knows some people."

"Let's try and wait until your second week before you start shooting people," I said.

"You going after the deadbeat dad?" T.J. asked.

"Yes. Since we've narrowed down his haunts, I think I'll find him today. I'll be in touch."

"Go get 'em, boss."

I headed down the stairs planning to do precisely this.

———

By mid-afternoon, I wondered if this asshole had a hideout we'd yet to discover.

John Argent and I were the same age—thirty-four—though in very different circumstances. He didn't own a business, but he held a steady job and could certainly afford to pay his delinquent and future child support. Throwing him in jail would make this less likely going forward. The state didn't always have the best solutions. His ex-girlfriend and mother of his daughter simply wanted him found and held accountable.

The police struck out in their attempts to locate him at home. Once they checked his house and work, they basically stopped. With murderers, rapists, arsonists, and other serious criminals out there, the cops needed to prioritize, and dead-beat dads fell pretty far down the list. I'd run a couple to ground before, though the last time occurred before T.J. came to work for me.

I figured our target probably hadn't been to his house in a week or two. Once we were on the case, T.J. and I built a profile of the not-very-esteemed Mister Argent. In the era of social media and the constant thirst for followers, people shared way too much of their lives. I'd written some scripts which scoured the various sites, extracted a list of likely associates, and dug for information on them. Unfortunately, we kept striking out on finding him at any of the most prob-able spots. We were scraping the bottom of the barrel in terms of likelihood by now.

I sat in my Audi S4 at the curb in Greektown. The rowhouse I kept in sight belonged to a second cousin of Argent. I'd already seen the other man pop in and leave again. If Argent still held a job—and if he stayed here—he'd be arriving soon. My phone buzzed on the passenger's seat, and I answered the call. "Anything, boss?" T.J. asked.

"Not yet. It's been kind of uneventful."

"You think he's there?"

"I think we don't have many more places to try if he's not," I said. "I want to wrap this up."

"I know we've gone past your one-case-at-a-time preference."

"We've been beyond it for months," I said. "I like the good publicity, but everything has a price."

"You need us to stay here much longer?" T.J. wanted to know.

"How about another hour? If there's nothing by then, you two can go home."

"Sounds good."

"How's our intern doing?"

"I've shown her a lot already." T.J. chuckled. "I think she wants to get out in the field."

"She'll need to wait in line behind you, then," I said. From my right, someone rounded the corner and walked toward the house. He wore sunglasses despite the overcast sky, and a baseball cap pulled low hid even more of his face. Long sandy blond hair peeked out around the ears. "I think I see him now."

"Nice. Kick his ass."

"If I have to." I ended the call and slipped the phone into my pocket. I put the windows up and climbed out of the car. Argent slowed as he noticed me. I stayed on my side of the street and moved in his direction. He paused. I didn't want to play cat and mouse with him, so I checked for traffic and crossed the road.

Argent watched me draw closer before turning and running.

————

"Why do they always run?" I muttered as I gave chase.

Traffic lights—which often went red or green in sequence—now let a lot of cars zoom up and down the streets. Argent looked to cross a couple times, was shooed back onto the curb by a loud horn and extended middle finger, and kept going instead. I closed the gap to about ten yards and settled in behind him.

Argent looked to be of typical build. Before I took a couple bullets almost three years ago, I was an excellent runner. Now, I was merely a very good one, having lost a little top-end speed and a touch of endurance along with one of the lobes of my left lung. Still, even ninety-something percent of what I used to be able to do put me well ahead of the average person. I still ran at least fifteen miles a week, and most of the people I needed to chase did not.

Argent was no exception.

He lacked the size to barrel into people and knock them down, so he avoided anyone who almost crossed his path on the sidewalk. We neared a restaurant with a large outdoor seating area. It dominated the whole corner, cutting the width of the sidewalk to about half in favor of rows of tables and chairs. Many of them were occupied. A short and simple barrier extended around the space, with a gap for entry and exit. Two women were headed out when Argent approached. He slowed, grunted, and kept going, making a right at the corner.

By the time I reached the makeshift gate, the women had

moved along. This meant I didn't need to go around the dining area. I dashed through the gap and plotted a course. The tables and chairs weren't arranged in precise rows, but through aggressive use of the Pythagorean Theorem, I exited the other side two steps behind my quarry. Argent turned, and his eyes widened when he saw me.

It made him slow a little, so I turned on the jets and dove at him, tackling him around the waist. "Get off me, man," he grumbled, trying to swat my hands away. I gave him a short jab in the solar plexus and listened to him suck wind for a few seconds.

"John Argent. You need to pay your child support."

"Christ, you ran me down over some money?"

"It's a pretty good sum," I said. After identifying myself, I rolled him over, zip tied his wrists, and hauled him to his feet. "You can explain it to the cops and eventually a judge." He scowled and leaned against the brick exterior of a nearby rowhouse. "You gonna run again?" Argent shook his head, and I called it in.

"How'd you catch up to me so fast?" he wondered once I finished talking to the police.

"I paid attention in geometry."

"Seating area must have been thirty feet a side."

I shrugged. "And it's about forty-two if you cut the angle like I did. If you want some actual back-of-the-napkin math, I can go ask the hostess for one."

Argent grumbled and fell silent. The police collected him a few minutes later. As I walked back toward the car, I called T.J. "There's now one fewer deadbeat dad roaming the mean streets of Baltimore," I said.

"Nice work, boss."

"No comment on my correct usage of fewer versus less?"

"Well," she said, "it's also one *less* case on the ledger, but we're still swimming in them. You sure you don't want to bring in another investigator?"

"Positive." T.J. asked me this at least twice a week, and my response remained the same every time. With an intern now in the fold, I might be able to offload the easier cases—especially those which could be worked online—to the two women. "Maybe you and Lexi can do some background work on some of them."

My secretary sighed. "Fine. I didn't think you'd change your mind, but I had to ask."

"I know. You wouldn't be you if you didn't."

"And you wouldn't be you without the stubborn refusal to bring in some help."

"We each have our charm," I said. "See you tomorrow."

"Yeah, yeah," she said.

CHAPTER 3

THE NEXT TWO weeks saw the agency hold the rhythm.

We closed our share of cases while only accepting a pair of new ones. Unfortunately, two new explosions rocked the city in this window. The first happened eight days ago, and the second a mere two. The press picked up the story after the second bomb blast, and now it dominated the headlines, talk radio, podcasts, and the like. We just needed cynical grifters on YouTube to try to sell something to complete the tragedy bingo card.

The spectacular nature of the incidents took center stage. Speculation—by sources both qualified and ridiculous —as to the bomber's identity came next. The actual victims received the short shrift, barely earning mentions in stories or segments which should have been about them. Apparently, all three men broke the law at some point in their pasts, and at least one podcast ran with the absurd idea of the killer being some sort of dynamite-powered avenging angel.

T.J. must have heard my grunt or seen me roll my eyes because she asked, "What?"

"Next thing we know, this asshole will get a catchy name."

"Adrian Brown never got one," my assistant pointed out.

"True," I said. Brown was a killer of women, and we caught him in early winter. His was the case whose storm of publicity spiked interest in our agency six months ago. "He definitely should have considering he was covering the story himself."

"You can't give yourself a nickname."

"Agreed." I remembered a less skilled player on my high school lacrosse team trying to pick his own moniker. "Sticks" because he thought he was some sort of wizard running with the ball. The rest of us thought it ludicrous and refused to use it. Then, when he forgot to wear a cup one practice and took a ball in a very unfortunate place, he became known as "Swells." He hated it, the team loved it, and the nickname stuck—as good ones do.

Lexi arrived right on time, travel mug of coffee in hand. We hadn't talked about her father since the first day. This was fine with me, and I got the sense she felt the same. T.J. again lamented the agency being behind on work. I didn't tell her I harbored no plans to bring someone else in. There was no need at this point. She and Lexi did good background work on several matters, and our closure rate picked up since the new intern joined us. No clients complained, and this was the metric I cared more about than the occasional grumbles of my secretary.

At about ten-thirty, footsteps rang on the metal stairs. There was one main entrance downstairs, and then a second door to the right provided access to the steps. With the addition of a sign on the second door, we almost never got accidental visitors. The door opened, and a slender woman walked in. She was short and white, and the dark circles under her eyes matched the color of her hair. "You're the detectives?" she asked.

"Yes," T.J. said. I didn't bother pointing out only one of us was an actual detective.

"It's been eight days." She sank onto a guest chair in front of my desk when T.J. gestured toward it. My stomach clenched as I nudged a box of tissues toward our new arrival. Many things could have happened in the city and the state eight days ago, but I had a feeling I knew what she meant.

"Take your time," my secretary said.

"I should probably start from the top." She sniffled and dabbed at her brown eyes. "I'm Margie Williams. My husband Walter died eight days ago."

"We're sorry for your loss," I said. I guessed the widow Williams to be a few years older than me, though an intense process like grief can add age to a person's appearance.

She nodded and continued. "He was on his way to work." A few tears ran down her cheeks. "You probably know the rest. He started the car, it blew up in front of our house, and he was gone."

T.J. glanced at me as she jotted a few notes. Margie Williams didn't need to know my limited involvement with the first bomb. I'd never appeared in any news story or blog post about the whole mess so far, and after the Brown fiasco, I preferred to keep it this way. "I presume the police have been investigating."

Margie stopped wiping her eyes long enough to snort. "Sons of bitches. Their investigation has been for shit, and I've got a theory. You wanna hear it?"

Despite having listened to quite enough people who had theories recently, we all said yes.

———

"Walter has . . . had a criminal record."

Margie Williams let her statement hang in the air. Clearly, she meant it as some indictment of the police and the way they'd handled things so far. "You think the police don't want to investigate a crime against someone they've arrested before?"

She spread her hands. "I don't really have another explanation."

"I'm not trying to be difficult here," I said, "but the BPD puts handcuffs on thousands of people a year. If they refused to do much when those people turned up as victims later, it would be a major scandal."

"You'll have to ask them the reason," Margie said. "Don't you have a cousin on the force? I think I read that over the winter."

"I do." This marked the first time a potential client asked about my association with the BPD and my cousin Rich. Fame came for us in strange ways.

"I'd be curious to see what he says."

I felt the same even though I didn't think the cops were shirking their duties just because the late Walter saw the inside of a prison. "What happened the morning your husband died, Missus Walters? Anything unusual?"

"No." She shook her head and plucked a fresh tissue from the box. "Walter's had a hard time getting a job. He caught on at a little bookstore. I think the owner felt sorry for him." She showed a quick smile, but it faded almost as soon as it appeared. "He was headed to his job last Monday morning."

"Was he convicted and released from jail?" Lexi asked.

"Convicted, yes," Margie said. "He never got sentenced, though. Some issue with the arrest." Her brows creased as she sneered. "Another fine job by the fucking cops." She covered her mouth after cursing. "Sorry."

"It's fine," I said. "They're both adults, and they've heard at least as much from me."

"Do you think the police didn't want to investigate your husband's death over whatever technicality got him out?" Lexi wanted to know.

"I like her." Margie pointed at our intern and nodded. "That's a good question." She turned to me. "Maybe you can ask your cousin."

"It's a serious accusation," I pointed out. "Even if it's true, he's not going to confess over coffee." Margie frowned but didn't say anything else. It was good to see Lexi—the recently-declared criminal justice major going into her third year of college—ask the question. "Have they told you anything since last Monday?"

"The usual shit," Margie said with a scoff. "'We're working on it,' 'The investigation is ongoing,' 'These things take time.' Platitudes. Someone hated my husband enough to blow him up. The medical examiner told me he probably didn't suffer. The force of the explosion got him before the flames did." Her eyes leaked again, and she paused to use another tissue. "Building a marriage *takes time*. Getting your life back in order *takes time*. Killing someone with a bomb is quick." She blew out a quick breath. "Fucking cops."

"People who are unhappy with the police come to us pretty often," I said.

"You take that cousin of yours to task?"

"When I need to."

Margie balled up the latest tissue and spiked it into the

small wastebasket beside my desk. "Well, you can tell him I said to eat shit."

"He's probably already heard it today."

"Either way . . . I want you to look into this. I've read about you."

"Unfortunately, so have a lot of people," I said. "We're still busier than usual."

"I can pay," Margie said. "Walter was murdered. He had life insurance."

"I appreciate your desire to get this solved," T.J. said. "We'll definitely let you know. If we didn't have quite a bit on our plate already, it would be an easy yes."

Margie frowned but stood and offered a curt nod. "All right. I'll wait to hear from you, then." She headed for the door, stopped, and faced us again. "You ain't the only agency in town." Before we could answer, she headed out the door and down the metal steps.

———

"What the hell?" I said.

"You were the one who told her we were busy," T.J. pointed out as she headed back to her own desk.

"To set her expectations. People think the cops are sitting on their hands or messing things up. We can usually do better, but it's not always fast. I know she thinks 'investigations take time' is some hollow platitude, but it's true."

"We're pretty busy. Since you're the only investigator, you still have a few cases waiting."

"None of them are murder, right?" I pressed.

"No," my secretary admitted.

"Then, I think we can find the bandwidth. When we

took these other jobs, our clients knew we had a backlog. They understood it might take a while."

"You might have a serial bomber," Lexi said. "Three dead now. I think it meets the definition."

"I didn't even think about it," I said.

"Look at all the press you got for stopping a serial killer six months ago. If we can figure out what's going on here and stop it, you'll be the most famous PI in the state."

I grimaced. "Not sure I want people to recognize me. I've tried to keep my picture out of the stories, but it's impossible. I think my days of going undercover are over."

T.J. pointed to herself and Lexi. "We can do some of these for you. None of those cases ever struck me as super complicated. I'm sure two capable ladies can power through a great deal of the work."

"You could finish up whatever else needs doing and sign off on it," Lexi added.

"I'm glad you know so much in your two weeks of experience," I said.

She flashed a fake smile. "Me, too."

"Would you be so eager to take this if you hadn't been nearby when the first bomb went off?" T.J. asked.

It was a good question, and I used a deep breath to think it over. "I don't know. Maybe not. Being near the scene definitely made it more real for me." I frowned. "The smell of someone burning up in a car. I hope he died quickly like Walter Williams."

T.J. crossed her arms. "We're taking the case, aren't we?"

"We are."

"You want to let Lexi and me handle some of the others?"

"So long as what you're doing is easy, yes. Don't endanger yourselves. I take the risks—"

"Because your name is on the door," they broke in and said in unison.

"As long as everyone's learned something," I said. "Let's get Missus Williams back in here so we can get to work."

MARGIE WILLIAMS RETURNED about an hour later. I explained we were taking her case because murder mattered a hell of a lot more than whatever else we had in the hopper. "I'm glad," she said as T.J. and Lexi presented her with our standard agreement. It was entirely my secretary's creation, laying out rates, what was billable, and a bunch of other information. At least once a week, I wondered how I made it over three years without her.

With a signed agreement on the books, I got to work on background for the bombings while the ladies looked for other cases they could handle in parallel. I started by looking for the most recent articles about the bombings. Baltimore has one major newspaper and a few smaller ones, plus a bunch of people with blogs, true-crime podcasters, and the like. I began at the top with the *Baltimore Sun*.

It didn't take me long to see the killer received a moniker from the press.

"Vox Populi" Strikes Again: Third Car

Bomb in Two Weeks Targets Convicted Criminals

By Sarah Jensen, Staff Reporter

BALTIMORE — In a city waging a constant battle with crime, a new and deadly menace has emerged. Two nights ago, a third car bomb in just over two weeks exploded in the heart of the city, killing its sole occupant. The victim, identified by authorities as Michael "Mikey" Granger, 44, had a lengthy criminal history but had recently been released from prison after his conviction was overturned due to a legal technicality. Granger's death comes just days after two similar attacks, and now, the city of Baltimore is grappling with the rise of a vigilante killer who has been dubbed "Vox Populi" by Internet supporters and the media.

Each of the bombings has been carefully executed, targeting convicted criminals who have been released from prison under controversial circumstances. While no group or individual has claimed responsibility for the attacks, speculation has run rampant. In some online circles, citizens have said the bomber (or bombers) is doing good work and represents a little-used voice of the people. Thus, the moniker "Vox Populi" has emerged.

Three Dead in Two Weeks

The first bombing occurred one week after Memorial Day, claiming the life of Thomas "T-Bone" Mallory, 39, a convicted drug trafficker. Mallory had been released from prison just weeks before, following the discovery of flawed evidence during his trial. His discharge, despite widespread protest, was considered *by some to be a miscarriage of justice. The second attack followed several days later, killing Walter Williams, 41, a convicted drunk driver who had similarly been freed after procedural errors were discovered in his case.*

The most recent blast, which rocked a quiet residential street in West Baltimore, killed Granger instantly. Investigators have confirmed that all three bombings involved car bombs of similar design, suggesting a single perpetrator or group with technical expertise. So far, the authorities have made little headway in identifying the person or persons responsible, and the lack of clear surveillance footage or witnesses has made the investigation difficult.

The explosions have also sparked widespread fear in Baltimore, as citizens worry over the possibility of further attacks. While each victim has been a criminal, there is growing concern that innocent bystanders could soon fall victim to the violent spree. Thus far, only one nearby person has sustained minor injuries.

A Divided City

As tensions rise, so do opinions on the vigilante killer. Some citizens see "Vox Populi" as a necessary force for justice in a legal system they believe has failed them. Others, however, express concern that such vigilantism will only fuel further chaos in an already crime-ridden city.

"It's about time someone did something," said Raymond Hargrove, 57, a local shop owner whose store was robbed just last month. "These criminals walk free because of some loophole, and we're the ones

who suffer. If the courts won't hold them accountable, then maybe it's time someone else did."

Hargrove's sentiments are echoed by several other residents, who see "Vox Populi" as a force for good in a broken system. Online forums and social media platforms have been buzzing with discussions on the vigilante, with some going as far as to call for donations to a "Vox Populi" legal defense fund should the killer ever be caught.

On the other side of the debate, however, many citizens are deeply troubled by the killings.

"It's terrifying," said Maria Sanchez, 34, who lives just blocks away from the site of the first bombing. "I understand people are frustrated with the system, but this isn't the answer. We can't let someone go around deciding who deserves to live and who deserves to die. That's not justice. That's murder."

Sanchez is not alone in her concerns. Civil rights groups and legal experts have issued statements condemning the attacks, urging the public to allow the justice system to function without interference.

"Vigilantism is a dangerous road to go down," said defense attorney Malcolm Weaver. "We have due process for a reason. Just because a case is overturned doesn't mean the person is guilty. The courts are there to protect all of us, and that includes making sure arrests and convictions are legally sound. This kind of violence undermines the very foundation of our justice system."

Police Scramble for Leads

In the meantime, Baltimore Police remain tight-lipped about the ongoing investigation. While officials *have not disclosed specific details, sources close to the investigation suggest that law enforcement is considering the possibility that the bomber is a former member of the military or law enforcement, given the sophistication of the explosives.*

"We're doing everything in our power to bring this individual to justice," said Police Commissioner David Ngo at a press conference late last night. "These acts of violence will not be tolerated, and we urge anyone with information to come forward. Baltimore is a resilient city, and we will not be intimidated by this kind of lawlessness."

Despite these reassurances, residents remain on edge, particularly in neighborhoods close to the bombings. As the investigation continues, many wonder when—or if —"Vox Populi" will strike again.

For now, the streets of Baltimore feel just a little less safe, as the city braces for the next move in a deadly game of retribution.

"What a crock of shit," I muttered. My fellow office occupants looked up from their work. "The bomber has a nickname now. I guess he's a real serial killer."

"What is it?" Lexi asked.

"*Vox Populi.*"

She snorted. "Voice of the people? A little bloodthirsty."

"Apparently, it started online, and the press picked up on it. If anything, it'll embolden this asshole to keep going."

"I guess we'd better stop him, then," T.J. said.

"I guess so," I said.

———

T.J. and I left Lexi at the office and headed downtown.

The Elijah Cummings and Clarence Mitchell Court-houses sat on opposite sides of North Calvert Street. We parked as close as we could and headed into the former. After passing through security and the metal detectors, I asked where I could find Judge Merrill Black. The guard directed me to the third floor but said the judge was most likely in court. Did I call his office to make an appointment? I did not. He told me it might be impossible to speak to the judge without one.

T.J. and I trekked up to the third floor anyway. Now after one o'clock, courts were in session. A harried-looking young man sat at a desk near the doors to three judges' offices. His hair needed a good brushing, but he dressed well, in stylish pants, a nice shirt, and a light cashmere sweater vest. The Movado on his wrist suggested he had money well above the salary of a court clerk.

"We'd like to talk with Judge Black when he's available," I said, showing the fellow my license and ID.

"He might be in court for a while."

"It's fine. We're on the clock."

The man frowned. "What's this about?"

"The three people who have died by explosion recently."

His brows remained knitted. "I'll shoot the judge an email. If he takes a recess, he might have some time to talk to you in his chambers."

"Thanks," I said. T.J. and I took seats in the surprisingly comfortable guest chairs nearby and waited. I pulled up some more articles and columns to read, quickly grew tired of the media fawning over someone who might be a serial bomber, and put my phone away again.

"How long you think we'll be here?" T.J. leaned in and whispered after we'd sat idle for about fifteen minutes.

"Don't know," I said. "I've been counting swirl patterns in the floor. You made me lose my spot, so now I have to start over."

"I'll count the holes in the drop ceiling."

"We'll know this place inside and out when we're done."

A female judge emerged from a nearby courtroom and walked past us. "Fabian, please come to my chambers," she said. The clerk got up, rolled his eyes, and followed her.

"I know I have no room to talk here," I said, "but you can't trust someone with a weird name."

"Okay, Coningsby."

"At least I have the good sense to go by my initials."

"Maybe this guy should, too."

"Depends," I said. "If his middle name is something like Uriah, he can't really go by F.U."

T.J. snickered, and Fabian emerged a moment later. After another quarter-hour or so, a courtroom door opened, and a tall, burly judge emerged. "Fabian, are these the people waiting for me?"

"Yes, Judge Black."

The judge waved a hand at us. "I can give you a few minutes. Fabian, please join us when you have a moment." As I walked past his desk, I could no longer see Fabian, but I imagined him rolling his eyes with Judge Black's back turned. T.J. and I sat in two guest chairs. For a judge's chambers, I wasn't impressed. It looked like a small office and was crammed full of furniture with a large desk, three chairs, two bookshelves, and a small table topped with a coffee maker. I liked the jurist already. "You're here about the bombings?"

"Yes." I showed Black my license and ID. "One of the families hired us after not getting very far with the police."

"Not surprised." Black shook his head. "I'm not some anti-cop hippie, but I can't imagine they're too motivated to solve these cases. Still, it's interesting I get to talk to another PI."

"Another?"

"Yes. Some fellow came in a few days ago about the same stuff. I don't know who he worked for." To my knowledge, I'd never been on a case a second PI also worked. Considering the potential scope of victims, it didn't surprise me, and I wasn't exactly keen on joining some local gumshoe society—if such a thing even existed.

"Let's talk motivation for a second," I said. "The cops might not be too interested, but we are. I understand these men all got let out on technicalities." The door opened, and Fabian walked in. He stood off to the side of where T.J. and I sat.

"Yes," Black said. "Each case is different, of course, but the state wields considerable power over any one individual. They need to do it correctly and responsibly."

"What about letting guilty people go free?" T.J. asked.

Black spread his hands. "I don't like it. Offenders, especially violent ones, belong in prison. The challenge is they need to get there the right way. If there are any shortcuts or problems in the arrest, investigation, or initial trial, then we owe those people a chance to get it right."

"Even if it means releasing them," I said.

"Even then."

"You talked about the police earlier, Judge. I can't imagine they're big fans of you letting a criminal walk."

"They're not," he said with a nod. "I can't worry about how they perceive it, though. We have legal standards to uphold. No one should go to jail because of a rushed investigation or some error by the police or a prosecutor. If they're already behind bars, the most common and fair remedy is to let them out."

Fabian wore a sour expression during the judge's explanation. "What do you think?" I asked him.

"Me?" I bobbed my head, and he blew out a quick breath. "I clerk for three judges. I don't have a lot of time to think."

"You must have an opinion," T.J. said.

He shrugged. "I guess I'm not a fan. I know the state needs to get things right, but there should be another remedy besides putting dangerous people back on the streets to prey on more victims." It struck me as a curious opinion considering his employer, but clerks probably didn't need to agree with the judges they worked for on everything.

"I wish we had some other solution," Black said. He handed Fabian a folder. The younger man glanced at it, nodded, and left the room. "I do the best I can within the system we have. It's not perfect, but we're not getting a better one anytime soon." He glanced at his watch. "Speaking of time, I'm afraid I need to get back to court."

"Thanks for talking to us," I said. T.J. and I left, taking the elevator back to the main level. "I don't know how much we learned," I admitted once we were back in the car. "Except we weren't the first investigators to make these rounds."

"Surprised?"

"Not really."

"I am," T.J. said. "Are we in a race to solve this?"

"No. We don't even know who else is snooping around. He might be a drunk."

"Or she."

I waved a hand. "Doesn't matter. We can't control it. Let's focus on what new information we learned today . . . which wasn't a lot."

"Didn't you used to tell me it all helps?"

"I did . . . and it does. We'll just need to find a use for it later."

"I hope we do," my assistant said.

CHAPTER 5

ONCE C.T. LEFT, Lexi and T.J. remained in the area for dinner.

T.J. suggested Brick Oven Pizza. It was a short walk, and the weather remained pleasant enough for early June. Both women wore shorts. The mercury rose into the low 80s earlier in the afternoon before settling at about 76. With a little breeze coming off the harbor, it made for a nice stroll. While Brick Oven Pizza drew a good lunch crowd and was packed on weekends, dinner on a Tuesday saw few patrons inside.

After reviewing the menu board, Lexi and T.J. each ordered a pizza and soda. "We'll have leftovers for lunch," Lexi said.

"And we won't share them with our boss," T.J. added.

Lexi smiled. "I'm glad my intern search led me to you."

"Me, too . . . and I think C.T. would say the same."

"You're interested in a lot of the computer stuff he can do, right?"

"Yeah. He's shown me some things already." T.J. remembered being hesitant at first. The idea of hacking sounded cool, but she felt her pulse quicken when it became time to press enter and execute a script or program in the real world. Her boss started her off with smaller tasks—mostly reconnaissance and information gathering. From there, she'd shown she could handle a more technologically interesting workload. "It's something I still want to learn more about. C.T.'s mostly self-taught, so he's not always the best instructor."

"I am, too," Lexi said. "Self-taught, I mean." She tugged at her auburn ponytail. Other than the difference in color, both women wore their hair in nearly identical styles. "My dad worked for a private security company after he left the Army. At some point, they gave him a laptop a bunch of red team guys put together." She chuckled. "He can turn it on and check email. That's about it. I've managed to learn quite a bit on it just helping him."

"He left that company, right?" T.J. asked. Lexi nodded. "Didn't they want the laptop back?"

"Maybe, but he told one of the owners to come and take it from him if he wanted it so bad. The other one didn't care."

"I've only met your dad a couple times, but I like him."

Lexi snorted. "Not many people do. He's never really been the warm and fuzzy type."

T.J. thought about her own father. He left when she was young, and only a few faint memories remained. Afterwards, her overwhelmed mother had a string of boyfriends, and a couple turned their attention to T.J. when the woman of the house was busy or asleep.

"You all right?" Lexi asked.

"Yeah." T.J. offered a quick smile. She figured it looked insincere. Lexi came from a much different and more stable background, but the pair got along very well. A cute waiter brought their pizzas and blushed when he flashed his pearly whites at the young women. Lexi ordered pepperoni, and T.J. chose mushroom and green pepper.

"Trade a slice?" Lexi returned a more genuine smile.

"Sure." Each took a piece of the other's plus one of their own and plopped both onto plain white paper plates. The cheese was appropriately greasy and gooey, and the steam carried the aromas of sauce, mozzarella, and the toppings. They chowed down in silence for a few minutes, and T.J. only broke it when her third slice started to make her feel full. "This case is a weird one."

"We can discuss them outside the office?" Lexi wanted to know.

T.J. shrugged. "As long as we're discreet about it."

"What bothers you?"

"The technicality thing. I would have loved to see something like that when I got hauled in front of a judge."

"You two talked to this judge. What did you think?"

"Seems like a straight shooter. A stickler for making sure things are done right. No matter what he says, I can't imagine it endears him to anyone else in the legal system."

"You think he might be the killer?" Lexi wondered, dropping her voice to a whisper.

T.J. could still hear her. While a few folks picked up carry-out orders, not many customers ate inside the restaurant, and none sat nearby. "I doubt it. He seems really committed to the idea that the system should treat everyone fairly even if it does so a little late."

"Not bad."

"No," T.J. said. "I think it's a core belief for him. He's not going to let someone out on a technicality and then blow them up a few days later."

"This is my first major case. Are they all so . . . squirrely?"

"No. We always have to do a ton of work, but you're right. Something seems a little off about this."

Lexi grinned. "We should keep investigating."

"You want to go back to the office?" T.J. suggested.

"We'd need to put these pizzas in the fridge." Lexi spread her hands. "What's a little more work while we're there? We don't even have to tell the boss."

"Just wait until you hear one of his lectures about overtime." T.J. snickered, and Lexi joined in. The same cute waiter dropped off two boxes for their leftovers. He remained silent, though not as much color rushed into his cheeks this time. T.J. and Lexi boxed up their pizzas and headed back to the office.

"I think we've found a pattern," T.J. said after several minutes of research.

Each of the three bombing victims got arrested for different crimes. None of the officers involved were the same. All were sent to the Central Booking and Intake Facility, but this was common in the city. The three men were arraigned before different judges, used three distinct public defenders, and went to trial before three different judges in the District Court. The common factor was getting into Judge Black's courtroom.

"Public defenders have to know what Judge Black thinks about technicalities," Lexi said. "Two women and one man filed motions for completely dissimilar things, and they all came before Judge Black."

"I can see why you thought he might be involved." T.J. frowned at her screen. "He strikes me as a real true believer in the system being fair . . . even if we sometimes have to force it. There's no reason he would let these men off otherwise. They'd never been in his courtroom before, and we don't see any indication he had contact with them afterwards."

"I'm going to send you an article I found," Lexi said. The link to the Maryland Law Review appeared in T.J.'s inbox a second later, and she clicked it.

Judicial Oversight and the Rule of Law: An Examination of Judge Merrill Black's Record in Overturning Criminal Convictions

By Jonathan H. Wade, Senior Editor

In recent years, Judge Merrill Black of the Baltimore Circuit Court has gained a reputation for overturning criminal convictions on procedural grounds, a judicial pattern that has sparked debate among legal scholars, law enforcement officials, and civil rights advocates alike. While Judge Black's rulings are rooted in established legal principles, including the protection of constitutional rights and the importance of due process, critics argue that his strict adherence to legal technicalities has led to the release of individuals who would—and perhaps should—otherwise be serving lengthy prison sentences for serious crimes.

Judge Black's approach highlights a crucial

tension within the legal system: the balance between the power of the state to prosecute offenders and the rights of defendants to a fair trial. In a number of high-profile cases, Black has reversed convictions on the grounds of improper evidence handling, lack of probable cause, or procedural errors during trial—decisions that have stirred both praise and controversy.

The Power of the State and the Role of the Courts

The authority of the state to investigate and prosecute criminal behavior is essential to maintaining public safety and order. However, courts are charged with ensuring that this authority is exercised within the bounds of the law. Judge Black, a former public defender turned jurist, has often emphasized the importance of the state following proper legal procedures when bringing cases to trial. His opinions frequently cite the need for law enforcement and prosecutors to "get it right the first time," arguing that cutting corners or mishandling evidence jeopardizes not only the integrity of a particular case but also public trust in the legal system.

Proponents of Judge Black's approach argue that his rulings are necessary to prevent abuses of power. "The police and prosecution must be held to the highest standard," said Professor Elizabeth Harkins of the University of Maryland School of Law. "When a conviction is overturned due to a violation of constitutional rights, it's not about letting criminals go free; it's about ensuring that the government plays by the rules."

Criticism and Concerns of Leniency

However, detractors believe that Judge Black's decisions often favor defendants at the expense of public safety. In several cases, individuals convicted of violent crimes, including drug trafficking, assault, and armed robbery, have seen their sentences vacated due to procedural errors—mistakes, critics argue, that did not negate the underlying facts of cases in question.

Law enforcement officials, in particular, have expressed frustration with what they perceive as Black's leniency. "No one is saying we should ignore the law," said a senior officer with the Baltimore Police Department, who asked to remain anonymous. "But when someone who was convicted of a crime based on overwhelming evidence walks free because of a minor technicality, it undermines the work we do to protect this city."

The issue has also sparked concern among victims' rights advocates. Convictions overturned on technical grounds often mean that victims and their families are forced to relive traumatic experiences during retrials or, worse, see offenders go unpunished. "We're not just talking about mistakes in paperwork," said Linda Shaw, a spokesperson for the Maryland Coalition for Victims of Crime. "These are cases where real people were harmed. There has to be some consideration for the victims, too."

Finding Balance: The Role of Judicial Review

Judge Black's record underscores a larger debate in the legal community about the role of the judiciary in balancing the rights of defendants with the interests of public safety. While the rule of law demands that trials be conducted fairly and without error, some argue that the courts should give greater weight to the substantive facts of a case rather than focusing on procedural missteps.

Ultimately, the question comes down to a fundamental legal principle: should a conviction stand if the process by which it was obtained is flawed? For Judge Black, the answer has often been no—a stance that, while legally sound, continues to raise questions about where the line between justice and leniency should be drawn.

As Baltimore and other cities face increasing challenges in maintaining public safety, Judge Black's rulings will no doubt remain a focal point of debate in legal circles, as courts, prosecutors, and law enforcement agencies strive to balance the need for accountability with the rights guaranteed by the Constitution.

"Pretty balanced take," T.J. said when she finished reading.

"It can be a divisive issue," Lexi acknowledged. "I want to see people put in jail for doing bad things, but I also want our system to be fair. It's a tough balance."

T.J. nodded. "Public sentiment seems to be behind the Vox Populi killer. I think we know which way the citizens are leaning."

"Sounds like we need to solve this before another bomb goes off."

"I knew you'd make a good intern," T.J. said.

———

The research made T.J. feel like she was in high school again.

She only went for three semesters before dropping out, so she never got to take the social studies class which dove into Maryland history, laws, and politics. It didn't sound exciting to her at age fifteen, and now, almost seven years later, it still lacked any real appeal. "You ever wonder how circuit court judges get to the bench?" she asked.

"Not really something that keeps me up at night," Lexi said.

T.J. smiled. "Me, either, though I might see boring legal articles flash before my eyes when I'm trying to sleep tonight."

Lexi rested her chin in her hands. "Please enlighten me, then."

"The governor appoints them from a pool established by each district," T.J. said. "Then, when the next election hits, they have to run or resign. Someone can challenge them. If they win, it's a fifteen-year-term, and they can seek re-election. They have to retire at age seventy."

"Is Black staring down a forced exit?"

T.J. shook her head. "No. He has two decades to go. I found an interesting opinion piece written by his opponent. Black just won re-election to his second term. The guy running against him didn't beat around the bush." She sent the *Baltimore Sun* op-ed to Lexi and then looked over it again.

Opinion: Judge Merrill Black's Dangerous Legacy of Leniency

By Douglas Pierce, candidate for Baltimore Circuit Court Judge

As Baltimore continues to grapple with rising crime rates and communities plagued by violence, we cannot afford to have judges who prioritize technicalities over justice. Yet that is exactly what Judge Merrill Black has done throughout his tenure. Re-election would be a victory for him but a significant loss for the people of Baltimore, who deserve better.

In the past several years, Judge Black has developed a troubling pattern: overturning criminal convictions on what he refers to as "procedural grounds." While it is true that all defendants deserve fair trials, it is equally true that public safety depends on the consistent enforcement of our laws. Time and time again, Judge Black has allowed dangerous individuals to walk free—not because they were innocent, but because of minor legal errors that, in many cases, had little to do with the actual guilt or innocence of the accused.

Take the case of Anthony Diaz, a convicted arms dealer. Despite overwhelming evidence linking him to illegal firearms trafficking, Judge Black vacated his conviction due to a technicality involving evidence submission. The ruling was a slap in the face to law enforcement officers who worked tirelessly to build a solid case and to the communities impacted by the flow of illegal weapons on our streets. Judge Black's decision sent a clear message: process matters more than public safety.

Some will argue that Black is simply ensuring that the government follows the law. But that argument conveniently overlooks the fact that his decisions have real-world consequences. When violent offenders are released due to procedural errors, they often return to their criminal ways, continuing to harm the very communities we are supposed to protect.

Baltimore is at a tipping point. Crime is on the rise, and residents are increasingly worried about their safety. Judges like Merrill Black who undermine the hard work of police and prosecutors only make matters worse. I'm running against Judge Black because I believe we need a judiciary that holds offenders accountable, not one that looks for loopholes to let them off the hook.

During the election, Judge Black and his supporters paint him as a champion of due process, as if that were the sole concern in our courts. But there is more to justice than technical adherence to the letter of the law. Justice also means protecting the innocent and ensuring that criminals face the consequences of their actions.

If Judge Black wins and secures another 15 years on the bench, I fear we will continue to see criminals exploiting these loopholes while our neighborhoods bear the brunt of the consequences. It is time for Baltimore to demand more from its judges—judges who will protect public safety, not enable those who threaten it.

"Welcome to the suspect pool, Judge Pierce," Lexi said. "Population: you."

"Bit of a leap," T.J. said, "but we have to take a look at him."

"We should all work on it tomorrow." Lexi stretched her

arms above her head and yawned. "I don't think I got out of bed before eleven last summer."

"But did you get to read legal articles and chase down shady judges back then?"

"Nope," Lexi said. "This is definitely an improvement. Want to call it a night?"

"Sure," T.J. said. "We'll get back after it with the boss tomorrow."

CHAPTER 6

IT WAS ALREADY humid when I ventured out for a morning run.

We stayed at Gloria's house the prior night. When we first got married, she wanted me to ditch my Federal Hill rowhouse, and we would then live in her much larger home in Baltimore County's posh Brooklandville area. As a city boy at heart, I balked at the move, and Gloria soon stopped bringing it up. It made sense to have one residence, but we both liked our houses and couldn't give them up. It may be the best example of a first-world problem in human history.

As compared to the mean streets of Baltimore, the meticulously asphalted roads of Brooklandville were tony and a little boring. Once you've seen a manicured hedge, the sixteenth no longer holds much novelty. I passed a few landscapers toiling away in the early morning heat, and I imagined their company passed several rigorous rounds of vetting from the homeowners association. When they complained about the height of Gloria's hedges, I suggested carving an expletive into the shrubs during the trimming process. This perfectly reasonable proposal did not meet a favorable response, however.

Three miles and change later, I headed back inside Gloria's house. I showered and dressed in the time it took her to do her hair and part of her makeup. She must have been meeting with a potential client or venue today. My wife, having dabbled in fundraising for a while, launched her own company over a year ago. Her job allowed her to work from the home office—an extra bedroom—most days, but others, she needed to be in the field.

Downstairs, I fried sausage patties and eggs, assembled breakfast sandwiches for the both of us, and kissed my beautiful wife goodbye. When I got to the office, T.J. was already there. She eyed my foil-wrapped meal. "Where did you stop?" she asked as I set my backpack down. I unwrapped the aluminum, and the aromas of eggs, butter, and sausage hit my nostrils again.

"Gloria's kitchen."

"Never heard of it."

"It's not a very well-known place," I said. "The chef, however, is very handsome."

"He seems to make small portions," T.J. said.

I grabbed a snack plate from the nearby coffee station and put half the sandwich on it. "You can have this if you share your pizza with me."

"How did you know I had pizza?"

"You paid with the company card," I said, "and you've either turned into a pig, or you took our intern to dinner, too."

"Why not both?" she wondered, accepting the sandwich. "Fine. You can have some of my pizza."

"Did you two work late?" I made a fresh cup of coffee

and carried it to my desk, where I sat and took a bite of my now half-sandwich.

"We thought something was a little squirrely about this whole case, so we did some research."

"And?"

"And it's still squirrely," T.J. said.

"You learned more, though. We need a different animal. It's chipmunk-y now."

T.J. rolled her eyes and disregarded my zoological suggestion. "I don't know if we have a suspect, but the guy who ran against Judge Black two years ago seems to think he's a commie who loves criminals."

"This guy was also a judge?"

"Yeah. District court, I think. The whole process is a little weird. I sent you both articles."

"It's not him," I said.

"Wow. You've really improved your speed reading."

"He's a sitting judge who ran against someone one level up. Apparently, he then went and trashed Black in an editorial. He'd have to be a fool to go around and kill people who walked out free from Judge Black's courtroom."

"He's a person of interest, then."

"'Interest' is doing some heavy lifting there," I said, "but I appreciate your initiative in doing all this after hours."

"We should at least talk to him."

I nodded. "We can. I want to sit down with some victims' families, too. Not just of the bomber. I mean the relatives of the original victims."

"You think one of them could be behind it?"

"Maybe. Someone either hates Judge Black, can't stand the three victims, or finds the whole technicality thing to be absurd . . . or some combination of those three."

"Makes sense," T.J. said. "You want to take Lexi into the field?"

"Do you think she's ready?"

"I do." T.J. bobbed her head, and her blonde ponytail pulsed on her shoulder, and as if on cue, footsteps came up the stairs. It was nearly ten o'clock.

"I guess we'll find out, then," I said as Lexi opened the door.

————

"I want to find a suspect today," I told the two young women once we'd all enjoyed some coffee.

"It's nice to have goals," Lexi said.

T.J. chuckled. "She's fitting in here already." After I rolled my eyes, she got more serious. "Where are we off to?"

"I want to drop in on the girlfriend of the first bombing victim."

"The drug dealer?" Lexi asked.

"He's the one."

"How do you know she'll be home?"

"She doesn't have a job, and she's in mourning," I said. "Odds are good she's at the house."

"Doesn't seem like a likely suspect," my assistant said.

"I'm hoping she can point us in the right direction from there. Maybe someone had it in for T-Bone. It's possible our killer stalked the house in the days before the bombing. If we strike out there, I have another idea."

"Are we all going?" Lexi said.

"You're supposed to learn as much as you can as an intern. Might as well see how we hit these mean streets and try to gather some information."

"Let's go, then."

We all headed to the S4. If not mean, it was certainly far from timid. T.J. climbed into the passenger's seat, and Lexi sat behind her in the back. T.J. scooted the bolstered bucket up a couple inches, and we were off. The drive from Fells Point to Federal Hill wasn't long in terms of distance, but despite the hour, we shared the roads with a lot of other cars. The traffic felt like an act of defiance from a city unwilling to part with its secrets so soon. As a resident of Federal Hill, my window decal allowed me to park on the streets at all hours. I found a spot a couple doors from our target and left the car there.

Keisha Smith, girlfriend of the late T-Bone Mallory, lived in an interior rowhouse they'd shared until recently. I remembered feeling the explosion which claimed his life. A few stray char marks still dotted the curb where Mallory's car exploded. I wondered if they would ever come out, or if the reminder of her boyfriend's passing would be painted on the concrete every time Keisha walked by. The brick exterior of the house looked dingier and more faded than its neighbors, and paint chips marred the blue door. Either could have come from the bomb blast or neglect.

Footsteps approached after I knocked. A slender Black woman answered the door, a cigarette dangling from her mouth. She wore a plain T-shirt and small shorts, and she seemed completely unbothered at how obvious her lack of a bra was to the three of us. "Miss Smith, I'm a private investigator." I showed her my license and ID. "We're looking into what happened to T-Bone and the other victims. Can we come in?"

Her narrowed eyes scanned the three of us. "Gimme a couple." She closed the door, and we waited. When she returned after a few minutes, Keisha wore a more complete wardrobe, and the cigarette was gone. She'd traded her earlier attire for a plain black T-shirt and cut-off jean shorts. Somehow, she'd even added some makeup, and it helped her look more pretty and less tired. "Come on in," she said. "Sorry about the mess."

We entered into the living room. This area didn't look bad, though all three ashtrays needed to be emptied long before our arrival. What I could see of the kitchen looked like a disaster area, with dishes and pans everywhere. I recalled my sister's death when I was sixteen. My best guess meant I'd been about twenty years younger than Keisha Smith. She had two decades of life experience on me. Grief, however, ruins both your plans and whatever self-image you've cultivated. Life can punch you really hard in the mouth, and getting up off the mat is rarely easy or quick.

"Can I get y'all anything?" our hostess asked.

"We're all right," I said. The three of us sat side-by-side on a shopworn couch. "I live a couple blocks from here, and I ran over when I felt the explosion. We're all sorry for your loss."

"At least it seems like you're trying to figure shit out."

"I take it you've talked to the police?"

"For all the good it did, yeah. There ain't no equal justice under the law when you're a criminal. I know T-Bone did some bad shit. Don't mean I didn't love him. Even if he did all they say, the cops should still try to catch whoever killed him."

"I agree," I said. "Did you know of anyone who wanted to hurt Thomas?"

Keisha snorted. "Lord, that might be a long list."

"Recently, then. Anyone hanging around the house? Messing with his car? Sending threatening messages?"

She shook her head. "Nothing like that. This came out of the blue. I was inside eating breakfast. He went out, started the car, and . . . " Keisha's eyes closed, and she couldn't finish. She didn't need to.

"The police don't have a suspect yet," I said. "You probably don't find this surprising. Another victim's family hired us, and we actually want to get to the bottom of things." I took a business card out of my wallet and left it on the cluttered coffee table. Hopefully, it wouldn't disappear under an empty cigarette pack. "If you think of anything, please call us."

"I will," Keisha said after composing herself for a moment. "Thank you. I hope you're able to find something."

From Federal Hill, we headed a few blocks west past the Camden Yards stadium complex. Another rowhouse, this one belonging to Bill Erickson, whom I expected to be home because his social media identified his job as remote. Sure enough, he answered the door and frowned at the three of us. Bill Erickson was short and wide, and his jowly face made him look unfriendly. "Mister Erickson, we have some questions." I showed him my license and ID. "It's about the recent bombings. Do you have a few minutes?"

"Private investigator?" he demanded.

"Yes."

"I don't have to talk to you, then." Before he could close the door, I stuck my foot in the way.

"True. I can't compel you to talk to me. However, the police don't seem to be on to you yet despite the fact you might have wanted to kill T-Bone Mallory. My cousin's a homicide lieutenant." I shrugged. "You can talk to me or to him. Not only am I younger, smarter, and better-looking, I'm less likely to come with a dozen brutes ready to pull your house apart. Your choice."

He scanned the three of us again and opened the door. "I guess they don't look very brutish."

"You should see us when we're out of coffee," I said as we filed in. The layout here was very similar to Keisha Smith's place, but Erickson kept a tidy home. His furniture looked new. He muted some business show on the TV, and we all sat in the living room. "How's your daughter?"

"Fine." He showed a brief smile. "Living on her own again and back to being herself." Helen Erickson bought drugs from T-Bone and fell into a coma. Her father spoke as a witness at the trial. If someone's poison nearly killed one of my relatives, I would also make a very good murder suspect.

"You can see how we might wonder what you thought of T-Bone Mallory."

"Son of a bitch," Erickson muttered. "He damn near killed my Helen." After a deep breath, our host continued. "I was happy to help get him convicted, and yes, I didn't like hearing he got out on some bullshit technicality. I wanted him to get what was coming to him . . . but not by getting blown up."

"You'd rather he got shanked in prison?" I asked.

Erickson shrugged. "I wouldn't have shed a tear. Still won't, but I don't think anyone deserves what happened to him."

"I presume you have an alibi for the morning in question."

"Out of town for work," he said. "Plenty of people can confirm this. You don't need to sic your cousin or his brutes on me."

"You won't mind us checking it out, then," T.J. said. His shoulders went up and down again.

"I'm sure Helen wasn't the only person T-Bone and his product hurt," I said. "You know of anyone else who'd want to get back at him?"

"No. We didn't have a support group or anything."

As before, I dropped a card onto the coffee table. This one would be a lot easier to spot, but I figured it would wind up in a trash can about a minute after we left. "If you think of anything, please give us a call." He grunted, and before we made it back out the door, Erickson had unmuted the TV.

"Seems like we were oh-for-two," Lexi said as we climbed back into the Audi.

"Yes," I admitted. "We didn't find a good suspect this morning. If you learn something doing these, they weren't pointless."

"What's next?" T.J. wondered.

"Let's go back to the office and see who else we might drop in on," I said.

———

We returned to an unwelcome sight.

Three news vans—one each for the major local TV stations—sat in the parking lot. With the Vox Populi killer gaining a nickname and random media attention, some of the scrutiny now shifted to us as the agency had already been mentioned in numerous articles about the bombings. "Shit," I muttered. I didn't bother to try and make the turn, opting to keep going instead.

"What are we going to do?" T.J. asked.

"My preference is not talking to the press . . . especially

not so early. We won't be able to tell them much, which will get spun into us being incompetent, and suddenly, no one can catch this Vox Populi asshole. Hard pass."

"Reporters often wait on public roads," Lexi said. "They're on private property."

"True." I called Manny, and learning he was unhappy with the situation didn't require my vast sleuthing powers.

"What the hell is going on out there?"

"Three news vans."

"I know," he said. "Why are they here?"

"You running a special on brake jobs?"

"No."

"Maybe you should be," I offered. "Look at all the free publicity you'd get."

"Is this about the bombings?"

"Yeah. We're working the case, and our involvement has made the news already."

"Nobody better plant a goddamn bomb at my shop," he said, agitation spilling into and sharpening his tone. "I think I've been pretty understanding so far, but I can only take so much."

"You have," I said, trying to placate him. Manny had, in fact, been a great landlord. He didn't ask questions when I sent goons tumbling down the stairs. When someone shot up the parking lot, he built a wall to better protect customers' cars. While I footed the bill, he paid up front, and I reimbursed him over the course of a year. The location was good, too. I didn't want to lose a good office. "I think you can get rid of them, actually. You own the place."

He grunted. "True. Didn't even think about it."

"We just drove by. Can you let me know when you've chased them off?"

"Sure. I work for you now." He hung up before I could offer a clever retort. I made a left with the goal of driving around the block for a few minutes until Manny sorted the reporter mess out. A short while later, he called back. "They're gone. Something tells me they'll camp out on the sidewalk next time."

"Thanks," I said, and again he hung up.

"You seem popular with the owner," Lexi said.

"Manny likes us. He's just crabby about things happening at his place." I headed back toward the shop. The last of the news vans headed away, its brake lights small red dots in the distance, as I pulled into the lot.

"We still need to find a suspect," T.J. said as we all climbed out of the car. "The press will be back."

Up until a few years ago, I sought out positive press coverage for my detective business. Now, with a more tradi-tional revenue model, I avoided it. "Remember our number one rule for appearing in stories," I said.

"Just keep going with, 'no comment'?" Lexi asked.

"No. Always look better than the cops. Usually, it's not hard."

CHAPTER 7

WITH LUNCH and coffee to sustain us, we kept working.

Thanks to the copious reporting of the killings—which had only gone up since the press gave the murderer his *nom de guerre*—we knew quite a bit about all three victims. None would win any awards for upstanding citizenship, but whatever their crimes, getting blown up outside the legal system seemed a poor solution. Of course, vigilantism often attracts people, and the more bloodthirsty, the better. It had become impossible to read about the killer without encountering a growing legion of drooling fanboys—and even some fangirls —hoping he would continue his work. Some even provided suggestions for future targets.

"This is disgusting," Lexi said.

Considering who her father was, I found her opinion on these extrajudicial killings curious, but we didn't need to pursue this. "These clowns always attract fans," I said.

"A bunch of deplorable people."

Knowing our three dead criminals also opened up anyone they'd victimized as potential suspects. So far, we'd struck out on two attempts to tie people related to T-Bone

Mallory to the bombings. Armed with police files, I knew we would find more possibilities. The cops could do this work, too. I wondered how seriously they were looking into things. My cousin—whose mistake of leaving me alone at his computer years ago still allowed me to access the BPD's resources—didn't lack for major crimes to investigate. At some point, it would be an issue of resource allocation, and even if he didn't mean to give dead criminals the short shrift, I knew it would be the result.

"I still like Judge Pierce," Lexi said.

"Me, too," T.J. chimed in.

"It's not him," I said.

"You told me we could talk to him."

"We can. The thing is we have to go with more than him writing an editorial after losing a close election. Was he in town when the bombings happened? What's his alibi? Judges are lawyers, too. If we don't go in there armed to the teeth with a good theory and a trove of facts to back it up, he's going to rip us apart."

Lexi frowned. "I'll look into him."

"You're a killjoy," T.J. said to me.

"I'm sparing you hours of frustration," I said.

"You really think we're going to find a suspect in these three guys' police files?"

"I know we won't find one if we don't start looking."

She grumbled but got to work while our intern ran down their pet theory. I figured it would hit a dead end. Scathing column aside, Judge Pierce didn't make a good suspect, and I wasn't going to hurl capital murder accusations at a well-regarded jurist without unshakeable evidence and an assist from the cops. "I'll keep looking into Mallory," my assistant said after she finished stewing.

Considering who hired us, I focused on anyone harmed by Walter Williams. I didn't realize how many times he'd gotten popped for driving under the influence. The fact he was still able to get a driver's license was something of a miracle. Williams first got arrested for blowing twice the legal limit on a breathalyzer when he was seventeen. As this was also four years under the minimum age to buy alcohol, he got charged with two crimes. However, the only victims of his driving were a mailbox and a fence, so he got tried as a juvenile, and not much happened as a result.

In the twenty-four years since, Williams committed the same offense five more times. On the subsequent occasions, he collided with other cars and injured people, though no one died. Accidents can lead to very expensive medical bills, missed work, and even permanent disability. Williams emerged lucky from his incidents, as no one ended up seriously injured. I doubted anyone wanted to kill him—not to mention two other individuals—over a broken arm six years ago.

This left me with Mikey Granger. If criminality were a grocery store, Granger pulled something from every shelf and aisle. Pimping out his cousin? Check. Selling illegal guns? Yep. Distributing weed before it was (mostly) legal? Of course. Looking through his smorgasbord of illegal activity, I realized many people might have good reason to cause Granger harm. He'd spent nearly half his adult life in prison and still couldn't stay out for more than a couple years at a time. He was in the middle of one such streak now.

From his record, I identified the five most likely to want to see Mikey Granger blow up in a car. Two of them were already dead. A third now lived over a thousand miles away. I looked into the remaining duo—someone shot with a gun sold by Granger eight years ago, and a man whose niece disappeared while in Granger's company and never returned.

Based on social media timelines, the first person was at work when two of the blasts went off. Despite this setback, I allowed a tiny amount of optimism to creep in. Maybe the last possible suspect—a man named Phil Kristoff—would pan out. He didn't keep much of a social media presence. To blow three people up, someone would need prior explosives experience or enough money to pay such a specialist. Kristoff never served in the military or worked in law enforcement— the most likely places to work with bombs—and in fact possessed a spotty job history. This meant he didn't have the money to hire an expert.

So much for optimism.

"I'm striking out so far," I admitted.

"Oh-for-three?" T.J. asked.

"Yes. I'm going to stop now and avoid the golden sombrero."

"Maybe we should reconsider the judge," Lexi said.

"Maybe we should consider this is going to be a tough case."

To accentuate my point, a set of footsteps climbed the metal stairs.

———

Unannounced visitors are rarely a good thing.

Sometimes, it's a potential client, though the majority of them either call or fill out an online calendar reservation before stopping by. Our most common uninvited guests were enforcers trying to intimidate us and discourage me from continuing the investigation. The only thing they succeeded at was going down the stairs much faster than they walked up. Before the door swung in, I'd opened my top desk drawer, taken out my .45, and pointed it at the person walking through.

He did not dress like a goon.

The man who strode in was tall—about the same height as me at six-two—and trim. Not everyone could wear a slim fit suit, but our guest nailed it. He was black, wore round glasses, and kept his hair in a short afro. "You don't need the gun," he said. "I'm a lawyer."

"Those two phrases don't go well together," I said, keeping the weapon trained on him, forefinger flexing along the slide above the trigger guard.

He put up his hand. "I work in the state's attorney's office. Can I show you my ID?"

I let the gun rest on the desktop but didn't release it. "Sure."

He reached into his front pocket and pulled out a well-worn brown wallet. Inside, a laminated ID card identified Amos Johnson as a prosecutor for the state's attorney. "Now, can you put the gun away?"

"I reserve the right to take it out again," I said, slipping the .45 back inside the drawer and shutting it. "You are an attorney, after all. What can we do for you, Mister Johnson?"

He glanced toward the side table. "Coffee fresh?"

"No, but it can be." Lexi got up and worked on a new pot. I appreciated T.J. delegating some tasks to the intern.

Johnson sat in a guest chair and crossed his legs. His socks matched the color of his suit pants exactly. If I were on the jury for a case he prosecuted, the style points might persuade me. "My office understands you're also looking into the bombings," he said.

"Can't believe everything you read in the paper."

"The reporters have been quite complimentary of your agency."

"Like I said . . . if it's in print, it must be true."

Johnson smiled. "I know you often end up working on the defense side of the house."

"Is that a problem?" T.J. asked as she wheeled her chair to the desk.

"Not at all. I believe everyone's entitled to a fair trial and a competent defense. If anything, I wish the other side used good investigators more often."

"Wouldn't that make your job harder?"

"I think I'd still do all right." Johnson shrugged. "Putting someone in prison shouldn't feel like shooting fish in a barrel." He waved a hand. "I came here because I want you to know what happens when violent criminals get let out on legal technicalities."

"Hang on," I said. "If you really believe in things like fair trials, then you also have to accept the state can make mistakes."

"Sure. We're talking about minor administrative oversights. Sometimes, we miss a T we should have crossed. It happens. When it does, it shouldn't invalidate everything the cops and my office did. Guilty people are still guilty, and they don't belong back in the communities they've preyed on."

"I sympathize. It's a tough balance. I think everyone wants to see real criminals put away for a long time. The majority of us want to see it done the right way."

"It was . . . in every case. The police did good work, and so did we."

I spread my hands. "It appears Judge Black disagrees."

Johnson snorted. "With all due respect to the judge, he's a big softie. Way too lenient on this stuff."

"Maybe we should start asking where you were when the bombs went off," I said. Johnson chuckled, but I didn't, and his mirthful expression turned to a frown.

"You can't be serious." He crossed his arms. "This is ridiculous. I had nothing to do with any of those events."

"They weren't 'events,' I pointed out. "No one sold tickets. They were explosions . . . carefully planned as far as I can tell. Three people are dead. Maybe they wouldn't be on the shortlist for Citizen of the Year, but I don't think they deserved to die in car fires."

"Honestly, I don't think they did, either," Johnson said. "It's just one reason why I'm not the guy who did it." He took a deep breath. "Look . . . here's what I'm saying. Whether we think those men deserved what they got or not, there's a strong public sentiment out there. Ultimately, I work for an official elected by the people of this city."

"Is your office going to endorse a vigilante?"

"'Endorse' is a strong word. I know you do good work. Maybe this time, you decide to back off the case. We don't want to open the floodgates here. I don't need to see Judge Black letting any more criminals go."

"Unless you think the judge is the bomber," T.J. said, "him releasing men on technicalities is part of the system. What the killer does isn't related."

Johnson put up his hands again. "I simply want to keep the killings down. Maybe this is a tantrum, and once it runs its course, things will go back to normal."

"Here's what we're going to do," I said. "My agency is on this case, and we're going to do our best. Our best, by the way, is pretty goddamn good. Once we figure out who this Vox Populi jackass is, we'll work with the cops to make an arrest. Assuming they take him alive, I expect your office to prosecute the killer for what he's done . . . no matter how many adoring fans he might have on Facebook. If you don't, I think it'll be the story of the year, and your boss will find herself bounced out on her ass at the next election . . . maybe sooner."

"Think about it," Johnson said as he got up and started toward the door.

"Already did."

He left without another word. "Did he just threaten us?" T.J. wondered.

"Sounded like he wanted to," Lexi said.

"Tempers are high," I said. "There's the perception the police don't want to find the killer because they want him to take out more criminals. While I'm sure a few feel this way, most don't. They want to catch people who do things like endanger citizens with car bombs. Prosecutors want to put them away." I waved a hand. "This guy is out over his skis."

T.J. wheeled her chair back to her own desk. "I hope that's all it is."

"Me, too."

CHAPTER 8

A FEW HOURS LATER, my cousin Rich called. "I know I caught the previous serial killer for you," I said, "but I can't help on every case."

"Somehow, I think we'll be all right. You heading out soon?"

"Probably. What's up?"

"Let's get some food. Want to meet me at Brick Oven Pizza in a half-hour?"

"Sure."

"See you then," he said and ended the call.

"What did Rich want?" T.J. asked.

"He was calling to check on your entry in the Nosy Secretary Awards."

T.J. stuck her tongue out at me while Lexi snickered. "He probably needs someone to bounce ideas off of."

"He has people who work above and below him to use as sounding boards," I said even though she was probably right. When I started working as a PI, Rich thought the idea was ridiculous. His opinion held for the first year or so, and then he started coming around. Now, having received several commendations for cracking cases I did a lot of the work on, Rich valued my input.

T.J. put her hand over her heart. "Are you complimenting the police?"

"Only a few members of the force."

About twenty minutes later, we all filed out, locked the door, and scattered to our cars. Lexi got into a blue Honda Accord coupe, and I could tell it was a manual by the sound as she pulled away. Score one for the intern. T.J.'s Mustang, on the other hand, was an automatic. My S4 hailed from a generation where shifting your own gears was an option, if a hard-to-find one. I found a spot around the corner from the pizza place and walked in to find Rich already there.

My cousin was six and a half years older than me. I would turn thirty-four in about six months, but he'd recently passed the big four-oh. When we were kids, the age gap felt huge. He went into the Army when I was still in middle school. As adults, though, it seemed smaller. I'd given him an appropriate amount of grief about getting old, of course. Working as a lieutenant grayed Rich's hair faster. The brown still held a decent advantage. He was a little shorter than me at six feet even and a little stockier at two hundred pounds. Even in a restaurant, Rich couldn't help looking like a cop.

We ordered our respective pies—pepperoni, mushroom, and onion for me and some multi-meat monstrosity for Rich —and took an unoccupied table. It was just before six on a Wednesday, so the crowd remained pretty light. "I know you're working on the bombings," Rich said.

"So much for small talk." I sipped some of my soda. "I'm fine, thanks. Gloria seems interested in gardening, which surprises me. I didn't think she'd want to get her hands dirty. How are you?"

Rich smirked. "She'll wear gloves. No way your wife is getting topsoil under those manicured nails."

"You're probably right," I said.

"Don't think you're off the hook. Who do you think is going to dig the holes?"

"She's bought a bunch of plant pots and some stands to put them on." I shrugged. "Plenty of space on her deck."

"As riveting as your wife's new botany hobby might be," Rich said, "I actually wanted to talk about what we're both working on." He kept his voice pretty low even though no one sat at the neighboring tables. I gestured for him to go ahead. "I'm sure you won't tell me who hired you." I let my silence answer for me. "If I wanted to take a stab at it, I'd have a one-in-three chance."

"Let me guess," I said. "You're going to regale me with tales of how hard-working cops and prosecutors shouldn't have their work thrown out because of minor clerical errors."

Rich spread his hands. "Basically."

"It's amazing how many people in the system seem to have no fucking idea how it's supposed to work."

"Who else have you talked to?" my cousin wanted to know.

"Some guy from the state's attorney's office came by today. Gave us the same song and dance. Innocent people should go free, but paperwork shouldn't get dangerous criminals out of jail."

"You think it should?"

"I think it depends on the paperwork. For an actual trivial clerical error? No. But something more serious? The state has an obligation to do its job completely and fairly."

"Who visited you?"

"Amos Johnson." Rich snorted. "Not a fan?"

"I have to be able to work with any prosecutor," he said. "Some, however, are preferable to others." He paused for a drink. "You ever been around anyone who tried to give themselves a nickname?"

"Actually, yes."

"It never goes well, right? Always seems forced. This guy wants everyone to call him Bulldog." He chuckled. "I don't think anyone does. He even signs his emails with it."

"Pretty sad," I said. A waiter dropped off our pizzas. I used the triangular spatula to put a steaming piece on my plate. A bunch of fantastic aromas washed over me, and my mouth watered as I added a sprinkle of hot pepper flakes. My nose still full of pepperoni, cheese, sauce, and vegetables, I took a bite even though the slice was a little too hot.

Rich put a piece on his plate, eschewed peppers, and fanned it with his hand to cool it. "I think he has an older brother with the FBI or something. Probably trying to keep pace at family gatherings."

"What do you think about the press coverage?"

Rich rolled his eyes. "What a bunch of shit. I know they have to sell papers and get clicks, but come on. Vox Populi? This asshole isn't the voice of any people I want to know."

"I wonder if he gave himself the nickname."

"You think someone at *The Sun* might know who he is?"

"Doubt it," I said. "It probably came in via some anonymous letter to the editor."

"When you give these assholes nicknames," Rich said, "they become bigger. Almost mythical." He finally took a bite. When he shook his head, I figured it wasn't because of the flavor of the pizza. "Sometimes, freedom of the press is overrated."

"Better hope no one quotes you there. *Disgruntled BPD*

Lieutenant Threatens First Amendment." I moved my hand in the air as if displaying the headline.

"Nothing quite so salacious," Rich said with a chuckle. "I know how to offer a good no comment."

"We had reporters come to the office," I said, moving a second slice onto my plate. "Manny got rid of them. I get the feeling they'll come back and stick to the sidewalks."

"You've gotten a lot of press recently."

"More than I've wanted."

"Well, if you have a hand in figuring this shit out, you'll be the most famous PI in the state."

"Does this mean you'll start picking up the tab for dinner?"

Rich grinned. "Let's not get ahead of ourselves."

———

When Rich took his leftovers—leaving me with the check—I ordered a pizza to take home to Gloria.

Considering her lack of aptitude in the kitchen, I figured she hadn't started cooking without me. If I didn't fix dinner, we ordered in from somewhere. Very occasionally, my wife got the urge to cook—often with the help of one or more dishes she'd purchased in advance. I texted her with the dinner plans, picked up her usual pie, paid for everything, and drove it back to my house.

I turned onto the parking pad from the alley running behind this stretch of homes. Gloria's red Mercedes AMG coupe already sat there. If its appearance didn't convey its rocketlike tendencies enough, the red color gave it away. I didn't get to drive it often, but I always enjoyed my times behind the wheel. I walked in the back door. Gloria sat on the couch with her laptop. She smiled as I came in through the kitchen, stood, and kissed me. "How's Rich?"

"Same as ever. A few more gray hairs."

"He ever talk about Jeanne?" Gloria asked. Rich broke up with his girlfriend of a couple years around the holidays—right when we were in the thick of the winter serial killer case. She also worked for the BPD, and I heard she transferred out to the county.

"Not with me." I walked back into the kitchen and set the pizza box on the counter. Gloria followed me, lifted the lid, and inhaled the aromas. "Extra cheese and green peppers. My favorite."

"I know how my wife likes it," I said, adding a lascivious wink.

Her cheeks colored as she got a plate out of a nearby cabinet. "Yes, you do." With two pieces atop the porcelain, we walked back to the living room. I sat next to Gloria on the couch. Mercifully, she didn't bring a knife and fork with her. A few years ago—before I got shot—Gloria changed her diet and eating routine for the tennis tournaments she used to play in. It helped her strength and fitness, and while she didn't compete anymore, the smaller portions and mousy bites remained.

We turned the local news on and caught three stories about the bombings and the person—I mentally presumed a man because they always were—dubbed Vox Populi. "I hate how these killers get names," Gloria said. "The Boston Strangler. The Zodiac Killer. Now, we have Vox Populi. It elevates them."

"Rich and I were discussing the same thing."

"No one takes Latin anymore, so what are the odds the folks reading about this know what Vox Populi even means?"

"There's normally a translation in every article," I said.

"Social media is a big driver of news. 'Populi' looks much more like 'Popular' than 'People.' I wonder if it's planting the wrong kind of seed."

She had a point. For good or for ill—and I felt the latter outweighed the former—social media ended up being how a lot of people got their news and learned what was happening. Of course, they often learned either from a grifter with an agenda or a useful idiot parroting what the grifters were saying. It was an angle I hadn't considered before she mentioned it. "I think those horses are already out of the stable," I said. "No point in closing the barn door now."

"It sucks. I almost wish you weren't involved in this."

I shrugged. "Someone has to help the police get it right."

Gloria took another small bite. She'd managed to eat maybe a third of her first piece. When we ate pizza together, I often finished four slices before she got halfway through her second. "It doesn't need to be you," she said.

"It does. Someone hired us."

"You could decline the case."

"You know I can't."

She bobbed her head and offered a wan smile. "I do. It's what I love about you . . . and sometimes find frustrating."

"Safe cases are boring," I said.

"They also bring you home to your wife every night."

"I haven't missed a night yet."

"I know," Gloria said. "I just have a bad feeling about this one. Your involvement is out there. What if there's a bomb hooked up to your car one morning?"

"I'll start checking it before I leave." My car ended up parked outside no matter where we stayed. Here, we both left our cars on the concrete pad out back. Gloria's house featured a one-car garage, so my S4 sat at the far side of her driveway. If Vox Populi wanted to wire explosives to my engine, he could do it at either location. "Yours, too, when it's here."

"All right." My wife took another small bite. She'd almost made it to the thicker crust at the back. "I hope you can wrap this one up quickly."

"Me, too," I said.

————

As usual, I was up before Gloria the next morning, and I went out for a run.

Things just felt different on the streets of Baltimore. Even when there were no explosions, I liked the vibes of being in the city. From Federal Hill Park, I could look across the harbor and see people walking into nearby buildings like ants herding into a colony. Tiny cars moved along Pratt Street in fits and starts. As I rounded the bend on another lap, I smelled coffee and bread from a nearby bakery. Horns honked a block or so away. The city came alive in a ritual every morning, and I missed it when I hit the streets of Brooklandville.

After showering, dressing, and whipping up a quick breakfast, I packed my bag. Gloria ate eggs at the kitchen table. I kissed her goodbye, promised to be careful when she told me to, and headed out the door. By the time I rolled into the parking lot and walked into the office, it was a few minutes after nine. T.J. did her usual glance at her watch. I shrugged, set my bag down, and poured a cup of coffee. "Traffic?" she asked.

"It wasn't bad. I enjoyed my run this morning."

We did some tandem background work on one of the non-critical cases in our backlog. At the end of about forty-five minutes, I felt T.J. had all the information she would need, and I told her to run with it. "Get Lexi involved, too," I said. "The more she learns this summer, the better. I don't know what her availability will be once the fall semester starts."

Our intern arrived a few minutes later. Lexi and T.J. worked on the other case while I kept digging into Vox Populi. No one jumped out as an obvious suspect, even going back to the families of original victims of the men freed by Judge Black. I really wanted to find an unhinged uncle with twenty years of explosives experience in the military. Of course, if such a person existed, the police would have already discovered him, and the Williams family hired us because the police had come up empty so far.

Three sets of footsteps on the metal stairs interrupted us. "Hired muscle?" Lexi asked.

"No," I said. "The steps are too light. Unless someone sent Charlie's Angels after us."

Sure enough, three women opened the door and walked in. Despite slight differences in hair color, all were some shade of brown, and they shared enough features for me to think they were related. All three came in jean shorts and looked pretty good wearing them. "We're Mikey Granger's family," one of them said. "I'm Monica, she's Madison, and that's Mitzi."

"I'm sensing a theme," I said.

Monica smiled. "Our parents are Marshall and Mary." Mitzi looked away at the mention of the parents' names.

"We're sorry about your brother."

"Thanks." T.J. dug a metal folding chair out of the small

closet. She offered one of the sisters her chair and took the uncomfortable seat for herself. I made a mental note to get a couple padded versions for the occasions we needed over-flow seating. Once we were all huddled around my desk, we got down to business.

"We've been working our way through everyone," I said. "Thanks for coming to see us."

"We don't really have much to tell you," Monica said, continuing to serve as the family spokeswoman. "Our brother wasn't a saint. We know that. We also know he hurt people over the years." Her voice cracked, and tears appeared on all three women's faces as if they'd arranged to start crying at the exact same time. "We can't imagine anyone wanting to kill him, though. Mikey was trying to do better. He didn't have any enemies."

"He got out on a technicality of some sort, right?"

"Yeah," Mitzi said. Her round face marked her as the youngest of the trio. I guessed her to be in her mid-twenties while the others were around my age or a little older. Considering her reaction to their parents' names earlier, I figured Mitzi was either adopted or came from a different mother. The resemblance between the sisters led me to the latter. "Something about witness tampering. His lawyer raised the issue, the judge looked into it, and he cut Mikey loose."

Considering Mikey Granger's status as a fairly low-level repeat offender, actual witness tampering or misconduct seemed unlikely. No one was trying to put a major criminal mastermind away. Still, bringing this up wouldn't help anyone, so I kept it to myself for now. "You told us Mikey didn't have any enemies," I said, "but he'd been arrested quite a few times. It's not unreasonable to think someone wanted to hurt him."

"Hurt him, maybe," Monica said. "Not blow him up."

"What did you come by to tell us?" T.J. asked.

Monica dabbed at her eyes. "I know we'll eventually figure into your investigation. We wanted to talk to you before you came to see us." She let go of a long breath. "We've been fending off the press for days. I don't want to add anyone else to the list of people we're trying to avoid. So here we are. We don't know who would've wanted our brother dead. Some people probably thought he was a career criminal, but we loved him." The last few words came out amid a fresh wave of tears. Lexi passed around the box of tissues.

"Thanks for coming in," I said. "We've had to chase reporters away, too. I think all the press coverage is going to get worse before it gets better."

"They're like sharks," Madison said, pushing her John Lennon glasses higher on her nose. "They smell blood in the water."

"It's definitely a feeding frenzy."

"If you find anything," Monica said, "I'd appreciate you keeping us in the loop. No offense, but we don't want to hear from you or the cops otherwise."

"Even though you're lumping me in with the BPD," I said, "no offense taken." After a short round of farewells, the three sisters left.

"You think they're telling the truth?" T.J. wanted to know.

I nodded. "Probably. Whatever Mikey was to the criminal justice system of Baltimore, he was their brother."

"What's up with the youngest sister?" Lexi said. "The dad totally had an affair."

"She was ten years younger than the other two," I said, "and she didn't seem to like the mention of their parents' names."

T.J. flipped her notebook shut. "None of that matters for our investigation. They came in to pre-emptively tell us they didn't know anything. Seems a little weird."

"Maybe." I shrugged. "People grieve in different ways. Let's rule them out for now. If we hit a long slump, maybe we can circle back."

My secretary sighed. "This is a damn weird case."

"Yes," I agreed, "it is."

CHAPTER 9

A FRESH ROUND of caffeine got the creative juices flowing. "I think we should focus on Judge Black," I told T.J. and the recently-arrived Lexi. "He's the common denominator in all these cases."

"He says he's not some hippie," my assistant said, "but the prevailing opinion of him is even less charitable."

"Cops and prosecutors won't like him." I shrugged. "He's making it harder for them no matter what someone might think about criminals walking out of the courtroom."

"Based on all the Vox Populi coverage," Lexi chimed in, "I'd say public sentiment is against the judge and in favor of the bomber."

"People look at train wrecks and car accidents," I said. "It doesn't mean they want them to happen. What if Judge Black is letting these criminals go for some reason other than a desire to see the state wield its power fairly and correctly?"

"You think he's on the take?" T.J. asked.

"Wouldn't be the first time someone in his position has been. Let's see what we can find out."

We all huddled over our respective keyboards and got to

work. I found a profile on Judge Black dating from shortly after his initial election to the district bench, so about fifteen years ago.

Judge Merrill Black: A New Voice in Baltimore's District Court
By Angela Hines, Staff Writer

BALTIMORE – As Judge Merrill Black takes his seat in the Baltimore District Court, many wonder how his unique background—first as a prosecutor and later as a defense attorney—will shape his approach on the bench. At 38, Judge Black is younger than many of his colleagues, but he brings to his role a breadth of experience that few in Baltimore's judicial system can claim.

For seven years, Black worked as a prosecutor in the city's State's Attorney's Office, developing a reputation as tough but fair, particularly in cases involving violent crime. During this period, Black was known for his methodical approach, his commitment to seeing justice done, and his diligence in bringing offenders to account. Colleagues describe him as "tenacious," "driven," and "relentless," a prosecutor who knew his cases inside and out and pushed for strong sentencing wherever warranted.

Yet after nearly a decade working with the prosecution, Black surprised many by leaving to join the ranks of the defense. The move raised eyebrows among peers and local media, sparking questions about his motivations. Some speculated that the switch was a career pivot, a bid to round out his résumé for a future judgeship. Others wondered if Black felt an obligation to understand the other side of the aisle before rendering judgment on his former colleagues.

For the past four years, Judge Black has defended Baltimore's accused, often taking on cases involving complex criminal matters. As a defense attorney, he represented a wide range of clients, from those charged with low-level drug possession to high-profile cases involving serious felonies. Friends of Black say his time as a defense lawyer made him acutely aware of the challenges and inequalities facing defendants, particularly those who may not have the resources to mount a robust defense.

"It's been important to me to understand the broader picture of justice," Black stated in a recent interview. "The system should work fairly for everyone, no matter which side of the courtroom they're on."

Now, Judge Black faces the challenge of integrating these two professional identities. In theory, his dual background positions him to bring a balanced perspective to the bench, one that acknowledges the need for rigorous enforcement of the law while also protecting the rights of defendants. Yet some critics question how impartial he can truly be, wondering if his years as a prosecutor might bias him in favor of the state—or if his recent defense work has made him too lenient toward those who find themselves on the wrong side of the law.

"Judge Black's experience on both sides is a double-edged sword," notes legal analyst Jordan Russell. "On one hand, he has insight into the challenges both prosecutors and defense attorneys face. On

the other, it's not yet clear where he will ultimately fall in terms of his philosophy on criminal justice."

As he settles into his new role, Baltimore's legal community will be watching to see how Judge Black interprets and applies the law. Will he hold steadfast to his prosecutorial roots, pushing for tough sentences in cases of violent crime, or will his more recent experience as a defense attorney temper his approach? Judge Black himself remains tight-lipped on his approach, insisting that he plans to handle each case as it comes.

In a city deeply divided over issues of crime and punishment, Judge Black's appointment brings both hope and caution. The next few years will likely reveal much about his judicial character. For now, Baltimore's citizens and legal professionals alike can only watch, wait, and wonder which side of the scale Judge Black's gavel will tip.

"He has an interesting background," I said once everyone read the piece. "Considering everything he's been doing, I'm surprised he was a prosecutor."

"There's nothing wonky in his investigation packet," Lexi said. "I just uploaded it."

"How did you find it?" I had a hunch or two—I knew how I would go about it—but I wanted to hear her process.

"The court system keeps things pretty tight. They have to. I searched for files and chose a specific extension . . . first Word and then PDF." She turned up her palms. "Even tight ships can have leaks. Someone didn't lock down those files correctly."

"Good work," I said. Her method was the same as mine. I checked the document she uploaded. Whoever left it available to anyone who can use Google in a semi-clever manner should have been fired. The dossier contained a lot of vital information on the judge. Most importantly, investigators found nothing fishy in his background, interview, or financials. There remained the chance Judge Black deceived whoever looked into him, but from what I could tell, the work was thorough.

"I guess he's not on the take, then," T.J. said. "I was hoping we'd wrap this up quickly. The cops might not have access to that file."

"They can probably get it through proper channels," I said. "Regardless, the judge doesn't seem like the problem. Let's keep digging."

———

Journalists and newscasters have long followed the credo of, "If it bleeds, it leads."

I wasn't sure how this translated to the world of explosions but figured a similar sensibility would carry the day. Sure enough, our city's recent spate of bombings made national news. I imagined Mayor Vincent Davenport grousing about how this would harm both tourism and his reelection chances, though his complaints would almost certainly be in the reverse order.

To see what national scribes had to say about the story, I browsed a popular article.

Baltimore Under Siege: A Wave of Car Bombings Tests City's Legal and Law Enforcement System

BALTIMORE — *In a city already grappling with persistent crime and a complex judicial system, an unprecedented series of car bombings has gripped Baltimore, leaving residents both fearful and outraged. Over the past two weeks, three separate bombings have claimed the lives of convicted criminals, each recently released on legal technicalities. The victims, all former defendants in Baltimore's criminal courts, had served time before being freed due to procedural errors or new evidence, only to meet a violent end within weeks or months of returning to the streets.*

The killings have stoked debate in Baltimore and beyond about justice, public safety, and the role of the courts in maintaining both. Law enforcement officials have confirmed that the bombings are connected but admit they have few leads, describing the devices used as "professional-grade" and noting that each was placed with a level of precision rarely seen in local cases. Local media has dubbed the killer "Vox Populi" —Latin for "Voice of the People"—after a letter to the editor of the <u>Baltimore Sun</u>. The name has caught on quickly in news cycles and online, with locals voicing mixed opinions on whether this is a dangerous vigilante or a twisted folk hero.

The bombings come at a time when Baltimore's judicial system is under renewed scrutiny. Recent coverage has highlighted the track record of Baltimore Circuit Court Judge Merrill Black, known for over-

turning convictions on legal technicalities. Though Judge Black has his defenders, many Baltimoreans feel that the courts' leniency allows too many dangerous individuals to evade justice. "It's bad enough when these guys are let loose again. But now someone's taken matters into their own hands, and everyone's at risk," said one Baltimore resident, expressing a common sentiment among community members who have grown increasingly wary of the city's crime rate.

In the absence of swift police action, families of the victims have taken the unusual step of hiring private investigators to look into the bombings themselves. Though the Baltimore Police Department has not commented on these efforts, sources suggest that the investigators are collaborating with family members frustrated by the pace of the official inquiry. This move has sparked debate among locals over whether these private parties will help or hinder the investigation, with many worried about the lack of regulation and oversight that often accompanies private security work.

At the same time, critics argue that Baltimore law enforcement is stretched too thin to handle such sophisticated crimes, and any outside help should be welcomed. "The police are working hard, but there's only so much they can do," said a source familiar with the situation. "If private investigators can help ease the burden, maybe that's what the city needs right now."

Despite the mounting pressure, officials are urging patience, emphasizing that these attacks require detailed and thorough investigation. "This isn't some-

thing we can rush," said a police spokesperson at a recent press conference. "We're committed to getting to the bottom of this, but it has to be done the right way."

As Baltimore remains on edge, many residents are wondering who will be next—and whether "Vox Populi" will continue to act outside the bounds of the law. The bombings have turned a grim spotlight on the city's criminal justice system and the difficult questions of where justice ends and vigilantism begins. For now, Baltimoreans can only wait, hoping their city doesn't become the stage for another violent act.

I narrowed my eyes as I scanned the paragraph about private investigators—plural—again. At the courthouse, T.J. and I learned we weren't the only gumshoes to pay Judge Black a visit. Considering we'd spoken to the other victims' families and none mentioned hiring anyone, I wondered how involved this other person was. Maybe not at all. Then again, it wasn't like local PIs had a union, and I wouldn't have joined or attended any meetings if they did. If another sleuth walked the mean streets looking for the same clues I hunted for, I'd be none the wiser.

I forwarded the article to T.J. and Lexi. "I know what we heard at the court, but you think someone else is working the case, too?" my assistant wondered a few minutes later.

"Do you know anyone who works for another investigator?"

She snorted. "It's not like we go out for martinis every week."

"Every two weeks?" I said.

"I've never met another PI's *executive* assistant." I heard her emphasis on the penultimate word there but didn't say anything about it. We ordered lunch while we worked, and a cheery fellow delivered our sandwiches and homemade chips about a half-hour later. He smiled a little too much when Lexi answered the door, grinned even more when T.J. came to take a bag, and lingered just a moment too long when the ladies closed up shop.

We'd recently finished our sandwiches when more footsteps came up the stairs. These were heavier, and sure enough, two large men walked through the door and stared us down.

———

"No comment," I said.

"What?" the one closer to me asked. Both were taller than yours truly and at least half again as wide. Both looked to be in their early twenties, and I wondered if the blond who stood nearer to me even started shaving yet. His dark-haired friend sported a goatee dyed bright red for reasons known only to him.

"We're not speaking to reporters," I clarified. Behind me, I heard the girls shift their positions. T.J. usually stayed away from any rumbles in the office, but a light pair of footsteps moved closer. I figured it was Lexi, and I hoped she didn't have a gun out right now. We didn't need to send a pair of goons away with gunfire.

"We look like the fucking press?" the one with the interesting facial hair demanded.

"I hate to make assumptions," I said, "but if you want me to figure you're a pair of idiots doing the bidding of some asshole, I'm okay with it." They stood behind one another in the sort of central aisle formed by the gaps between everyone's desks and the coffee station.

Blondie apparently couldn't live with me besmirching his character because he rushed forward. I blocked three punches, backed him off with a short jab, then put him down with a left cross and right elbow to the jaw. As he covered his face, the light danced on his expensive watch. Not something I'd seen on the wrists of many enforcers before.

I stepped over the fallen goon as the other one readied himself for my advance. He threw the first punch, and I let him, as I preferred playing defense early. You can learn a lot watching how people strike. Some don't turn their hips and get enough power from their legs. Others go on a flurry but tire themselves out quickly. This guy fell more into the latter camp. Standing closer to him, I could see he carried more weight than the man currently on the floor. I questioned him while I still had the chance. "Who sent you?"

"Piss off," he grunted.

"Did the bomber tell you to come and try to discourage us?" He frowned but offered no verbal response. Even if Vox Populi put them up to it, these two idiots might not know the man who gave them their orders had also murdered three people. When my larger foe's punches slowed, I deflected one more, backed away enough to give me room to throw a kick, and put my shoe right in his gut.

When Red Goatee folded in half, I gave him an elbow above the ear and snapped his head back with a knee to the face. He dropped to the carpet. Behind me, I heard the sounds of a renewed skirmish and turned to see Lexi squaring off against the much larger blond muscleman. Even as I moved toward them, she showed me she didn't really need my help by punting him first in the balls, then the gut, and a final under the chin to send him horizontal again.

I offered the intern an appreciative nod before turning my attention back to the groaning goons. "This is the part where you tell us whose bidding you're doing."

"Go to hell," the goateed one said.

"Have it your way." I hauled him to his feet. "Stairs hurt a lot more going down. Sure you don't want to talk?" His stony silence spoke for him. We got to the door, and I made sure to ram his face into the frame. While he shook his head to clear the cobwebs, I guided him through and gave him a hard shove. He went head over heels at least once on the way to street level and landed with his left arm pinned under his body at a strange angle.

"He might need a cast," I said as I approached the other. "How about you? You going to be smarter than him?"

"I'm not saying shit," he grumbled.

"Did your benefactor buy your fancy jewelry?" Before he could cover his arm, I kicked him in the gut, grabbed his hand, and took the watch from his wrist. The metal band was a mix of gold and silver, the face black and more gold. "A Movado Eight Hundred," I said. "I had one of these in college. They must be fourteen hundred dollars or more by now." I crouched and saw his sour expression from a little closer. "You don't seem very good at intimidating people, so I don't think you bought this with your leg-breaking money." I turned it over and saw an inscription on the back. *KK, graduation day.* "Nice grad gift. I'm sure Mom and Dad are proud of your career choice." I snapped a photo of the timepiece but held onto it.

"Fuck you," he said and sat up. "Gimme my watch back."

"You want it?" I walked toward the door. A quick glance showed the other goon still lying in the same position. Occasionally, I wondered what happened if someone walked in the main entrance to Manny's shop, looked through the door on the right, and saw some big oaf splayed out. "I wonder if you'll pick up your watch or your friend first." Despite Blondie's protests, I drew my hand back and fired the Movado toward the ground floor. It landed near the fallen man, and the tinkling sound it made told me it did not survive the trip intact.

"Goddammit." He hustled past me and down the steps.

"You show your faces around here again," I called down, "and a lot more than your fucking watch will get broken." I closed the door in time to see T.J. and Lexi exchange a high-five. "Nice strikes back there."

"Thanks," our intern said. "I've been taking kickboxing for a few years now." She jutted her chin toward the door as an engine coughed and revved outside. Screeching tires told me our two would-be goons were beating a hasty retreat. "What the hell was that?"

"Welcome to someone trying to get us to back off."

"It ever work?"

"No," I said.

CHAPTER 10

KK, *graduation day.*

I looked at the inscription in the photo. A swirl of possibilities served as the response to what the initials KK might stand for. T.J. posed it anyway. "Part of this job is challenging assumptions," I said. My secretary had heard this more than once, but I went into it for Lexi's benefit. "We can assume the Movado belongs to the goon we just sent packing, and this makes his initials KK. What if it's not his?"

"How?" Lexi wondered.

"Maybe he took it from someone. These two weren't very good, but their tough guy act will work against easy marks. He could have taken it from someone as part of roughing him up or shaking him down."

"Now, you're assuming the big idiot has done this before," T.J. pointed out.

I nodded. "I am. You can't avoid presuming things not in evidence. It's part of the job. You just can't get attached to a particular theory because it's convenient."

"Most likely, though, it's his watch," Lexi said.

"Most likely, yes." We all looked at the photo on one of

my monitors. "The metal is in good condition, so the watch is either new or he takes good care of it. At the risk of making more assumptions, I get the impression these two didn't make the dean's list anywhere, so the fancy timepiece is a high school graduation gift."

"Nice one, too," Lexi said.

"What did you get?"

"My dad helped me buy my car, and we fixed it up together."

"Probably cost more than the Movado."

She bobbed her head. "More useful, too."

"I don't think these guys are very old," T.J. added. "Definitely younger than twenty-five. Regardless of academics, these two may not be old enough to graduate college. They could still attend for all we know."

"Not many people in their line of work wear fifteen-hundred dollar watches," I said. "They either can't afford them, or they don't want to risk their valuable stuff when any day might require you to do something dangerous."

Lexi crossed her arms. "He had other nice stuff. When you were hauling him toward the door, I saw a Hilfiger logo on his jeans."

"Damn. I'm starting to like this guy now."

The intern rolled her eyes. "We get any pictures of these two?"

"No. There's a security system for the whole building. I basically configured it for Manny. When we're here, it's offline, so it's not taking photos."

"Maybe we need something else, then. Even a basic camera above the door."

"Good idea," I said. "They didn't do so well today, so whoever sent them might ask them to come back."

"If they come armed, I'm prepared," Lexi said.

"Excellent. As the intern, you get to clean up the blood." I stared at the photo again. Showing it to local jewelers and pawn shop owners might turn up a hit. Even if it did, however, knowing who bought it didn't necessarily connect us to the man blowing people up. I filed it away as an avenue to pursue if we got stuck. With three of us able to make the rounds, we could cover quite a few businesses in a single day. "The watch isn't getting us anywhere right now," I said. "Let's see what else we might be able to find."

———

"Found something new, boss."

Lexi looked up from her laptop and smiled. We'd been plugging away for a couple hours. Our intern would need to leave soon, and I wanted to have dinner at home with my wife one of these nights. "What is it?"

"Interesting blog post from a couple days ago. I'll send it to you." The link appeared in my inbox, and clicking on it took me to an online journal called *Silent Operator*. The layout was garish, with the theme apparently chosen by someone who was both a masochist and colorblind. Reds, black, and camo patterns dominated the page. The text was in white because of course it was. If I didn't run the risk of sounding so old, I might have complained about my eyes hurting trying to read it.

———

***"Justice Served: Baltimore Bombings Send
a Clear Message"***
By ShadowBravoSix

Listen up, America. It's time to face some hard truths about what's happening in Baltimore. I'm not a cop, a lawyer, or a judge. I'm a retired soldier who spent decades learning how to handle threats, eliminate them, and make sure the bad guys never got up again. And when I see what's going on in Baltimore, I can't say I'm disappointed. Quite the opposite—I'm relieved. Finally, someone's taking action.

Three criminals have been blown off the streets by these recent car bombs. Literally. These aren't your average everyday scumbags, either. We're talking about convicted felons—drug dealers, drunk drivers, parasites who should have rotted behind bars. But no, they managed to slither their way out thanks to so-called "legal technicalities." Good old Judge Black and his merry band of bleeding-heart defenders seem to think these "technicalities" are worth letting killers, dealers, and destroyers back into our neighborhoods. It's pathetic. So, if the courts won't keep these people where they belong, I'm glad someone's stepping up and making sure justice still gets served.

People in this city are afraid, and who can blame them? The law is more interested in protecting the guilty than protecting our families. This so-called "Vox Populi" vigilante is doing what we all know needs to be done but most of us are too afraid to admit out loud. They're taking the kind of decisive action that's long overdue. Car bombs may be extreme, but let's be real: these scumbags didn't deserve to slip back into their old lives like nothing happened. Explosions don't leave room for appeals or "technicalities." There's no loophole or sympathetic judge waiting at

*the end of a detonator's wire. Just justice—quick, effec-
tive, and final.*

*Now, I can hear the faint-hearted whining from
here: "But what if an innocent person gets hurt?"
Newsflash: innocent people have been getting hurt for
years because of guys like these! You think a couple of
criminals popping off in a parking lot is some tragedy?
Tell that to the families destroyed by their drugs, their
guns, and their violence. Baltimore's on fire already—
someone just decided to control the burn.*

*So, to Vox Populi, if you're reading this: Keep up
the good work. This city's been begging for real justice
for years, and it looks like you're the only one with the
guts to deliver.*

ShadowBravoSix, signing off.

"Well," I said when I finished, and it looked like T.J. did
as well.

"Maybe it's him," Lexi suggested. "The wink-wink stuff
about 'Vox Populi, if you're reading.'"

"It could be." I shrugged. "It's more likely whoever wrote
this is nuttier than the Planters factory."

"Both could be true," T.J. chimed in.

"Fair enough." I turned to our intern. "It's a hideous blog
which doesn't appear to feature any obvious signs of attribu-
tion. I'll bet I could figure out who's behind it in under a half-
hour. How about you?"

"Might take me a little longer." Lexi grinned. "I'm up for
the challenge, though."

"Go for it." My email dinged again. T.J. forwarded me

two calendar invites for meetings happening in about ten minutes. "What are these?"

"Clients coming in to pay their bills." She put a hand up and spoke over my follow-up question. "Yes, I sent them the link to pay online. Some people still love writing checks."

Lexi snorted. "My dad's one of those people."

"As long as we're getting paid," I said, kicking my feet up onto the desk. "I'm not the one who goes to the bank anymore. What a waste of time."

"I do it online . , , and we might use the money better if we brought in another investigator or two."

"Too much management overhead," I said. "The two of you are the limit of what I can handle."

The pair glanced at each other and snickered. I knew what they were thinking, so I didn't bother asking.

———

The first clients—a nice couple who looked like age peers of my parents—stopped by a few minutes after T.J.'s heads-up. They were concerned about their daughter and young grandson who had apparently cut off communication with no prior notice or warning. I found them and delivered the agreed-upon message as promised. Anything else was out of my hands, and I made sure the clients knew this. Lines of communication were now frosty but open.

"Thank you," the woman said, her eyes welling.

"I had a falling out with my parents a few years ago," I said. After I got shot, they ended the successful arrangement of their foundation funding my cases with no fee for clients. Since then, I'd greatly overhauled my business model to be more traditional, and most of the ice fell away from my relationship with Mom and Dad.

Most.

"What happened?"

"We're in a pretty good place now." I smiled. "Let's just say they objected to some of the dangers of the job. It doesn't matter. I'm glad your daughter is open to talking to you again." They settled their bill and left. I endorsed the check, and T.J. would take it to the bank in the morning.

"They were nice," she said, "but I'm glad we looked into them first." I had no problem helping a couple try to re-establish ties with their daughter—unless the daughter fled for the kinds of reasons no one wants to think about. A couple hours of research convinced my secretary and me our prospective clients were on the up-and-up.

The next clients who stopped in were a little younger and clad in fancier clothes. Their case was one of cyber stalking. Some ruffian kept harassing the wife, I figured out who he was pretty quickly, and the stalking stopped under threat of a legal action. While I would miss out on the chance to wear an Armani in court, the swift resolution benefited everyone. The couple thanked us profusely, T.J. collected their check, and the total of both would keep the lights on and the juice flowing for another year or more.

"Not bad additions to the bottom line," T.J. said.

"Are you angling for a Christmas bonus already?"

"*Angling* is a little strong." She grinned. "Let's just say I'm making sure you're aware the holiday is coming."

"Sure," I said, "in six months and three weeks."

"I have something," Lexi said. We huddled around her screen. "The writer is ex-Army. I have my dad's credentials, so I was able to do a little digging. This is an unclassified and redacted file, but I think we can conclude he has some experience with explosives."

I scanned the record of former Staff Sergeant Joseph Thormann. While he did work with bombs, he specialized in disabling them and rendering them inert. This probably meant he knew how to make something blow up, of course. Still, it was a leap from being on the Army's version of the bomb squad in Iraq to a vigilante killing people in Baltimore a decade later. "What do you think?" Lexi wanted to know when T.J. and I finished reading and straightened up.

"Maybe," I said.

"Maybe?"

"I'd say he has the relevant knowledge. At the risk of sounding like an acting coach, though, what's his motivation?"

"Haven't gotten that far yet," Lexi said.

"We might be able to find something," T.J. added.

"Another late night with pizza and gossiping about boys?" I said.

Lexi snorted. "Could you be any more cringe?"

"Probably. I try to go for both sus and cringe at the same time. We can call it *singe*."

I snapped my fingers. "Get it trending on TikTok. I want royalties starting tomorrow."

"Okay, boomer."

I headed back to my own desk. "Anyway, if you want to look into this guy a little more, go ahead. I'm going to try and have dinner with my wife. Don't land yourselves in trouble."

"We won't," T.J. said, and the two young women shared a look.

"Why don't I believe you?"

They remained silent as I slung my bag over my shoulder and headed for the door.

CHAPTER 11

"COME ON," T.J. said. "We can sit outside his house."

Lexi pursed her lips. "I don't know."

"You know who this guy is, right?"

"Yeah."

"And his address?"

"Yeah."

"Let's go, then. What is he . . . twenty-five minutes away?"

"Probably a half-hour in traffic," Lexi said.

"Whatever," T.J. said. "I'll drive."

Lexi remained still for a minute, and then a smile slowly spread over her face. "Fine. I'm in. It beats doing a pile of the usual intern work."

T.J. took her keys out of her purse and pressed a button on the fob. The Mustang fired up in the parking lot. "I got the remote start added a couple months ago," she said. "The car really didn't have any options. It got used for rentals before I bought it. With summer coming up, I want the AC to run before I get in."

"Makes sense. I wish I could get it sometimes. It's hard to add something like that to a manual."

The two climbed into the freshly-cool Mustang and headed down Eastern Avenue. Including a trip through a McDonald's drive-through, they arrived in northeast Baltimore about thirty-five minutes later. Thormann lived on Gardenwood Road, a side street off of Cedonia Avenue. The houses were duplexes and all stood on one side of the road. The opposite side was a large field with two baseball diamonds, a couple marked soccer pitches, and a playground. Thormann's address—5426—was about halfway along the street. T.J. curbed the car in front of 5422. She would have preferred to stop on the other side, but with no other cars there, her Mustang would have stood out for reasons other than its yellow color.

Lexi pulled a laptop from her bag. An additional card mounted on the side showed tiny flashing red and green LEDs. "It uses cellular," she said. "As far as I know, my dad's old company still pays the bill. The service has never stopped working."

"What are you trying to do?" T.J. wanted to know.

"A couple things. I want to see if he's posted anything else. The blog I found generated a lot of reactions . . . way above what his posts normally get. I also want to find out if he's home. There are a couple lights on, but that doesn't mean anything."

"The laptop will tell you if there's traffic going out his router?"

Lexi nodded, and her auburn ponytail shimmied. "Even if he's just watching something on a streaming service, I can pick it up. Most traffic is encrypted these days, but I'm not trying to break into anything." She paused, and T.J. watched as a couple application windows popped up, and colored bars filled one of them. "He's definitely home and online."

T.J. returned her attention to the house. "You think he's the guy?"

"I hope not."

"Why?"

Lexi sighed. "I was pretty young when my dad retired from the Army. I think I was ten. I remember him going overseas at least once. When he got out . . . he was different. He did four combat deployments. At least eight years in different warzones all around Afghanistan. I can't imagine how many times he got shot at, kicked in a door, killed someone. It wears on you. No matter who you are, it wears on you."

"He came back with PTSD," T.J. said. It wasn't a question.

"Yeah. At first, he just seemed kind of . . . withdrawn, I guess. Like, I would see him, but it didn't seem like he was all the way there. My parents were split up at this point, and I know now that my mom was trying to turn me against him." She let out a humorless chuckle. "What a piece of work she turned out to be. Anyway, I remember her saying my dad was crazy. The war turned him into a lunatic."

"Jesus Christ."

"Things were bad between them," Lexi acknowledged. "I didn't see any of what she tried to tell me. He was a little different, but he was still my dad. I knew he wasn't a nut. Even then, I could tell. Eventually, he found the right therapist at the VA and got into a painting program. It lets him get all the stuff in his head out onto a page. He still does it, and he's even a little less protective of the output than he used to be." She sighed. "My point is . . . lots of people come back different. War changes you, and not everybody gets the help they need. I hope this guy isn't the killer because I don't want him to become another grim statistic about former soldiers."

T.J. didn't know what to say. "Wow. Your dad seems so well-adjusted and . . . even."

"He's way better now." She chuckled. "He can shoot a bunch of people and doesn't always need to sit down with his watercolors later. I'm really proud of the progress he's made." Her voice cracked. "I probably should tell him that one of these days."

"I'm sure he knows." T.J. patted Lexi's left hand and got a small smile in return.

Lexi wiped at her eyes and got back to the laptop. "We're here for surveillance. Might as well surveil."

———

"Wow, he just made a new post."

Lexi pointed at the screen, and T.J. leaned in to see. The app showed traffic going out over port 443—which T.J. knew was the encrypted way to reach the Internet—to the man's blogging platform. "I hope he didn't double down because his last entry ended up being popular," T.J. said.

Lexi opened a browser and visited Thormann's blog.

I Said What I Said: Baltimore Needs Justice, Not Sympathy
By ShadowBravoSix

Well, it looks like my last post hit a nerve. Some of you are cheering me on, saying "Finally, someone gets it." And to those folks, I say thank you. You know what it means to stand up for justice. But then, we've got the other half—the hand-wringers, the faint-hearted, the "moral authorities" telling me that I'm unhinged or out of line for supporting what's happening in Baltimore. To all of you, here's my response: I said what I said, and I stand by every word.

Look, I'm not here to sing "Kumbaya" and pretend like everything's fine. Our so-called justice system is broken. We've got criminals walking free, slinking back into society like they're reformed, all because of some "technical oversight" or bleeding-heart judge. The lives they destroyed? The families they left in shambles? Guess that doesn't matter much when there's a loophole to exploit, huh? Well, if the courts won't deliver justice, then maybe it's time we admit we're glad someone else will.

For those whining about "due process," let me ask you this: where was the due process for the people who had to pick up the pieces after these criminals ripped their lives apart? Where's the justice for the kids who got hooked on drugs? For the innocent people whose lives were ruined by their violence or recklessness? These are people who were found guilty, convicted by a jury, and now they're back out on the streets because some judge has a soft spot for technicalities. Tell me, how is that fair?

I know the critics are saying I'm endorsing vigilantism. Well, maybe I am. Perhaps it's time we admit that Baltimore—and cities like it—need more than sympathy and empty promises from their so-called leaders. You call Vox Populi a vigilante; I call them a warrior. They're delivering what we've been waiting for while everyone else wrings their hands, schedules vigils, and does nothing of consequence.

To those who support me, know this: we're on the same team, and I appreciate every message, every like, every share. To the critics, here's a little advice: you don't have to read what I write. Stick your head back in the sand, pretend the world is nice and safe, and leave the hard truths to those of us who can handle them.

This city needs action, not excuses. If you don't like it, then maybe you're part of the problem.

ShadowBravoSix, signing off—still here, still unfiltered.

"So much for not doubling down," T.J. said and sighed.

"Still doesn't mean he's guilty," Lexi pointed out. "He likes a vigilante's approach. That's a little disturbing, but it doesn't mean our guy here is a criminal."

"I know you don't want him to be."

"I don't . . . for a bunch of reasons, really . . . but the personal one is because it'll make for a really shitty conversation with my dad."

"I think it's time we figure this guy is a person of interest," T.J. said, trying to keep her tone gentle. "It would be stupid for the killer to write a blog series praising himself, but we've all read or seen stories of murderers who got too impressed with their own handiwork. The arsonist who's always at the scene of a fire he started. That sort of shit."

"I know," Lexi said in a small voice. "You're right." She clicked on the *Reply* option below the post.

"What are you doing?" T.J. wondered.

"What I hope someone would do for my dad if the roles were different." Lexi's fingers flew over the keyboard as she typed a reply.

You don't know me, but I'm the daughter of a soldier. Your post is getting attention, and it might be the kind you don't want. People are starting to take an interest in what you write, and they might come around asking questions. Think what you want about what's happening, but you're putting yourself on the investigative radar here.

"If he's the guy," T.J. said, "you might have just tipped him off."

"I don't think he's the killer," Lexi said.

"Even though we need to check him out, I don't, either. We'd better hope we're right."

Lexi chuckled. "We definitely can't tell our boss about this little trip."

"We can't. I even paid with my own debit card at McDonald's. Last time, he knew we got pizza because I used the company card."

"Does he let you do much investigating?"

"Some," T.J. said. "When I started, I was just the secretary. He didn't have systems in place for *anything*, so I had to build all that. Once I finished, he started working with me on the easier aspects of what he does. I've definitely learned some things. I'll do background work and help out with the online parts of our investigations. Sometimes, we interview people together. If he thinks something might be dangerous, though, C.T. goes by himself. You've heard him say his name is on the door, so he takes the risks, right?"

"Yeah," Lexi said. "Sounds like he wouldn't approve of our little trip."

Another light went on in Thormann's house, and a bulb on the porch soon glowed. T.J. started the car as the front door opened. "Shit," she muttered. She wondered if the man had any cameras or simply spotted them from a window. Without tinted windows, he could have seen through the windshield into a car—one not regularly parked on his street. T.J. hoped the former soldier wasn't armed as she threw the car in drive and hit the gas. No bullets chased the vehicle as it accelerated from the spot toward the intersection at Cedella Avenue.

CHAPTER 12

ON FRIDAY MORNING, I hit the decidedly not-mean streets of Brooklandville for a morning run.

It was scenic in its own way, far more manicured hedge and pine tree chic than the awakening city vibe I enjoyed in Baltimore. Here, the area woke up with the sounds of landscaping equipment and crews hollering at one another in Spanish. The nearest coffee shops and eateries were too far away for their aromas to carry to the pavement surrounding Gloria's house. I headed back inside after about three miles and did another half-hour with weights.

Once I finished, I drank water in the kitchen. Gloria's enormous stainless steel fridge dispensed cold water and ice cubes measuring precisely one inch in all directions. Considering how much she paid for it, I hoped the water came from unicorn tears. It tasted like what came out of my tap in Federal Hill, so I doubted it. My wife walked into the kitchen still wearing her pajamas. Both the top and shorts were small and tight enough on her to be interesting. She held her nose and theatrically fanned her hand in front of her. "Pee-yew!"

"You get your tickets yet?" I asked.

"To what?"

I set my glass down, flexed my bicep, and slapped it with my other hand. "To the gun show."

Gloria chuckled. "I must have missed the deadline."

"Great seats are still available."

"You need a shower," my wife said.

"If you come with me, I can hook you up with a back-stage pass."

She grinned. "How can I say no to such a unique offer?" We headed upstairs. When we came down later, dressed in proper clothes for the day, I hit the button on the coffee machine and started the process of brewing a pot. I'd definitely be late and catch the side-eye from my secretary this morning, but I had a very good excuse. While the magic morning juice dripped into the pot, I scrambled a few eggs and made toast. Gloria and I ate together at her dining room table. "How's the case coming along?" she asked.

"Slowly. We don't really have a suspect yet."

"Anything promising?"

"Not really," I said. "I'd like to catch a break before someone else goes boom."

"I still don't like you working on this one."

"Rich says I'll be the most famous PI in the state if I can crack it." My wife's expression didn't change. This factoid would not win her over to my side. "I'm already the most photogenic. Might as well have the recognition to go with it."

"You don't want to be famous," she said.

"Depends how much I can charge for autographs."

She smiled, and it was good to see considering how nervous I knew she was about this case. "You're still checking your car?"

"And yours when it's at my house."

"I hope you don't have to much longer," Gloria said.

"If I make enough money selling autographed photos," I said, "we can outsource it."

Gloria shook her head, and we finished breakfast.

———

When I walked through the office door at nine-twenty, I caught a serious case of the hairy eyeball from T.J.

"If you keep practicing, you might be able to see behind yourself," I said.

"I'm going to start coming in late, too."

I shrugged. "I've never required you to be here at eight-thirty every day." She didn't say anything else, so I set my bag down and pored myself a mug of coffee. "Anything new and interesting?"

"No," T.J. said, and I thought she answered a touch too quickly. I left her and Lexi here alone last night. The two of them probably got mixed up in something under the guise of helping the investigation. T.J. looked fine physically. She wore short sleeves and khaki capris, and I couldn't see any injuries on her. Her face featured the usual minimal makeup she favored. Before I could inquire further, a single set of footsteps came up the stairs.

I opened the desk drawer and put my hand on the gun as the door opened. Rich walked in. He noticed my hand and cocked an eyebrow. "Expecting someone else?"

"You can never be too careful."

"Pretty sure you don't need artillery," he said.

"I don't know. Some of your brethren are really pushy when they ask for donations to the Police Athletic League."

Rich rolled his eyes, I shut the drawer again, and my cousin poured coffee into a disposable cup while he and T.J. exchanged morning pleasantries.

Once we all had our morning beverages, Rich dropped onto one of my guest chairs. "I talked to Judge Black again," he said.

"And?"

"And he's not changing how he does things. He's still going to be a stickler for getting things right. I respect it, even if I think he takes it a little far sometimes. It's a good reminder to my detectives about getting the details right . . . including the paperwork side of things."

"I'm sure they're thrilled," I said, and T.J. snickered.

Rich's expression suggested he added a generous pour of lemon juice to his coffee. "You making any progress on finding a suspect?"

"We have a lead or two."

"A lead? Wow. You must have watched some cop shows recently. Next, you're going to start talking about vics and perps." T.J. snickered again. I did not appreciate the neutrality of her amusement in the moment.

"Who are you looking at?" I asked, not taking Rich's bait.

He shrugged. "Just a guy. He might be a rabble rouser . . . or he might be the killer. He seems very complimentary of Vox Populi and wants him to keep going." Like me, Rich presumed our bomber was a man. Considering the statistics on these types of killers, it was a more than reasonable guess.

I shrugged. "Even assholes have fans. An unfortunately large number of people seem to endorse vigilantism right now. They're not all killers."

"No, but this guy has the experience someone would need."

"Military?"

"Yep," Rich said.

Before I could answer, T.J. chimed in. "He could just be a soldier who's still adjusting to life after his service."

When Rich remained silent, I added, "Not everyone gets a job with the police right away." Following a decade in the Army—and a medical discharge following a knee injury—Rich landed with the BPD shortly after coming home.

My cousin narrowed his eyes. "I'm well aware. I was lucky. A lot of men and women I know weren't. You think I want it to be some ex-soldier? The reality is the guy makes for a good suspect. We're looking into him." His eyes flicked to T.J. "Maybe you already have, too. We don't have to be in agreement on this."

"It sounds circumstantial," T.J. said.

I pointed in her direction. "I'm not the only one watching *Chicago P.D.* reruns."

"Whatever." Rich finished his java with a big swig, got up, and tossed the cup in a wastebasket. "I guess we'll see what the investigation turns up. Thanks for the coffee."

I harbored no plans to say, "You're welcome," but Rich opened the door and left before I could have.

———

A suspicion nagged at me as we got back to work.

When I left yesterday afternoon, T.J. and Lexi gave me the impression they were going to dig into Joseph Thormann AKA ShadowBravoSix. I knew Lexi had a soft spot for ex-soldiers, so her sympathies were easy to predict. My assistant, on the other hand, was supposed to be the unbiased one who asked questions and dug for the truth. This morning, she seemed happy to write Thormann off as a suspect and steer Rich toward someone—anyone—else.

What happened?

I looked up a few things and then asked her as much. "What do you mean?" T.J. wanted to know.

"You've done a one-eighty on this guy. Yesterday, you and Lexi were going to look into him because he was at least a person of interest. This morning, you're trying to nudge Rich away from him."

My secretary shrugged. "I guess we're figuring he didn't do it."

"Out of the blue?" I pressed.

Her shoulders bobbed again. "Lexi and I did a little more research."

"I thought you did." I went back to a different tab on my browser and read what I found. "You don't know me, but I'm the daughter of a soldier. Your post is getting attention, and it might be the kind you don't want. People are starting to take an interest in what you write, and they might come around asking questions. Think what you want about what's happening, but you're putting yourself on the investigative radar here. It's a reply to a new post on Thormann's blog, and it's signed with the handle LotusTesla."

"So?"

"Someone could be a fan of electric vehicles and British sports cars," I allowed. "The other possibility is it's a joint *nom de plume* for an assistant who likes getting into trouble sometimes and the daughter of a car guy. L.T. for Lexi and T.J."

"Could be lieutenant," she said.

"Do you know how many Army lieutenants are women?"

"No idea."

"About twenty-three percent," I said. "I looked it up because I thought you might try to deflect. My guess is the odds of this coming from the two of you are a lot higher than twenty-three percent." T.J. didn't say anything. "We'd better hope he's not the guy. You might have given him a heads-up."

T.J. sighed. "Fine. It was us."

"I know. Lexi's soft spot for this guy is understandable, but I expect you to try and find the truth even if it's uncomfortable. I also expect you to fess up when I've caught you doing something questionable."

"Sorry," T.J. said, pursing her lips. "Lexi told me things about her dad and how getting out of the service was for him. I hope Thormann's not the guy, and we don't think he is."

"Whatever your opinion, he makes a convenient suspect. The cops are going to—" The sound of a distant explosion made me stop talking. T.J. and I looked at each other and then both rushed to the window bisecting the wall behind my desk. To the west, a plume of dark smoke twisted toward the sky like a malevolent snake slithering away from a kill.

"Another bomb?" T.J. asked in a quiet voice.

"Hard to say for certain, but I think so, yeah."

We kept staring out the window in silence. I wanted to mention how important it was for Joseph Thormann not to be Vox Populi now, but it seemed unnecessary. T.J.'s loud breathing told me the same thoughts were occupying her mind.

CHAPTER 13

THE EXPLOSION ORIGINATED from the neighborhoods near the Camden Yards stadium complex.

We watched coverage on one of the local news stations. They interrupted a game show to air a special report. Two solemn anchors sat at the desk while a reporter covered the evolving story from the field. Behind her, smoke still rose even as the fire department doused the car and two nearby houses to which the flames spread. As before, the unfortunate person in the vehicle—it looked like the blackened husk of an SUV—was charred and dead. Despite nearby property damage, reports suggested no one else sustained an injury.

"Just wait," I said. "People who are supporting this asshole will take it to mean he's carefully planning these attacks to not cause any other casualties."

"It's just luck," T.J. said.

I nodded. "Probability is wasted on the stupid. Everything's a conspiracy when you don't know how shit works and can't do high school math. A woman got hurt in the first bombing. I was there. Her head was bleeding, and she had a concussion. Someone else in a nearby house got hit by flying glass when their window blew in. Nothing serious, but there's another example of luck. This killer doesn't care about anyone else. Luck runs out at some point."

"You're concerned he's going to get made into some kind of hero."

"He already is," I said. "The name was the first step. Now, people who are inclined to support him will latch onto every positive nugget they can and ignore everything else. It's how myths get made."

T.J. didn't say anything else, which was fine with me. The whole topic made me salty, and I really didn't want to keep the conversation going. The on-site reporter said the SUV in question was parked on a pad behind the house. Besides a simple chain-link fence, the property also had a cinder block wall separating much of the backyard from the alley. The blast decimated the partition, but the wall absorbed a lot of damage which might have other-wise spread. A few flying cinder blocks wreaked some havoc, but the situation could have been a great deal worse.

We watched the coverage a little while longer. At some point, with a paucity of new information coming in, everyone started going over the same things. I muted the feed. "We've already seen reporters here," I said.

"No doubt we will again," T.J. grumbled. "They'll probably confine themselves to the sidewalk, but still."

"If this asshole gets painted as a hero in some circles, we'll be the people trying to stop him from doing the Lord's work in the eyes of a few . . . interesting characters."

"What are you saying?"

"You might want to see if you can join your BFF in getting a carry permit."

T.J. blew out a long breath. "Let's hope it doesn't come to that."

"I'm sure we could make it happen," I said.

"I know we'll be seen as unpopular. The cops would bear the brunt of it first, though. Right?"

I shrugged. "Maybe. They're more visible, but people also expect them to be armed. Killing a cop also provokes a disproportionate response. We're a private investigative office. Muscleheads can wander in the door and hurl threats around."

"We might need to start locking it," T.J. said.

"Yeah. Let's do it and get a camera. We'll screen our entries . . . at least until this case is wrapped up." I unmuted the news long enough to hear the same information for at least the third time. "We need to know more about what happened today."

T.J. returned to her desk. "Who the victim is would be a good start. Maybe he's another guy who went before Judge Black and got his conviction tossed."

"I think the judge will have a docket full of questions to answer if the pattern holds again," I said.

The pattern held again.

Sean Boyle made it forty-three trips around the sun when similar men in his chosen profession died earlier. He got arrested on numerous occasions for buying and selling stolen guns, and while he wasn't operating on the scale of arming some overseas rebellion, the weapons he put or kept on the streets definitely got used by people to do bad things. Somehow, Boyle got convicted only three times. The second should have ensured he only left prison on a slab, but instead, he got out in eight years.

To the shock of no one, Boyle went back to his old ways and got popped again. This resulted in his third conviction—one overturned by Judge Black on the grounds of something wonky in the surveillance requests. This seemed like something to chide police or prosecutors for but not to let a dangerous criminal like Boyle back onto the streets. Even if he wanted to start arming the gangs and criminals of Baltimore again, a car bomb cut his efforts short.

"This guy was a grade-A asshole," I said as I read a recent news story while T.J. drove us to the courthouse. "Getting people like this off the streets permanently is going to keep our killer popular."

"What about the judge?"

"He'll get seen as some bleeding heart who wants to let the worst of the worst back into society."

"Sounds like he could be a target," she said.

"It's one of the reasons I want to talk to him again."

"The police have to know he's on the killer's radar."

"I'm sure they do," I said. "However, people hire us to fill in gaps the cops can't cover. Who knows? This might be one of them."

Once T.J. parked the Mustang as close as we could get, we made our way into the courthouse. I could hear the buzz of conversations even before we got to the shared office area Judge Black used. Several uniformed officers milled about, talking into their chest-mounted radios and trying to look both busy and important. Carrying clipboards would have completed the look. My ID allowed me to remain in the area, though the officers were leery of letting us into Judge Black's office until the man himself blessed the endeavor.

"We'll be all right," he said as he shooed out the last cop. "I've talked to Mister Ferguson before."

Fabian the clerk stared around with wide eyes. His hair, neat last time, now looked rumpled, and his tie sat askew atop a dress shirt untucked on one side. "Stressful day?" I asked.

"I guess I'm not used to such a big law enforcement presence," he said.

"Neither am I," Judge Black added, "but we'll adapt. I've already talked to the police, Mister Ferguson, but I know you're investigating all this, too. I haven't had court yet today, and I probably won't now. Might as well ask your questions."

"By now, I'm sure you're aware who the victim was." I didn't phrase it as a question, which would win me no points on *Jeopardy!* but seemed all right here.

"I've heard, yes." The judge glanced to his black robe still hanging near the back of his door. "He was in my court not so long ago. I'm sure it'll get blown out of proportion in the press, but the prosecution made some key errors when they requested surveillance. They exceeded the scope of their warrant in my opinion. It rendered a great deal of evidence inadmissible, and the only just action was to let Mister Boyle go free."

"Of all the people your technicalities have released," I said, "he might have been the worst."

"These are not *my* technicalities, Mister Ferguson. I understand I'll be painted as responsible by some, but the law exists both to protect and restrict, and we need to treat both sides equally. Just because someone is a bad person doesn't mean the state gets to run roughshod over them without a care for getting things right."

I didn't come here to get into a legal argument with

someone who could trounce me in the subject, so I put up my hands. "You get my point, though. Whatever people may have thought of you before, the sentiment is going to be even stronger this time."

Judge Black bobbed his head. "The BPD and I have been discussing this. They told me to expect more negative coverage . . . I presume in both volume and tone even though I think they only meant the former . . . and worked with the county to offer police protection. I'm not a fool, so I took it."

Fabian frowned. Maybe he didn't want to see a cop or two parading around the area constantly, but he would have to get used to it. "I'm sure you've also been over it all with them," I said, "but do you have any idea who might be doing this?"

"No. The police don't have much in the way of a suspect pool as far as I understand it. I asked not to be involved. I'd rather not know. Whoever it is will move through the legal system at some point."

"They're looking at a former soldier," T.J. said, "but we don't think he's a good fit."

"I get a few of those. Inevitable in a state like Maryland with so many bases." The judge paused, and his brows furrowed. "None jump out at me, however."

T.J. shrugged. "We're hoping they move on to someone else."

A loud knock filled the room, causing Fabian to nearly jump off his chair. A cop with an angular face poked his head in and told Judge Black the deputy commissioner was here to see him. "I'll be out in a moment," Black said. "I wish you luck, Mister Ferguson. Those in your profession fill an important gap in the legal system. Now, I have to talk to someone who can pull rank on just about anyone here. Please let me know if I can be of any help later."

We thanked the judge and left, weaving through a phalanx of uniforms on the way back down the corridor.

———

Later in the afternoon, when T.J. and I were back in the office, Rich called.

"We got our guy," he said as soon as I picked up.

I got my assistant's attention and put the call on speaker. "What do you mean?"

"The former soldier. Thormann. We went to his house." Rich fell silent for a couple seconds like he expected me to add something. Maybe I was supposed to confess to visiting the place—which I hadn't. Something gave me the feeling the same could not be said for my secretary and our intern, however, but I refrained from saying anything. "He's in Gardenville," my cousin eventually continued. "We had a bit of a standoff."

"Most people don't enjoy being arrested," I said.

"Innocent people don't hole themselves up for two hours."

"I think you'd be surprised . . . and it sounds like you were."

"He's the guy," Rich said. "He has the right history and experience. No alibis for any of the bombings. He lives alone and doesn't socialize much, so no one can place him anywhere. Not even his house."

"What about his phone?" T.J. asked. "Or his car's GPS?"

"We think of these things, too. His phone stayed at his home, but he could have left it behind."

"And you think he walked to all these places from northeast Baltimore?" I said.

"Of course not," Rich said. "Thormann doesn't use any ride-sharing apps. His GPS stays put. Pretty easy to get someone to give you a lift, though, or slug your way across town in exchange for cash."

"Good luck getting a prosecutor to prove all this beyond a reasonable doubt." I scoffed. "I don't think you could even manage an unreasonable doubt here."

"He's not the guy," T.J. added. "Thormann didn't do it. He's a convenient suspect."

"Sometimes, the convenient ones turn out to be guilty," Rich said. "I presume you've read this guy's blog? Even after some commenter told him to tone it down because the cops might be onto him, he didn't. Left all his entries up. Didn't delete anything from his socials."

"Maybe because he's innocent," I suggested.

"You want to defend him so fucking bad, go work for the public defender. He's the one. You don't have to stay on the case."

"And yet we will."

"It's your time," Rich said and ended the call.

"Goddammit," I groused as I set my phone back down.

"Your cousin and his cops are so predictable sometimes." T.J. walked back to her desk and sank heavily onto her chair. "They can't see past the low-hanging fruit."

"This is the part where I remind you we don't work for Thormann, and we aren't responsible for his defense. As much as you and Lexi might not want him to be guilty." She frowned at me. "Do you really think I don't suspect anything? Let me guess . . . you drove over there, and one of you used a personal credit card so I wouldn't see it on the company account." She remained silent, so I kept going. "From there, you sat on his house, saw a new post, and tried to warn him. Nothing happened, so you left. Now, because Thormann is a convenient suspect, the police have zeroed in on him."

"We didn't have anything to do with that," T.J. said.

"I know. They bungled it all on their own. Am I right about the rest?"

She sighed. "More or less."

"I'll go with more," I said. "You're lucky. If he really was the guy . . . or just ended up an unhinged gun nut . . . you two might not have made it back."

"We did, though, because it's not him. We need to prove it."

"Logically, we can't prove a negative. No one can. We'll need to give the cops a better suspect."

"Let's get on with it, then," T.J. said.

CHAPTER 14

SATURDAY MORNING, I sat at home pondering whether to go into work.

I hadn't heard from T.J. yet. If she were on her way into the office, she would have called or texted. She took her laptop home most nights and weekends, however, and could have been toiling away from her apartment. I'd recently finished breakfast and now worked on my second cup of coffee. Gloria remained asleep upstairs. As soon as I dug out my laptop and put it on the desk, Rich called. "Turn on the TV," he said.

"I haven't watched Saturday morning cartoons in ages," I said. "Are they still a thing?"

"Local news."

"You're just going to leave me hanging about the Ninja Turtles?"

"Just put on channel eleven," he barked.

"All right, all right." I sat in the extra bedroom Gloria converted to an office. It was mainly for her use, but a second desk accommodated me when I wanted to work from her house. A forty-three-inch TV—the smallest in the house—

hung on the wall. I turned it on and found the local station he specified. A throng of people stood outside Central Booking, most of them masked, and many holding signs. *Crowd Protests Arrest of Vox Populi Suspect*, the chyron informed me. "Looks like you've got a situation on your hands."

"No shit," Rich said. "We have some cops out there to make sure things don't get out of hand. The commissioner doesn't want to arrest anyone yet. So far, they've been loud but mostly peaceful."

"You arrested the wrong guy," I pointed out. "This is a self-created problem. What am I supposed to do about it?"

"You keep telling me Thormann's not our killer."

"Yep."

"You got any other suspects?"

"Sorry," I said. "I didn't hear you over the sound of your flimsy case falling apart."

"I'm not in the mood to dance with you," Rich said. "This situation is a powder keg. If it turns violent, we'll be outnumbered and have to arrest a shitload of people. At least we won't have to take them far for processing. I'm willing to admit the possibility there could be other suspects out there."

"You think accusing someone else will mollify the crowd?" I snorted. "They're not upset because you arrested Joseph Thormann. They don't give a shit about him. I bet most of them don't even know his name and couldn't pick him out of a three-man lineup. They're pissed because you arrested someone they see as the symbol of everyday people taking back the justice system and dealing with criminals. Hauling a better suspect in there won't change anything."

Rich sighed. "You may be right. Still, if there's a chance Thormann didn't do it, I want to know who did."

"Good thing you're a lieutenant, then. You can order a bunch of cops to investigate. Have you tried it yet?"

"We're looking into things." Annoyance crept into Rich's tone. I knew I was pushing his buttons, but I enjoyed it—and I was aware he knew this, too. "You've been involved so far, and I know you're not going to stop just because we made an arrest."

"So you'd like me to come up with someone who's a better fit for Vox Populi," I said.

"Yes."

"So you can ride my stylish coattails to another commendation from your boss and the mayor."

"I'll give you a shout-out this time," Rich said.

"No, you won't."

"You're right. I won't. Let me know if you come up with anything." He broke the connection.

Soft footsteps heralded my wife's arrival. She stood in the doorway, and as much as I wanted to work on the case, the way her small pajamas hugged her body in exactly the right places tested my resolve. "Duty calls?" she asked.

"I think so."

Gloria stretched, forcing her already short top to ride up farther over her midriff. This did not improve my situation. "I'm gonna get some coffee. I think there are some things I could knock out today, too. You make breakfast?"

"There's a plate for you in the fridge."

She smiled. "Thanks."

As Gloria walked away, I realized I'd rather get Lexi and T.J. together and work in our actual office. If nothing else, I'd be less distracted. I put my laptop back in its bag, slung it over my shoulder, and headed downstairs.

———

Of the two young women in my employ, T.J. arrived first. It made sense because she had the shorter commute. She asked me if we needed coffee on the weekend, I shot her a look which I hoped suggested she'd recently sprouted two additional heads, and she got things going. Once the pot finished, Lexi arrived. "Any of you watch the local news this morning?" I asked. Both shook their heads, so I brought up the live broadcast and put it on one of my large screens.

"Wow," they both said at the same time.

"Central Booking?" Lexi wanted to know.

"Yeah," T.J. said before I could.

After a swig of my coffee, I said, "Rich called me earlier. He's open to the possibility they might have the wrong guy, but I think the BPD is still trying to assemble evidence against Thormann. The mob out there doesn't care who's in custody. They're upset because the cops hauled in someone they think is Vox Populi. Even if we make an airtight case against a different person, fans of this psycho are going to be pissed."

"We also don't work for Thormann," T.J. said.

"I know your sympathies lie with him." Both pursed their lips. "It's fine. I hope he didn't do it. We need to come up with someone who's a better suspect. It won't make the crowd hold hands and break out in song, but there's always the hope people will see the killer for who he really is. Thormann's a guy a lot of folks will like . . . or at least feel sorry for. Ex-soldier comes home, maybe he struggles to readjust to life as a civilian, and the cops haul him off to jail."

"I thought your theory was that people don't care about this guy," Lexi said.

"They don't," I said. "They care about the narrative. It's what the media is going to spin. Others will, too, probably in different directions and for their own purposes. If we can find someone who's a lunatic *and* an asshole, he's a far less sympathetic figure even if his real value is as a symbol."

Lexi sipped her coffee and nodded. "All right. I'm in."

"Me, too," T.J. added. "You got any ideas for where we can begin?"

"We're basically starting from scratch." I spread my hands. "I know we might have been able to do this remotely, but I like collaborating in person."

"Okay, boomer," T.J. said.

"Also, Gloria was wearing really tiny pajamas." T.J. chuckled while Lexi wrinkled her nose. "Fewer distractions here."

We didn't have much of a plan, but we got to work.

———

"The crazies might be coming for us, too," Lexi said a little while later.

A link appeared in my inbox. It went to a blog whose owner dropped no hints as to his identity. Like most people who thought they were anonymous online, he almost certainly left some breadcrumbs somewhere. Rather than go down the mental rabbit hole of figuring out who the mysterious scribe was, I read the post our intern sent.

Another Threat to Justice: Ferguson Detective Agency Meddles in Vox Populi's

Mission

Let's talk about obstacles. Just when it seems like we've finally got someone willing to stand up for the people and deliver real justice in Baltimore, the vultures start circling. We knew the cops would be there. They always are. "To protect and serve"—our paid-for overlords. Enter C.T. Ferguson and his little detective agency. That's right, Ferguson's been hired to snoop around and "pick up the slack" left by our police—who, let's be honest, haven't exactly made strides toward stopping the violence tearing this city apart.

Vox Populi is a hero. Three criminals dead in as many weeks, plus one more who thought he'd dodged justice. All of them had hurt people, broken lives, and walked free because our so-called legal system failed. And now Ferguson, who's clearly on the wrong side of this, is doing everything he can to bring down the one person who's actually making a difference. The sad reality is, Ferguson's just another tool of the system, getting paid to poke his nose where it doesn't belong and disrupt the only real justice we've seen in ages.

I'll tell you one thing: people like Vox Populi don't need interference from smug private eyes looking for a paycheck. Every minute Ferguson spends tracking down our city's protector is a minute that could endanger real justice for Baltimore. Maybe Ferguson should consider that before he digs any deeper.

"The author seems to know I'm smug," I said. "He could've added handsome and well-dressed, too."

T.J. and Lexi rolled their eyes in unison. I wondered if they practiced the move when I wasn't around. "It's not exactly a threat," my secretary said, "but it walks up to the line."

"I think it walks up, leans over, and spits on the other side."

"What are you going to do about it?" Lexi asked.

"It's probably nothing," I said. "People write bullshit like this every day, and ninety-nine percent of it doesn't go any farther than a screed. In case this is the one percent, however, let's see if we can figure out who wrote this. Or at least who owns this site."

"I'm on it."

I stared at the post for a couple minutes before getting back to work. About a half-hour later, I heard voices from outside. Manny and crew weren't working today—the shop generally opened every other Saturday—so no one would be here to drop off or pick up a car. I looked out the window and saw about eight guys in the lot. They looked like an offshoot of the crowd at Central Booking. One even carried a sign, though he held it at an angle where I couldn't read it.

"What's going on?" T.J. said.

"We've attracted a few protesters of our own."

She joined me at the window, and her eyes widened. "Jesus. What the hell is up with these people?"

"They probably read the same post we did," I said. "Finding our address isn't hard."

"What are we going to do?" she asked. By now, Lexi joined us in looking out the window.

"I'm going to talk to them," I said.

"What?"

I opened the top drawer of my desk and handed T.J. the

9MM. It offered less stopping power than the .45 I favored, but it also came with less recoil. She wasn't an experienced shooter. "You know how to use it?"

"I've been to a range a few times," she said.

"Good. Try not to shoot me in the back." I looked at Lexi. "I presume you brought your own?" She nodded. "All right. You two take up position here. Hopefully, we can resolve this without any gunshots."

"What if we can't?" Lexi said.

I shrugged. "These idiots made their choice." I opened the door, made sure to lock it behind me, and headed down the stairs.

CHAPTER 15

AS SOON AS I pushed through the main door and stepped outside, two phones focused on me.

If I'd retained any chance at anonymity before, it was gone. No more undercover work for yours truly. It had been dangerous but ultimately rewarding. Nine men in total stood in a rough semicircle in front of me. I'd never fought off more than three at a time before. If this group was dumb enough to come at me in trios, I might be able to take them all down. I didn't glance up at the window to avoid giving away Lexi and T.J.'s position. "You all get lost on the way to Central Booking?" I said.

"Fuck you!" one of the ones holding up his phone shouted.

"Eloquent. This is private property. We already had to chase reporters away earlier."

"We ain't the press."

"Being a PI means I can puzzle out the facts on my own. If you insist on trespassing, is there something I can do for you guys?"

"Stop investigating," another one said.

"It's kind of what I do. It's even in the name of the company."

"We could make you stop."

I shrugged. "You might. You all certainly have a numerical advantage on me." They drew in a little closer. I pointed at the one who talked about making me stop. "I promise I'll break every bone I can before someone pulls me off you. You won't be able to walk or wipe your own ass for three months." He frowned, and his bravado melted like a wax figure on a hot day.

"Stop investigating Vox Populi," the cretin who cursed at me before demanded. "He's the hero of the downtrodden."

"The downtrodden? You look up the word on your drive over?"

"It's people like me!"

"Right. You're so 'downtrodden' in your Nike shoes and brandishing your new iPhone Pro. What is this, amateur hour? Go home, guys. You're rooting for an asshole, and you're out of your depth."

One man broke from the pack and rushed me. I sidestepped his first punch. No one looked to be joining him, but still, I wanted to end this as quickly and as brutally as possible. Putting this idiot down hard would hopefully discourage anyone else. I blocked the second punch, stepped outside the third, and caught my foe's right arm. Before he could pull it back, I used my right hand to turn it ninety degrees and drove my left palm through his elbow, breaking the joint with a snap loud enough to silence the mob.

My adversary clutched his arm and howled in pain. He stood with straight legs, so I kicked him in the side of the right one. It wouldn't break his knee, but it would probably cause ligament damage. The more immediate effect was his leg buckling and the moron toppling to the asphalt. I spread my hands. "Just like I thought . . . amateur hour."

A couple members of the crowd helped the wailing man back to his feet and made sure he could hop out of the fray. Six others still stared at me with the intent to intimidate. "Not bad against one person," a burly blond guy said. "We're a lot more than one."

"Let me give you another variable for the equation, Einstein," I said. "You willing to risk injuries like his in defense of some murderous asshole you've never met?"

"Sure."

I jerked my thumb over my left shoulder. "Let me direct you to the window up there, then. You'll see two young women holding pistols. My guess is we're somewhere between fifteen and twenty yards away depending on where you're standing. One of them is a so-so shot. She might aim for center mass and end up putting a round right in your balls. The other could shoot a fly off your forehead at twice this distance."

"Which is which?" another asked.

I shrugged. "Fifty-fifty chance, guys. You might get lucky and survive to run out of here, or the world might very suddenly fade to black. If you stay much longer, *someone's* going to shoot at you, and I promise the bullets-to-assholes ratio is definitely in my favor."

"We could rush you."

"You could. There are six of you here right now. Eight if we count the two who helped Braveheart hobble away. I'm good for three or four. My money's on the girls with guns to take care of the rest."

I waited as the crowd spent a minute looking at each other. My pulse pounded in my ears. I wanted them to leave peacefully, but if they insisted on staying and escalating, I was ready to fight dirty and let T.J. and Lexi handle their share. After a long moment, the assembled jackasses started a strategic advance to the rear. "You should drop your investigation," a voice hurled back as they skulked toward the sidewalk.

"And you should have the courage of your convictions." The comment didn't change things. With one man still helping the injured guy limp away, the nine-person throng dispersed to the sidewalks of Eastern Avenue. I released a breath and walked back inside. "It's me," I announced as I unlocked our office door.

Lexi and T.J. lowered their weapons. "What a shitshow," my assistant said.

"Yeah. I wonder if Manny will give us a break on the rent after this."

"Probably not considering our investigation drew them here."

"I guess we won't mention it to him, then," I said.

———

Two things happened in short order following the Great Parking Lot Altercation.

First, videos taken by a few cretins ended up online. Despite one person getting badly injured and the rest losing face, they still posted the video. It cut out shortly after I dispatched the guy who stepped forward. This was designed to make me look like an aggressor who responded to peaceful protestors with violence, of course. A few such comments already came in. While the video and commentary track didn't mention a location or address, someone could spend thirty seconds on Google and get it.

Second, the cops came. We didn't call them, and I don't think the assembled jackasses did, either. The incident happened on a Saturday just off a major road in Fells Point. Multiple people could have seen it driving by, and it only took one to grab a phone and dial 9-1-1. The responding uniforms—one officer and a sergeant, both men—asked us what happened.

"We were working when they came into the parking lot," I said. "Nine by my count."

"What did they want?" the sergeant asked.

"Same thing the assholes outside Central Booking want. They think the bomber is a hero and basically demanded I drop the investigation."

"I'm going to guess you said no."

"Yes, and one of them didn't seem to like it."

"What happened to him?"

"He's going to be on his team's injured list for a while," I said, "and for his sake, I hope he knows how to use a fork left-handed."

"Nothing else happened?" he said.

"No. After I took care of one, I guess the rest of the crowd lost their nerve."

"They still would have held a big numerical advantage," the officer pointed out.

I shrugged. "They lacked the courage of their convictions. Ginned-up idiots like them usually do. They'll froth at the mouth if someone tells them to, but their hearts aren't in it if there's a chance they're going to get hurt."

Following a few more questions, the pair left. There wasn't much to investigate. Lexi's gun was legal, and so was mine—even though I let T.J. handle it. The cops didn't ask about weapons, instead focusing on the brief standoff in the parking lot. I doubted any member of the mob would come forward short of hiding behind their social media handles. This meant they wouldn't try to press charges, and if they did, I had a good case for self-defense.

We were back to work a short while when Rich called. "I wish we could treat these so-called protestors the way you did," he said.

"It was kind of refreshing," I admitted. "Next time you come by, maybe you can drop off a set of riot gear just in case."

"You know the helmet and plastic shield makes it almost impossible for people to see your face, right?"

"Never mind, then. Handsomeness is its own shield."

Rich chuckled. "Everybody all right?"

"Yeah, we're fine. Something like this isn't going to stop us."

"Your agency has gotten called out pretty regularly on this one," Rich said. "Contrary to what marketers like to tell you, not all publicity is good publicity."

"I know. A couple of these geniuses uploaded some videos. We might end up with a few additional visitors before this is over."

"Let's try and get the right guy behind bars, then." Before I could pounce on this, Rich added, "I'm not saying we have the wrong guy now, of course."

"You do."

"If we do, we'll cut him loose. The commissioner and the mayor both want this wrapped up before someone else dies."

"I was wondering when the mayor would insert himself. Surprised it took so long. Aren't we in an election year?"

"I forgot . . . you don't vote."

"I do try to work, though, and I'd like to get back to it. Thanks for checking in."

"Sure," Rich said, and we ended the call. I thought about another group of ne'er-do-wells coming to the office, and a few even testing their courage by coming up the stairs. With two additional employees to protect, I couldn't be cavalier about these things. I left T.J. and Lexi to keep working while I drove to an electronics store. There, I bought a couple security cameras and a gently-used TV. Back at the office, I set up the electric eyes, made sure they worked with the recommended app, and set everything to display on the TV. It was a forty-two-inch model—not the latest tech, but certainly good enough for what I needed. We could mount it on the wall later.

"Why not just add to the security system?" T.J. wondered.

"This is our problem," I said. "The main system can still let us see some exterior angles, but we don't need to bother Manny with this."

"Let them come back," Lexi said. "We're armed."

I appreciated the sentiment, but I hoped we didn't get any more unexpected guests.

———

My hope didn't last long.

The first camera I configured caught a car pulling into the lot and parking near the main entrance. A woman got out. She came in, made the turn, and we lost her when she opened the interior door. Her footsteps rang on the stairs, and the camera outside the door picked her up again. It didn't feature the best resolution, but I guessed her to be in her later forties. Probably not an assassin sent to kill us. The door remained locked, so after trying the handle, she knocked.

I got up, unlocked the door, and opened it enough to peek out. The woman on the other side stood about five-five, was slender, and her hair was a mix of dark red and some gray. Dark circles showed under her eyes. "Can we help you?" I asked.

"Actually, I hope I can help you."

"With what?"

"The bombings." She patted her large purse. "I might have information you can use. My husband is . . . was . . . a PI like you."

Considering how quickly she corrected herself to the past tense, I declined to say there were no PIs like me. I opened enough for her to walk past me. Once she was inside, I scanned the entryway, saw nothing of note, and locked up again. "I'm Jane Graves. My husband Duncan was a private investigator, and he was looking into this mess."

I remembered seeing a tidbit about multiple PIs working the case. Considering how many people were potentially affected, it made sense. Her husband's name also sounded familiar. "I think I met your husband once."

Jane nodded. "Yes." A small smile appeared on her lips and then disappeared as quickly as it came. "At the risk of being too honest, I don't think he liked you very much. He thought you were a young hotshot who didn't know what he was doing."

"Your husband might have been right." I gestured to our round table, which currently had the new TV sitting atop it. "Sorry, let me move this." I lifted it and set it on the floor out of the way. "This is my assistant, T.J. and our intern, Lexi." After a three-way round of introductions, we all sat at the table.

"Anyone want coffee?" Lexi asked. I shrugged and nodded, never one to refuse a cup under most circumstances. She went to the sideboard and started working on brewing a pot.

Jane sighed. "You might have inferred that my husband is dead."

I nodded. "We're sorry for your loss. I don't remember hearing his name in connection with the bombings, though."

"He got run over by a car." Jane's voice cracked at the end. I grabbed the nearest box of tissues and slid it toward her. After a moment to compose herself, she continued. "I don't know if it was an accident or not. It happens every day, right?"

"Unfortunately, I'm sure it does."

"Anyway, Duncan had done some work on this Vox Populi." She snorted. "What a name. We never talked about what to do with his case notes in the event he died, but I want you to have them. Someone needs to stop this son of a bitch, and if Duncan can play a small part in it, I think it would really help."

I got the impression she referred to herself as the entity being helped, but I couldn't turn down the chance to make a break in this case. "I think it would really help, too," I said.

CHAPTER 16

OVER COFFEE, Jane took two things out of her bag: a small Moleskine notebook and a flash drive.

"Duncan originally worked for T-Bone Mallory, the first bombing victim," she said. "His girlfriend and family thought something was wonky in his arrest and conviction, and the public defender never took it up. When they had the money, they hired Duncan, and he found something. T-Bone got released, and . . . well, you know the rest."

"All too well," I said. "I heard and felt the first bomb. Even ran over to see what was going on, but it was way too late by then."

"Duncan felt terrible about what happened." Jane wiped away a stray tear. Crying accentuated the dark circles under her eyes. When my older sister died eighteen years ago, I didn't sleep well for weeks. The insomnia and bad dreams were no doubt worse for Jane. "I told him he wasn't responsible, of course. He probably knew it on some level, but he kept telling me if he didn't get involved, T-Bone would still have been alive. In jail . . . but alive."

"Did Keisha hire him?" I asked.

Jane shook her head. "He reached out to her and offered to look around *pro bono*. Keisha didn't blame him. I think that was good for Duncan."

"What's on this drive?" Lexi wondered as she picked it up.

"Case notes, I guess," Jane said. "Duncan rarely told me anything about what he worked on." She paused for a dry chuckle. "I think he was worried people would come after me if they knew about his investigations. It was silly, really. He wasn't protecting state secrets or chasing down terrorists."

"Is it encrypted?" I said. Jane nodded. "Do you know the password?"

She spread her hands. "I wish I did. It was one of the things he never discussed with me. I remember he told me you were a computer guy and not a real investigator at some point. Sorry."

"It's fine."

"That's part of the reason I brought it to you. I figured you could use his notes, but I also hoped you'd be able to crack his password."

"Did you try?" Lexi wanted to know.

"No."

Our intern popped the drive into a USB port on her laptop. When she tried to access the folder representing the device, a new window filled the screen, and she called us for a look-see. It was a medium blue background with white lettering and a black box with a blinking cursor.

Property of Duncan Graves
Confidential Investigative Information
Encrypted with AES

Any attempt to copy these files to an unencrypted drive will result in erasure.

Enter password below. You have three attempts before the information is gone forever.

"Any idea what he would use?" I asked Jane.

"No clue."

"We'll have to try and figure it out, then." I tapped my finger on the notebook. "I hate to ask, but . . . how long ago did your husband die?"

"Six days," Jane said. "His funeral was yesterday. Why?"

"I was wondering if he had any thoughts on the man the police have arrested. We're of the opinion he's not the killer."

"I can't say for certain, but I'm sure Duncan would have felt the same. He didn't tell me much, but I know he was concerned about former soldiers being demonized. He didn't think there was a military connection. At least not an American one."

This supposition probably went over very well with our intern. "People often pick significant things in their lives as passwords," I said. "What can you tell us about Duncan?"

It took Jane a minute and a couple tissues to answer. "We met twenty-five years ago in Columbia. I'd like to say it was love at first sight, but it took a while to get there. Duncan worked as a Howard County cop before he left the job and went private. We wanted to have kids, but . . . it was hard. I finally got pregnant a few years ago. Duncan was preparing to scale back his business and maybe even find someone to take it over." She paused again to wipe her eyes. "Our son ended up stillborn. We grieved for a while, and then Duncan threw himself back into his work. I told him he needed to dial it back a little. He wasn't as young as he used to be. He kept going, though. I'm not sure how he had the bandwidth to try to help Keisha with T-Bone's murder, but he swore he did."

"We'll do our best to get the information," I said. "Thank you for coming in."

Jane said her goodbyes and left a moment later. A pall hung in the air. We had many reasons to want to solve this case, and another PI's widow walked in and added one more to the list.

———

"I don't want to enter a password until we know more," Lexi said, her eyes focused on the warning message.

"Agreed," I said. "We'll need to have a few really good guesses lined up. The challenge is I don't want digging into some other PI to derail us. We don't know what's on the drive. He might not have anything of value to add, and then we'll just be wasting a bunch of time for nothing."

"There are three of us now," T.J. pointed out.

"True." I pointed to her. "You and I will keep seeing if there's something we can find out about the case. Either a better person of interest or a detail we can use to get Thormann off the hook. Lexi, you look into our recently deceased PI."

"I'm on it," the intern said.

After a while, I hoped her progress outpaced mine. We'd been trying to find good suspects for a while. Thormann—thanks to his incendiary experience and rhetoric—made a solid one. If we were now operating from the opinion he didn't do it, I couldn't come up with anyone to nominate in his place. Maryland held plenty of military bases, and many former service members called the state home. A decent percentage possessed the right experience to be interesting. Nothing tied any of them to the victims, the crimes, or anything we knew about Vox Populi.

I understood why Rich and the BPD arrested Thormann, and I grudgingly admitted I understood why they still held him. This was a red ball of the highest order. The commissioner and mayor would be making promises to the media and demands of the rank and file officers. If Thormann wasn't the guy, and they cut him loose without another realistic suspect, it would be a feeding frenzy in the local and national press. I hated when politics intruded on things like murder investigations, but they were unavoidable here.

"Anything?" I asked T.J. after another half-hour.

She shook her head. "I wish. So far, we have an incredibly shallow suspect pool."

"Unfortunately, only one guy's been swimming in it."

"I don't have anyone better," she said.

"Me, either." I turned to Lexi. "Any good intel on Duncan Graves?"

"He's had a pretty long career," she said. "A few milestone cases. Some personal things to celebrate along with a couple to mourn." Lexi shrugged. "His life is basically like anyone else's except for what he did. There are several things I think might be worthy of making a password or passphrase out of, but we only get three cracks at it."

"At some point, we're going to reframe those options as two free chances plus the final one we need to be really careful about." I glanced at my watch. "Maybe not today, though. You're not supposed to be working full-time."

"I do need to get going soon." She frowned. "Kind of hoped I could make some progress here, but there's nothing jumping out at me."

"Don't worry about it," I said. "Thormann's not going anywhere. This will be an interesting test. If the bombings stop, it'll add fuel to the idea the police actually arrested the right guy. If another explosion happens, I get the feeling he'll be cut loose."

"It would be nice if we could get him out in the meantime," Lexi said.

"I agree, but our priority is finding who the killer is, not who it isn't."

She packed up her stuff. "I'll see you both Monday . . . unless something major breaks and we're all back here tomorrow, I guess."

"Let's hope not," I said. Lexi headed for the door and squeezed T.J.'s shoulders in passing. As our intern's footsteps faded down the stairs, my assistant looked up from her work.

"Are we packing it in, too?"

"I have something else I want to look into," I said.

"What about Thormann?"

"We'd have to come up with an ironclad suspect in short order. Even if we handed such a person to the cops and wrapped it all in a bow, they would need to check our work and come to the same conclusion. It sucks he's being held, but we're not springing him today."

"All right." T.J. crossed her arms. "Despite being twenty-two, I don't have much else to do on a Saturday. What do you want to look into?"

"I think we need to go back near the beginning," I said.

———

T.J. gave me a puzzled look. "What do you mean?"

"These are all Judge Black's cases," I said.

"Yeah . . . and?"

"And how many more do you think he's overseen? The guy clerking for three judges struck me as a hamster stuck on a wheel. There could be a bunch more explosions coming if the cops have the wrong man in jail."

T.J. jiggled her mouse and logged back in to her laptop. "What are we looking for, then?"

"Patterns. What else besides Judge Black do these cases have in common? Prosecutors, pub—"

"Not prosecutors," she broke in. "We looked there already. Even counting the most recent bombing, three different people in state's attorney's office for four cases."

"All right," I allowed. "We'll remove them as a variable. What about public defenders? Investigators working for the state's attorney's office? Arresting officers? There has to be something we haven't found yet. Let's see if we can unearth it."

After a half-hour of solid research, the nugget I sought remained buried well out of unearthing range. None of the factors I rattled off ended up being the same. I even came up with a couple others on the fly and whiffed there, too. Whoever Vox Populi was, he didn't have an obvious involvement in the legal process which put four convicted men back onto the streets.

"All right," I said. "I think we need to consider Judge Black himself."

"You think he's letting people out of jail and then blowing them up?" T.J. demanded. Her crossed arms and incredulous expression told me her thoughts on the matter.

"Honestly? No, but we're running out of ideas. Remember what Sherlock Holmes said about eliminating the impossible."

"I don't see it."

"Me, neither. I think he's a true believer when it comes to the system treating people fairly. I know he doesn't have the right experience. Maybe the judge feeds info to someone who does."

"So he's not the killer, just an enabler?" My secretary shook her head. "I think we should pack it in for the weekend. You need some rest or a good meal."

"Maybe both." I frowned and powered off my laptop. "You're spot on. We'll table Black for now. I reserve the right to come back to him and remind you how correct I was if we find something definitive, though."

"Somehow, I think I'll be okay," T.J. said.

IN MY YOUNGER DAYS, I routinely slept past ten on the weekends.

The realization I was pondering my "younger days" at the ripe old age of thirty-four was prominent in my mind as Gloria shook me awake. Even more prominent was the fact this shaking occurred at nine-twenty. I meant to ask her what the hell she was doing, but it came out like a mumbled mess.

"I'm waking you up, silly," Gloria said as if she'd understood me the whole time. "Come on. We have the charity brunch today."

"I'm not hungry."

She scoffed. "You're always hungry when you wake up."

"Not on Sundays," I said, rolling over again.

Undeterred, my wife moved to the other side of the bed and kept up her attempts to rouse me. "It's a fundraiser I organized. 'Where's your husband?'" she asked in a higher-pitched tone. "Oh, he's sleeping because despite being thirty-four years old, he's really seventy-five."

"Old people get up early," I pointed out.

"All the more reason for you to be out of bed."

Considering I'd walked right into her comeback, I gave up the struggle. We were at my house, so Gloria would have fewer options in terms of what to wear. This would not save us a single second, of course. I made coffee while she began the complex ritual of getting herself ready for an event. My wife was a beautiful woman and could look like a knockout in no makeup, a T-shirt, and cutoff jean shorts. She knew it because I told her often enough—for all the good it did.

I ate a granola bar with my coffee. This served both to tide me over until the food came out and give me a few more minutes away from the hurricane of Gloria getting ready for an event. When the time was right, I ventured upstairs. Because I completely forgot about the event, I needed Gloria's attire to clue me in to the dress code—with a small allowance for deviation considering she would always want to look like the belle of the ball as the organizer.

Instead of a gown or something fancy, Gloria wore a bright yellow sundress. The hem stopped an inch or so shy of her knees, and the neckline just low enough to be interesting. My expression must have been quizzical because she smiled and said, "This one isn't super formal, and it's outside."

"We're going to need to hurry home," I said, grinning as I very obviously checked her out.

She slapped my shoulder. "Let's see how good you look first. I'm going to do my makeup."

For a black-tie event, Gloria starting her makeup would give me at least an hour to get ready. Considering the more casual nature of today's soirée, I figured I still had at least thirty minutes. I wouldn't need more than half the number. Shorts struck me as too informal, so I chose a pair of chinos and a freshly pressed green button-down. Rolling the sleeves up to my elbows if it got hot would lend me a rakish look. I shined a pair of brown loafers and slipped them on to finish my business casual appearance.

"Not bad," Gloria said when she saw me later. "I thought you might pick a polo and cargo shorts."

"What am I, the boatswain on a water taxi?"

Gloria grinned. "The shirt goes with your eyes."

"It's almost like I picked it for a reason," I said.

We left a few minutes later with me driving Gloria's rocketlike coupe after inspecting it for incendiary devices. Our destination was the Saturday Morning Cafe, which sat on the border of Harbor East and Little Italy. I thought it was a couple blocks too far north to claim the fancier Harbor East distinction, but no one consulted me on unofficial neighborhood boundaries. I didn't know how much outdoor seating the place normally set up for Sunday brunch, but white canopies surrounded the building and allowed seating for at least eighty people. As I handed the keys to a valet, I guessed half the spots were full.

Attending an event as the organizer's arm candy meant I didn't see my wife for huge swaths of time. She steered me to the table we'd be sitting at—centrally located like I expected—and then disappeared to check on any of a hundred things. This left me at the round table with three middle-aged couples who paid a premium for the prime location. Despite being an outgoing person, I've never cared for the forced nature of these situations. One of the women swore she recognized me. Her husband pooh-poohed the idea, but she insisted I was some sort of famous detective.

"Guilty as charged," I said.

"How famous?" the husband wanted to know.

"Benedict Cumberbatch is clearing his schedule to play me on TV." The husband's brows knitted in apparent skepticism. "I think he has the wrong look, too. He's great, but I'm more handsome in the conventional sense."

This earned me a snort, but I didn't care. A waiter in a white shirt and black jeans dropped off a pitcher of mimosas. I would need a few to make it through this event. As I poured my first, the lady who recognized me asked, "Aren't you working on those bombings?"

"I am."

"What do you think of them?"

This seemed like a trap question, but I answered anyway. "I was a couple blocks away when the first explosion went off, so I've seen them up close. I've smelled the burning flesh, seen someone else injured, and witnessed the property damage firsthand. Whoever's doing this is no hero."

"Really?" The husband folded his arms under his chest. A few tuts from other people at the table told me mine was the minority opinion. "Sometimes, people need to act outside the system. What about Batman?"

"Batman is a fictional character," I pointed out. "Also, I must have missed the issue where he blew up the Joker with a car bomb."

"Sometimes, the system lets us down."

"Sure. People hire folks like me when it happens. They don't run around and blow other people up."

The conversation petered out. I downed the rest of my mimosa and poured another. If this chat continued, Gloria would need to drive us home. Thankfully, the waiter returned with a menu card and golf pencil, telling me I should check off my selections. I picked a waffle, bacon, and fruit, chose slightly more healthy fare for Gloria—knowing she rarely ate much at her own events—and handed him the cards.

Thankfully, no one seemed to want to debate Vox Populi with me any further. As the event filled up, Gloria returned and sat beside me. "I always feel bad leaving you for a while at these things," she said before she kissed me. "How are you?"

"You know me," I said, "making friends wherever I go."

———

Later, after the rest of the brunch passed uneventfully, Gloria and I headed back to my house.

She declared the event a success, with a nice sum raised beforehand and more onsite. With nothing else on the docket, I enjoyed a lazy Sunday of baseball and trying not to think about the current investigation. Following the Orioles game, Gloria sashayed around in her sundress and shot me a lascivious look. The dress came off the moment we got upstairs, and afterwards, we put on more sensible clothes and adjourned to her house. We didn't strictly alternate nights, but spending more than two in a row at either place was rare.

I tried to stay out of the home office. Through dinner, my resolve held. A news alert made my phone buzz, however, and while I could have used it to check things out, I've always preferred more screen real estate. The local papers—the *Banner* looked to be the lone holdout—published an editorial claiming to be from the Vox Populi killer himself. Of course I had to read it.

"A Message from Vox Populi: True Justice
Is Coming"

This is a message to the people of Baltimore—and to those who think they can stop me.

Yes, I am responsible for the four bombings that have rocked this city. Each one was a carefully calculated act of justice against criminals who walked free because our broken legal system put technicalities over safety, over the lives of the people these offenders destroyed. Men who sold poison to our children, who armed killers, who profited from the suffering of others —these were not victims. They were guilty men released by the courts because a judge decided their rights were more important than the safety of our communities. So I stepped in. I delivered what this city has been denied for too long: true justice.

Many of you already understand. Your support has been loud and clear, and I am grateful for jt. You recognize Baltimore cannot thrive if the worst among us are allowed to walk free without consequence. You know criminals who exploit the system don't deserve to live their lives in peace, as if the harm they caused can simply be forgotten. And you know I am not finished.

To Judge Merrill Black and those who uphold this failed system: you are complicit in this chaos. You create a world where killers and drug traffickers find loopholes, where prosecutors and police are forced to fight with one hand tied behind their backs. You tell the people of Baltimore that their safety is less impor- tant than the technicalities in a courtroom. You send these criminals back into our neighborhoods with no real consequence. But understand this: I am providing another remedy besides putting dangerous people back on the streets.

Some of you think you can stop me. You think your investigations, your private detectives, and your endless press conferences will slow me down. They won't. I will not stop until every last criminal set free by this system has been held accountable. I will not be intimidated by those who are paid to protect this failed system, who care more about due process than they do about the innocent people affected by crime.

I understand what many of you are thinking—this is dangerous, this is extreme. But ask yourselves this: what is more dangerous—one man taking action to protect a city, or an entire legal system that keeps putting violent criminals back on the streets? Every bomb I've set, every target I've chosen, has been selected with precision. These men were guilty, they knew it, and they knew they wouldn't escape justice forever. There is no coming back from the lives they destroyed, the families they tore apart. If you want to live without fear of people like me, then demand better from your courts, your judges, your system. Until then, I'll continue to do what I have to do.

To the criminals Judge Black has set free: your time is coming. I'm not interested in your excuses or your lawyers' arguments. I don't care about the technicalities that got you out. All I care about is justice— the real kind. And I promise you it's coming sooner than you think.

Baltimore deserves better than what Judge Black and his colleagues have offered. And as long as they

continue to fail this city, I'll be here, providing the justice they refuse to.
        —Vox Populi

"Christ on a bike," I muttered as I sent the op-ed to T.J. At some point, the *Banner* would bow to pressure and run the piece, too. The only question was would they do so before the national press picked up on it? A couple phrases the killer used stood out to me, and I turned them over in my head to no avail. My phone buzzed with an incoming text from my assistant.

> What the actual fuck?

> The media is carrying water for this guy now.

> You pick anything up reading it?

> No. A couple sentences caught my eye, but I can't make any connections. Whoever this is took care not to reveal anything.

> Agreed. Maybe Rich will let Thormann out now.

> I admire your optimism.

> We young people aren't old and jaded like you.

I smiled and slipped my phone back in my pocket. This editorial going live meant nothing for Thormann. He could have written it and configured his email program to send it at a specific day and time. Still, I wondered what would happen to my cousin's side of the investigation as I logged out and walked back to the main floor of Gloria's house.

———

The next morning, I got an early start in an attempt to catch Judge Black before he left for work.

He lived about ten minutes from Gloria. A police Explorer sat at the curb outside his house. I left the S4 across the street and a couple houses short. Lights were on inside the residence, but I couldn't see much else. Judge Black lived in a common two-story home, and most of the others on the street looked similar. There must have only been a few options in the cookie cutter when the neighborhood went up. The houses were nice but bland and not much separated any of them. Maybe the homeowners association discouraged interesting color palettes.

I hoped Judge Black would check in with the police. It would give me time to ask him a couple questions. By now, I presumed he knew about the editorial attributed to Vox Populi. Maybe the jurist would recognize something in the writing. Whoever penned the op-ed really had it in for Black and his judicial history. The two men must have known each other. The cops might have danced carefully around Black in the event one of their cases landed on his docket. I didn't have the same concerns.

A few minutes later, the garage door went up. Once it rose to the top, Judge Black stepped into the driveway, waved to the officers in the Explorer, and climbed into a black Audi A8 I could see the rear half of from my vantage point. He had good taste in cars. I knew I liked the man for a reason.

Unfortunately, my chance to catch the judge before he drove downtown seemed to have evaporated.

I looked up in time to see an explosion blow the garage apart and take out half the house.

The county police Explorer rocked at the curb and then flipped onto its side. My car shook but remained planted. Windows blew out on homes nearby. Debris from the house rained down into the yard, and a few scattered bits landed on the cops' SUV. I got out of the S4 and dialed 9-1-1 as I ran to check on the officers. There was nothing else I could do for anyone.

CHAPTER 18

I'D NEVER APPROACHED a car tipped onto its side before.

Owing to the shorter height, I went from the roof side, which was closer to me anyway. Only a few stray shards remained of the side window. The two officers inside were both men and they seemed awake and alert. Glass covered both of them, particularly the driver closer to the asphalt. A few spots of blood covered his face. "You both all right?" I called into the cabin.

"I think so," the passenger said.

I climbed atop the Ford. "I can help lift you out." The cop closer to me unbuckled his seat belt. I thought about using the door, but keeping it open at this ridiculous angle would probably be harder than just using brute force. Finagling himself to climb out while not stepping on his partner proved a bit of a challenge. Once he oriented everything properly, he used the center console for a foothold and put one hand on a section of the window frame not covered by a jagged piece of glass. I grabbed his free hand and pulled, grunting with the effort. The guy was about my size.

Together, we got him out and onto the upturned side of the Explorer. The pair of us then helped the driver climb free.

"Thanks," the passenger said. "You live around here?" A few other people stood on their front porches to take in what happened. What was left of Judge Black's house still burned and smoldered in spots. Sirens drew closer. The man who served as the commonality between all the cases was dead. I hoped the end came quickly. The force of the blast probably killed the judge right away. It felt odd to think of this as a mercy, but these were odd times.

"No. I'm working on the bombings." I showed the pair my ID. "I was hoping to catch Judge Black before he left for the courthouse."

More police cars and three fire trucks rolled onto the scene. I went back to my car and waited. The cops would probably want to talk to me once the scene was less chaotic. I texted Rich to let him know what was going on. He replied and told me the county let him know right away. He and Paul King were en route. "The more, the merrier," I said under my breath. I also texted T.J. to let her know I'd be in late because of the morning's events.

With hoses connected to nearby hydrants, firefighters worked on dousing the blaze. One man from the engines—I presumed him to be an arson specialist—joined a pair of BCPD detectives in checking out the garage. Another text from Rich informed me he was five minutes out. One of the cops I helped pull out of the Explorer pointed me out to a detective. He was a tall, slender black man with a full mustache and thin-framed glasses. Something in his move-ments as he walked across the street told me he was a wiry and tough fighter. "You saw what happened?"

I nodded. "I got here a few minutes before the bomb went off."

"I'm Detective Traylor." He did not offer his hand. "You private?"

"Yes." I showed him my ID. "I've been working on the bombings."

"Seems like you haven't made very much progress."

"Neither has anyone else," I said. "Two homicide cops from the city are coming. The judge works there, and the first four blasts all happened within the borders."

"We don't mind looping them in," Traylor said. "What brought you to this street so early?"

"I wanted to catch Judge Black before he left."

"Why?"

"An op-ed went live last night. It's supposedly written by the killer. I was hoping the judge read it and might have picked up on something."

"Don't the city cops have someone in custody?"

"He didn't do it," I said.

"You seem pretty sure." Another car arrived. Rich and King climbed out, flashed their badges to the officer blocking the road, and approached.

"I think I won't be the only one who is." My cousin and his sergeant approached. King was probably somewhere between the two of us in age. His long mop of sandy brown hair and generally unkempt appearance made him look like he flunked out of a Rolling Stones cover band before trying the police as a career.

"What the hell happened here?" Rich wanted to know.

"The bomber stepped up his targeting," I said.

"Why are you on scene?"

"I came here to try and talk to the judge before he headed into the city."

"You get a chance to?" King asked.

"No," I said. The fire department extinguished the car blaze. The house still smoldered in spots. Thankfully, flames didn't spread, though some nearby homeowners would soon be testing the flexibility of their insurance policies. I imagined a lot of disappointment in their futures. The dissipating black smoke allowed me to see into what remained of the garage. The rear wall was in tatters, but the frame of a door was clearly visible. If cops sat on the house all night and never left their vehicle, they wouldn't have seen someone entering the garage via the rear. "I saw it happen. The explosion knocked the county Explorer on its side. I dialed nine-one-one and helped the two cops get out."

"Probably not much else you could do." King frowned as his eyes took in the ruins of the Black house. "I guess the killer wanted to send a strong message to the judge."

The BCPD contingent pulled me aside for a few questions. I explained what went on for at least the fourth time, reiterated it for a fifth, and demurred on a sixth when a senior detective joined the crew. "You can verify my story with your colleagues in the city," I said. "If you want additional proof I'm not a psycho, call Sergeant Gonzalez. He's the person I've dealt with the most when I've worked up here."

"We're definitely going to check you out," the detective said in a gravelly voice suggesting he started chain smoking in kindergarten and never stopped. "Don't leave the state."

"I'll go where I want," I told him as I walked away. Rich and King were busy conferring with their counterparts. I lingered to try and hear something useful, but it was too early in the investigation for anything but the obvious. With the morning a failure, I climbed back into my car and left the county for my office.

———

By the time I rolled into the parking lot, it was nearly eleven.

"Did you bring fresh coffee?" T.J. asked once I'd secured the door behind me.

"No."

"Donuts?" Lexi added.

"No. The faint smell of smoke in my clothes is the only souvenir I'm carrying."

T.J. smiled. "I'm glad you're all right. We both are."

"You'd just be gladder if I brought donuts," I said.

"Duh."

"Fair enough." I unslung my bag and set it on the desk.

"Sounds like it was chaos this morning," Lexi said.

"Pretty much. Judge Black had a couple cops in front of his house. I don't know if they were there overnight. There's a back door into the garage, so our killer could have snuck in."

"What about lights?"

"The door was solid," I said. "No windows or anything. I would imagine someone who's good at doing things like planting car bombs can work by flashlight."

She nodded. "Probably."

"You think this will stop the attacks?" T.J. wondered.

"I don't know," I said. "On the one hand, Judge Black was the linchpin of this case. All the victims passed through his courtroom. On the other hand, it's clear Vox Populi has it in for the judge. Murder might not be enough. He might want to keep shitting on the man's legacy."

"I hope not."

"Me, too, but there are other people out on technicalities. Still a few targets. The cops know who they are, and they might even get to arrange protection."

"Might?" Lexi asked.

"You can't force someone to accept it," I said. "Considering what some of these people went away for . . . and might still be doing . . . they may not want a couple of uniforms hanging around."

"Sounds like we're going to keep working on this," T.J. said.

"I think it's the best course of action." I got up and checked the coffee station. Enough to pour a cup remained in the pot, but its freshness came and went while I watched the county firefighters extinguish a car with a murder victim inside it. I used enough coffee and water to make a half carafe and inhaled the aroma of the brewing java before I sat down again. "Any progress on the flash drive?"

"No." Some color appeared in Lexi's cheeks. "Not the good kind at least. I made an attempt to guess the password and struck out."

"So we're down to two." She nodded in confirmation.

"Do we each get a try?" T.J. said.

I shook my head. "This isn't some egalitarian endeavor. We have a hard limit. Whoever can make a good guess should try. We have to be really protective of the last one."

"If there's even anything good on it."

"We can try making some progress on our own," I suggested. "Then, even if we manage to get in, we may not need whatever notes my colleague was able to assemble."

"We'll need some luck, then."

The coffee finished brewing, and I got up to pour a mug. "We make our own luck."

———

By the time lunch rolled around, there was a dearth of luck in the office.

We still butted into the wall of a poor suspect pool. By now, news of Judge Black's murder had spread far and wide. It received copious coverage from all the local outlets and got significant coverage in national papers and major news sites. Most of the pieces pointed out how the judge got blown up despite being under police protection, calling into question the BPD, BCPD, and however they needed to hand things off when Black transitioned between the two locales. I imagined Rich with steam coming out of his ears. Commissioner Ngo's short hair was probably on fire. I thought he was an asshole—he felt the same about me—so I enjoyed the thought.

The quest for a good decryption password to use on the flash drive met similar results. Because bad things tend to come in threes, I happened upon another editorial supposedly written by the bomber.

"A Warning to Baltimore's Criminals and the System That Shields Them"

Baltimore, you're welcome.

As many of you know, this morning, Judge Merrill Black was removed from his position of so-called authority. Yes, it was I who orchestrated the car bomb that ended his reign. Judge Black was the man responsible for flooding our streets with criminals, putting technicalities over justice, and allowing dangerous men to slip through the cracks. His misguided rulings brought violence, drugs, and suffering back into our neighborhoods, and for that, he paid the ultimate price.

Judge Black sat at the heart of a broken system, protected by police who failed to keep our city safe from him and his dangerous rulings. Early today, he faced the justice he so often denied the victims of Baltimore. Under police protection in two jurisdictions, surrounded by every safeguard the law could offer, Judge Black's life ended not in a courtroom but in the house he built by taking our tax dollars. Let his death serve as a reminder that no one—not even those who hide behind badges or robes—is immune to true justice.

To those who call me a vigilante, I say this: I am a necessary correction in a city that's lost control. The public has spoken, and their support for my actions grows louder each day. I know that many of you see what I see—a city abandoned by its leaders, laws that cater to criminals instead of protecting the innocent, a justice system that has failed its people. And so, with the removal of Judge Black, I am one step closer to my mission of cleaning up Baltimore for good. But make no mistake: my work has only just begun.

There are still criminals out there . . . walking our streets, hidden by technicalities, and protected by the very system that claims to seek justice. These are men who think they've escaped. They look over their shoulders, confident that police, private detectives, and layers of laws will shield them from the consequences of their actions. But I am here to tell them, as I tell all of Baltimore: no one is safe from the justice they deserve.

I am aware that law enforcement and hired private detectives are working around the clock to stop me. They waste resources, scrambling to protect the criminals who have escaped justice and to investigate the means by which I deliver it. But they won't catch me. I know this city as well as they do—perhaps better. And I know the anger that simmers beneath the surface here. I am not the enemy. I am simply the answer Baltimore needs. For every innocent life Judge Black's rulings endangered, I will bring the guilty to justice, one by one.

To the people of Baltimore who support my mission, know that your voices fuel my resolve. You understand that this is about more than just a handful of convictions. This is about reclaiming our streets from those who would poison them. Judge Black's death is only the beginning, a necessary purge in a system that needs to be cleansed. I know I am not alone. I see it in the messages, the support, the quiet nods from those who wish to see their city truly safe again.

As long as this city's leaders and courts continue to fail its citizens, I will remain. Baltimore deserves a future without criminals hiding behind legal loop-holes, without judges who prioritize procedure over safety. The so-called justice system may try to hunt me down, but I'm not afraid. I have a mission, and I have the support of those who see through the lies, who

know that the real enemy isn't me—it's the system that's protected the guilty for too long.
    —Vox Populi

I sent the piece to Lexi and T.J. They both read it and shook their heads. "He killed a judge, and now he's going to become even more popular," my secretary said.

"It's pretty fucked up," I agreed.

"What can we do now?" Lexi asked.

"We've seen the other case reports," I said. "We need Judge Black's."

"Isn't it with the county?"

"They're investigating, but they've looped in the BPD because of shared jurisdictions and all."

"Can we get the case file?"

I smiled. "Of course."

CHAPTER 19

I'VE HAD an in on the BPD's network for years.

During my first case, my cousin Rich—then a uniformed sergeant—made the mistake of leaving me alone at his computer for a couple minutes. It was more than enough time to capture some very relevant information. Since then, I've been able to get the BPD's network to accept a basic Windows virtual machine as one of its own. I didn't have an easy way to access the county's resources but could probably break in if we needed something.

I downloaded the case file to my main laptop and shared it with the girls. We all looked it over. Most of the investigative work came from BCPD cops and detectives I didn't know. Rich and King each contributed a few notes, and the BPD had made only a few other entries in the file since receiving it.

The bomb required a high level of sophistication and experience to construct. It was a powerful shaped charge designed to blow out and up. Damage to the back wall of the garage came from the force of the blast and also stemmed from the main structure being compromised. Judge Black died instantly, and officers and crime scene technicians recovered his body in many parts of varying size. A few still remained embedded in the car or the wood of the house and garage.

Police speculated an experienced person could have entered via the rear door and rigged the explosive to the starter with minimal light. A tall fence ringed Judge Black's yard, so anyone who made it past the gate could have escaped prying eyes. The bomb itself went off when the engine turned over. Construction was consistent with what people learn in the military, intelligence agencies, and similar organizations. This would not help our search for a suspect, and it made me wonder if poor Joseph Thormann still sat behind bars for a crime he obviously couldn't have committed from a cell.

"This is gruesome stuff," T.J. opined.

"Yeah." I frowned at the contents. "Kinda glad I had an early breakfast. I skipped some of the more grisly bits about the effects of the bomb on the judge's body."

"I wish I had," Lexi said, wrinkling her nose.

"It sounds like our killer needs knowledge no one in our suspect pool possesses." I brought up my VM again and used the BPD connection to check on Thormann's status. He got released a few hours ago. "Thormann's back out, by the way. Pretty obvious he's not the killer when he's sitting in a cell while Judge Black gets blown up."

"A very tiny win," T.J. said.

"Sometimes, those are the only ones we get," I told her. "Nothing wrong with celebrating for a moment. I know you both believed he was innocent from the jump. We need to keep digging, though, and we need a much larger field of potential suspects."

"What are you thinking, boss?"

Before I could answer her, the phone on my desk rang.

———

Our actual wired phone didn't ring more than a couple times a day.

It was a Voice Over IP line which came with the business-class internet service. I didn't really want it, but it cost almost nothing per month, gave us a number other than a cell phone, and worked for clients who were used to calling potential landlines. We didn't give the number out often, but it was in whatever scattered electronic directories passed for a phone book these days. Before T.J. could answer the one on her desk, I shook my head and picked up the handset on mine. "Ferguson Detective Agency."

The line remained mostly silent for a second. A faint electronic buzz came through as background noise before someone finally spoke in a distorted voice. "You need to drop your investigation."

I got the ladies' attention and put the call on speaker, setting the handset down as quietly as I could. "We're a busy agency. Which investigation did you have in mind?"

"You know exactly which one." While voices can be electronically altered like this one, people's speech patterns normally remain identical. They don't think to change their cadence or the way they say certain words. I didn't recognize any of those factors in this caller. I mouthed for Lexi to try and trace the call even though I figured it would be futile.

"Why don't you be specific, Lord Vader?"

"You think you're funny?" the presumptive killer demanded.

"My mom laughs at all my jokes except the off-color ones."

"You're getting some good press riding my coattails. Congratulations. Now—"

"Thanks," I broke in. "Free publicity is the best kind."

"You need to take this seriously. I'm not going to stop. So far, I've only focused on violent criminals out on technicalities . . . and the man who saw fit to set them all free. I could expand the scope of my work. You're not exactly a hard man to find, and I know you're not in the office alone."

"Come visit us, then. We can have a chat, you tell us who you're working with, why you're both such psychos, and then we can have the cops take you away. What do you think?"

The man I presumed to be Vox Populi let out a short laugh. It sounded menacing under electronic distortion. "Tell you what. I'll keep doing what I do. You keep doing what you do. So long as those two paths don't cross, we're good. If you keep nosing around, though, you or someone close to you might get hurt. And by 'hurt,' I mean vaporized. I heard they didn't recover all the bits and pieces of Judge Black. Could be you or someone you love next." Lexi and T.J. both glowered. "What do *you* think?"

"I think you can fuck right off," I said.

"You made your choice," he said and hung up.

"Prick."

"We telling the cops?" T.J. wanted to know.

"Depends if we get anything on the call."

"The number resolves to a burner," Lexi said. "It pinged off three different towers while you two were talking."

"So he was in a car," I said. "Any more precise info?"

"The phone is off now. I would guess it either stays off, or he tosses it onto a cargo train. With a little time, I could get more precise locations."

"I doubt they would tell us anything. Out of curiosity, where did the call come from?"

"I can only give you a generality," Lexi said. "From the tower data, it started in Lutherville and eventually moved into Towson."

"He was most likely going around the Beltway, then," I said. "Probably riding in the back. Whatever distorter he was using did a good job of masking the background noise. Even so-called quiet cars are about seventy decibels at highway speeds." Maybe the electronic hum I heard was how the distortion box processed and spat out the road, tire, and wind sounds happening outside a vehicle going sixty-five.

"You want me to keep digging for a better location?"

I shook my head. "I don't think anything will come of it. Send what you have to Rich. Let the cops dedicate their resources to it. I have a different idea."

———

"We need to expand our search," I told Lexi and T.J.

"How?" my secretary asked.

"We've been focused on a few people close to the victims. Let's branch out. Include family members. It has to be someone in the orbit of a person killed by the bombings."

"Including Judge Black?"

"Sure. His legal tendencies weren't always well-received in the general population. It stands to reason some people close to him would disagree, too."

"They'd need to disagree pretty sharply," Lexi pointed out.

"No argument here. Let's see who did . . . and keep in mind we need someone with the experience and training to make these explosives. The bomb planted in Judge Black's car was different than the one in T-Bone Mallory's."

"We're on it," T.J. said, and we all got down to business. Rather than throw a dart at someone's family tree, I focused on what we'd heard directly from the killer. Vox Populi kept himself in the news through his actions, but he also spoke directly to everyone via a pair of editorials. I pulled up both and combed through them for something I could use—some familiar saying or a phrase I'd heard in a prior conversation.

After a few minutes, I found something which met the criteria.

I am providing another remedy besides putting dangerous people back on the streets.

It was from the first op-ed. The line didn't jump out at me originally, but now, something tugged at my memory. "Remedy" didn't come up in many conversations. Where did I hear it? I closed my eyes and thought about the people we'd visited since this whole mess began. The realization hit me. My eyes went wide open, and I must have gasped because T.J. and Lexi both shot me quizzical looks.

"Fabian," I said. I remembered the first time we went to see Judge Black. Fabian, the harried clerk who juggled working for three jurists, popped into the office. When we were getting into the consequences of releasing people on technicalities, I asked him what he thought about it. After trying not to answer at first, he eventually said something I now realized was telling. *I know the state needs to get things right, but there should be another remedy besides putting dangerous people back on the streets.*

"The clerk?" T.J. wondered.

"He's the one." I mentioned what he said on our first visit and how the same line appeared verbatim in the first Vox Populi screed the news sites ran with.

"I don't know." She frowned. "I see it, but it might be a little flimsy."

"Who uses 'remedy' in a sentence these days?" I said. "Maybe charlatans like homeopaths, but no one else does." T.J.'s furrowed brows didn't lift. "Fine. I think this is another brilliant deduction, but you think it's flimsy. Let's shore it up, then. Fabian himself doesn't strike me as the type to break into a garage and wire a carefully-crafted bomb into the starter of a car. Who's he working with?"

A couple minutes later, we had an answer. Fabian Charles had an uncle named Frederick who worked for the Maryland State Police on its bomb squad. Another uncle—the late Stanley Charles—did the same work but died on the job. I knew there was more to the story, so we kept digging. Following a settlement paid out to the family, the criminal charged and convicted for Stanley Charles's death got released on a technicality.

The judge in question? Merrill Black.

The killer met his end a few months later when a car ran him down. The driver was never found. Frederick Charles had an alibi—provided by nephew Fabian—but he ended up leaving the state police shortly after. "He has to be the one," Lexi said. "I wonder if the other PI came to the same conclusion. Maybe he got too close to the truth. Didn't he get hit by a car, too?"

"He did," I said. "Good thinking. You two work on Fabian and his uncle. I'll see what I can find about my deceased colleague." I didn't like splitting the investigation at the moment, but confirmation would help us convince the police. Most people pick something personal to use as a password, especially for something important. I dug through the life of Duncan Graves for significant milestones, personal triumphs, and things he might use as motivation. A few things loomed as possibilities, so I ran them against what I remembered his widow talking about when she dropped off his notes and the flash drive.

Our son ended up stillborn.

I couldn't imagine the level of grief two people would experience in this scenario. After months of hope and expectations, the Graveses would have probably set up a nursery in their house, bought a crib and supplies, and picked out a name.

A name.

Twenty seconds later, I found the records of Maximillian Graves. I tried *Maximillian* as the password on the flash drive and got in. Today was the day for epiphanies. "I'm in," I said. Lexi and T.J. wheeled their chairs closer, and we pored over the notes Duncan Graves had assembled before his untimely death—likely a murder. He'd covered a lot of the ground we did, including fruitless hunts through the initial victims. Eventually, he settled on Fabian as the most likely suspect considering what happened with his uncles. It turned out Graves was the PI who visited Judge Black's chambers before we did. The notes referred to Fabian as "harried and squirrely."

"Looks like he got there, too," Lexi said.

"And died for it," T.J. added.

"This asshole isn't getting to us," I said. "We're taking him down. Let's call Rich."

CHAPTER 20

A COUPLE HOURS LATER, I rode with Rich and Paul King as we headed toward Fabian's house.

He lived a short walk from Patterson Park in East Baltimore. On the drive, I checked property records. Fabian was the sole owner of the property, and nothing on his social media suggested he lived with roommates. I couldn't imagine clerks for the city courts took home a huge salary. This was a lot of house to afford on one honest person's middle-class income.

"What do you think we'll find?" King asked from the passenger's seat of the city-issued Dodge Charger.

"Probably not Fabian," I said. "Before we left, I called the office. Things are obviously in chaos after what happened to Judge Black. Fabian put in for bereavement leave. He's not going to get it because it's meant for family members, but he's not at work. My guess is he's already hiding somewhere else."

"Makes sense," Rich said. "With Thormann released, he probably knew the focus of the investigation was changing."

Two other police vehicles followed us—another Charger

and an Explorer much like the county used. The bomb squad was also en route and would meet us there. If we were right, and Fabian had already cleared out, it stood to reason he wouldn't want the cops to search his house. No matter how smart they think they are, most people leave some sort of evidence or clue behind.

A few minutes later, Rich curbed the car, and we all climbed out. Like many areas of Baltimore, the streets surrounding Patterson Park were packed with rowhouses. They stood in clusters of ten or more, with gaps leading to alleys running behind the homes and offering off-street parking. My neighborhood—Federal Hill—was the same, and I'd turned most of my meager backyard into a concrete pad to fit two cars. Some residents here no doubt did the same.

The challenge was Fabian's house stood smack in the center of a group of rowhouses. "If he's wired the place to blow," I said, "a blast will take out a lot more than just his place." While measures like firewalls should have existed between individual homes, most of the structures dated back a century or more. History often came with modern code violations.

"We're going to wait for the bomb squad," Rich said. "Officers will be prepared to evacuate the neighbors if we need to."

Two even larger SUVs rolled to the scene. A squad of cops in heavy armor climbed down. A few carried specialized equipment I didn't recognize. The one item I knew was a wheeled robot the bomb squad would deploy into unknown areas. Its cameras and other gear would tell officers what threats—especially explosive ones—waited inside a building. One member of the team conferred with Rich before half approached the front of the house and the rest headed around to the rear.

Rich, King, and I waited in the street. I remembered occupant safety information from college—something about being a distance away from the building equal to three times its height in the event of collapse. I took a step back and still felt we were on the border. Rich and King's radio crackled with a bunch of chatter and numbered codes I mostly didn't know.

A moment later, something clear came through. "We have a tripwire."

———

The bomb squad found a second tripwire at the rear entrance as well.

We waited in the street while a half-dozen uniforms evacuated residents in the cluster of townhouses and the specialists went to work on making Fabian's place safe to enter. Some people gathered in the street. When asked what was happening, Rich gave a noncommittal answer. "You'll make captain before long if you keep working politics in so easily," I told him.

"I'm happy where I am."

"Just like you were in your sergeant days . . . until your lieutenant turned out to be on the take." Rich's supervisor—a loudmouthed boor named Gannon O'Malley—got arrested on a case my cousin and I worked together. Never trust anyone who shares a name with a video game villain.

Rich grunted but didn't offer another response. Whatever his ambitions, we had more pressing concerns in the near term. The afternoon sun made me sweat as we waited for the bomb squad to finish. After another half-hour, they reported both tripwires as disabled, and no other threats prevented the police and a handsome private investigator from entering the house. Both had been rigged to an impressive pile of explosives capable of leveling three rowhouses and damaging at least as many more.

I hoped this would be the only bomb.

Even with the immediate threats offline, officers on the bomb detail went into the place first. Rich, King, and I entered via the front door. One step up got us into the living room. Wood paneling on the bottom half of the walls matched the color—but not the quality—of the flooring. A black fabric sofa, coffee table, and large bookcase were the only furnishings, and a massive TV hung from the wall. The bookshelves were full. I couldn't see a speck of dust in the room. Fabian must have used it regularly.

The other team entered via the rear, and we saw them in the kitchen. A shallow dining room with room enough for a table and two chairs spanned the width of the building between them. The kitchen itself was a decent size, with counters running the perimeter in sort of a U shape. There wasn't enough room for an island. The appliances fell somewhere between new and ancient. A coffee maker, microwave, and toaster oven took up some counter space. I breathed a sigh of relief at seeing the stove was electric.

"We'll head to the basement," the sergeant who led the second team said. They carefully inspected a door between the dining and living rooms before determining it was safe. A couple bomb technicians accompanied Rich, King, two uniforms, and me upstairs. Two cops stayed behind and conducted a more thorough search of the main level.

Before we reached the second level, the ordnance crew

checked the floor for things like pressure plates, nearby doors for tripwires, and the like. "All clear," one of them said a few minutes later. Other than the footsteps of the BPD crew, I didn't hear anything which would mean another person occupied the house. As expected, Fabian cleared out. The questions remaining were did he leave anything useful behind, and would there be a bomb waiting for us?

I hoped we were out of the woods on the second part, but I made sure to step cautiously just the same.

———

The upper level held three bedrooms and two bathrooms.

One bathroom lay directly across the hall from the steps. It was small and cramped, the kind you foisted on guests because the main one would be nicer in every way. A sink, toilet, and tub somehow managed to fit inside the walls, but a person using the space would find little room to turn around. People tend to hide things—especially drugs and weapons—in toilet tanks, but we found nothing of interest there.

A compact extra bedroom was off on the right. The only furnishings were a twin bed and nightstand on the left side. Three rolled-up yoga mats and a rack of dumbbells stood along the far wall. I didn't recall Fabian being especially tall, so he probably had enough room to exercise in this small space even with a bed. The closet was empty. We moved on.

The main bedroom was on the other side of the modest hallway bathroom. It was probably twice the size of the guest space with enough room for a queen bed, two nightstands, a dresser, and a chair. Like most older houses, there was no en suite attached nor a walk-in, but the closet was a good size. It was also full of clothes and shoes. Before anyone could snoop around, a member of the bomb squad checked wall-to-wall and gave the all clear. One of the uniforms sorted through everything in there while the rest of us examined the room itself.

We didn't find anything one wouldn't expect to happen upon in the bedroom of a man in his late twenties. As before, a uniform stayed behind to keep up the search. Rich, King, and I followed two bomb techs and the last uniformed officer into the lone remaining bedroom. This was configured like an office and a gaming room. A small desk sat in the corner. An octagonal table took up most of the square footage. Drink holders and slots for poker chips were carved into its surface. I'd spent many an evening in college and grad school around tables just like this one.

The closet was empty save for a large cubby serving as a bookcase. It was packed with Dungeons and Dragons books spanning multiple editions of the game. Fabian's table would also serve well as a D&D surface—there was room for all the players plus space in the center for the map. I'd dabbled in the game enough to appreciate Tony Stark rooting for a secret door in the second Avengers movie.

Speaking of hidden panels, something about the room seemed a little off. The closet looked shallower than the ones in the other bedrooms. Fabian didn't hang any clothes in here because he couldn't. Even a button-down shirt would stick out too much to slide the door shut. "I wonder if there's some kind of panel in the closet," I said.

"Like a hidden door?" Rich asked.

"Yeah. Look how shallow it is. The only thing in the way would be the cubby."

The officer—a woman with Hairston inscribed on her

nameplate—approached. "I think I see some faint drag marks."

"Wait for the bomb squad," Rich said.

She didn't.

When the cubby slid a few inches, I saw a tiny red light flash. Rich and I both hollered for everyone to get down. I took a step toward the entry, turned, crouched, and covered my head.

The explosion still knocked me flat.

CHAPTER 21

I COULDN'T HEAR myself cough past the ringing in my ears.

A few books landed on me when the blast went off. I shook one off my arm and rolled onto my side. Rich and King looked about the same as I did. The bomb squad guy was across the room when the explosion happened. He seemed all right, too. Poor Hairston took the brunt of the blast. She lay on her back, bits of shrapnel sticking out of her face and neck, and blood covering most of those areas.

"Call an ambulance," Rich ordered King as my cousin and I both moved to check on Hairston. She was unconscious but had a pulse, albeit a weak one. When she slid the large white Ikea cubby aside, it must have tripped an explosive. Books and wood lay around her. The closet doors, already open, collapsed to one side. Considering the damage was confined to such a small space, the charge must not have been powerful, but Hairston was directly in its path.

"Ambo is on the way," King said, and sirens announced its arrival a scant couple minutes later. Paramedics assessed Hairston and loaded her onto a gurney for the drive to the hospital. When they headed downstairs and back to the ambulance, Rich sighed and looked around the ruined room.

"We don't have much of a crime scene anymore," he said. "Let's secure what's here." He pointed to the bomb technician. "Make sure nothing else will go off. I want to see what's in the area behind the bookcase." With the cubby reduced to kindling, we could see a recess behind it. It was maybe five feet tall, three wide, and three deep. The bomb wreaked havoc back there, too, but a small fireproof safe sat on the floor.

"I guess Fabian left something behind," I said.

"You think he wasn't planning on coming back?" Rich asked.

"Hard to say. He knows the bomb is there, and we can presume he also knows how to avoid setting it off. My guess is he didn't think we'd find his little stash spot."

"I wonder what's in the safe," King said.

"Let's get everything photographed first," Rich said. "Then, we can worry about it."

A crime scene team worked on processing the area. They took copious pictures, checked many surfaces for prints, and filled a dozen or more plastic bags with various bits of evidence—including some parts of the actual explosive device. As techs processed the scene and removed more debris, we got a better look inside the closet and the hidden compartment.

Nothing remained in it except for the safe. It looked like a really bulky briefcase and was made of black metal. It came through the explosion without so much as a scratch. I wondered what Fabian and his uncle might have hidden inside. It was the right size to hold a trove of documents. Considering the police owned the scene, I knew they would collect whatever we found inside the fireproof walls.

"We need to pop this safe," Rich announced a few minutes later when the room finally stopped looking like the scene of a recent meteor strike.

I offered, but the BPD had someone for the task. He used a snap gun on the lock, and even though it differed from the kind typically found on doors, it was mechanically the same. The black box popped open to reveal a flash drive and two manila folders stuffed with papers. "Dibs on the drive," I said.

"Bullshit," Rich said.

"I'll analyze it faster than your people will."

He shrugged. "Maybe you can. Doesn't change how we're doing things. You want to see what's on it? Read the case notes. I know you can."

I knew I wouldn't win this one, so I said, "Fine," and watched one of the uniforms bag the small device as evidence. All I could do was hope Rich made sure his technical folks worked on it right away. With no signs of Fabian at his house, we needed alternatives.

———

We were still looking for alternatives the next morning.

"Is the officer okay?" T.J. asked.

"I heard it was touch and go at first," I said. "It wasn't a big bomb, but it went off right in front of her. She lost a lot of blood. Her vest probably protected her from some of it. Rich told me she's stable as of a couple hours ago."

"That's good."

"I wish you could've gotten the flash drive," Lexi said.

"It wasn't for a lack of trying." I sipped from my coffee mug and checked the BPD's case notes. Still nothing about what they might have found on the USB device or in the manila folders. "They're taking their time with it, too."

"Maybe the drive had a password like Graves's did."

"It could have. The papers should've been processed by now, though. Considering this case is a massive red ball with a judge getting blown up, the commissioner should have deployed a team to read and analyze everything as quickly as possible."

"You a speed reader?" T.J. wanted to know.

"I've always processed things quickly." I shrugged. "Most 'speed reading' techniques have always seemed like glorified skimming to me. I know at least one person who swore he could do it even as he kept getting bad grades on tests."

Lexi shook her head. "This is bullshit. I've seen a few articles this morning that talk about a house being raided, the cop getting hurt, and all that. None of them mention *whose* house it was. Ridiculous. Why not name the suspect?"

"I don't know," I said. "Maybe they're gun-shy after running with Thormann being the bomber and having to watch him get cut loose a couple days later. Any kind of responsibility in reporting would surprise me."

"This Fabian asshole is the suspect . . . both him and his uncle." Lexi scowled. "Does this always happen?"

"We don't usually get much press on our cases," T.J. said. "The serial killer in winter and now this are unusual."

Before I could chime in with my agreement, the phone on my desk rang. It was the VoIP unit again, and I had a strong inkling as to the caller's identity even though the display told us the other party was unknown. I picked up the handset and put the call on speaker right away. "Hello?"

"You made it personal," the same distorted voice as before said.

"I had the higher ground, Anakin."

"Make your Vader jokes. Laugh it up."

"Do you think we don't know who you are, Fabian?" I said. "The local papers might be too chickenshit to call you out, but I'm not. I had a feeling something was off about you the first time we walked into the courthouse. Never trust anyone who has a weird name and lacks the good sense to go by their initials." Fabian's sigh came out as a mechanical hiss. "If you don't want me making Darth Vader cracks, maybe you shouldn't go out of your way to sound like him."

"It doesn't matter," he said, keeping the distortion on even though we knew who he was. "What's important here is you've made it personal. You went to my house."

"Did you really think no one would?"

"How's the lady cop?" It was hard to pick up tone thanks to the device Fabian used, but I swore I still detected some mockery.

I wondered if he had any cameras in the house. We didn't see any during the raid, and there was no record of a contract with any alarm company. Still, Fabian could have hidden a small electric eye or two around the place and monitored them remotely. "She'll be fine. Why don't you make things easy on yourself and tell me where you are? It'll save us all a lot of trouble."

"I don't think so. The cops were doing their jobs. You could have backed off. You should have."

"Why?" I pressed. "Because you sent a couple idiots after me? You want me to drop this, you'll have to do a hell of a lot better."

Fabian laughed, and the electronic scrambling lent it a

menacing tone. I fought against the shiver running up my spine but eventually acquiesced. "I'm going to. Remember, asshole . . . you brought it all on yourself." He hung up.

I set the receiver back onto the base unit. "What do you think he meant?" T.J. asked.

"I don't know," I admitted. "We've seen what he and his uncle can do, though. They got into Judge Black's garage and wired his car to blow up. Let's all be careful. Keep an eye out for people following you . . . strange vehicles hanging around. Make sure you check your cars before you get in and turn the engine on."

"We really need to catch this prick," Lexi said.

"Yes," I said, "we do."

———

Later in the afternoon, Rich called.

I hoped the cops had made a breakthrough, but his tone quickly dashed my optimism. "Nothing on the flash drive yet," he grumbled. "There's a password to get into it, and our techs are pretty sure the files are encrypted on top of everything."

"So you might need more than one password?"

"Basically."

"If only you knew a clever and handsome fellow who made his bones as a hacker," I said.

"You think our people aren't good?"

"Good? Sure. When you're ready to raise the bar a level or two and bring me the drive, you know where to find me."

"We hit the uncle's place," Rich said, changing topics. "With the county. He rents an apartment in Perry Hall. They brought their bomb squad, and I made sure we took our time and didn't have a repeat of what happened to Hairston at Fabian's place."

"How is she?"

"Better," Rich said. "Eager to get back on the job, which probably won't be happening for a while. I worked with your buddy Gonzalez on this one."

"Did he ask about me?"

"No."

"He must have been distracted by the gravity of the situation," I said.

"Must have been."

"I guess you didn't find anything in the apartment?"

"Nothing," Rich said. "It was neat and tidy. Nothing out of place. No hidden compartments or dresser drawers with false bottoms."

"Fabian's clearly spiraling," I said. "Maybe he wanted to be named by the press at this point. I don't know. He called here again and issued threats."

"Do you know where he called from?"

"No. It was a burner each time. He used some kind of voice distorter. Sounded like someone doing a mediocre Darth Vader impression. Even when I pointed out we knew who he was, he didn't drop it."

"And you couldn't help but poke the bear a little," Rich said.

"Well . . . I think *poke* might be a little strong."

"It's not just you anymore. I know you throw yourself into these frays come hell or high water, but you're not paying the price alone. You have a secretary and an intern now."

"I told them to be careful," I said.

"Plus parents with the Ferguson surname. And a wife."

"You think this maniac might come after Gloria?"

"Her fundraising has made her something of a public figure. Your recent cases did the same for you. If someone really wanted to get to you, do you think he wouldn't use your wife? This prick killed a sitting judge, for Christ's sake."

"All right," I said. "I'll make doubly sure to check Gloria's car before she gets in it. She can work from home, so I'll convince her to stay put until all this shit is over."

"You have to take this guy seriously," Rich warned. "He's killed four people already, and the last one was a hard target."

"I understand."

"Make sure you do." Rich ended the call. It was a sobering reminder of what we faced.

CHAPTER 22

T.J. GOT UP EARLIER than usual to hit the gym.

One of the reasons she wanted to live in The 501 was the onsite exercise facility. It featured a range of cardio machines, room to do things like yoga and Pilates, and the usual free weights and benches. It wasn't as big as an actual gym, but anyone using it lived in the building. It cut down on backwards-hatted bros taking selfies while doing biceps curls and then leering at every woman in tight pants.

T.J. had been leered at more than enough in her life. The irony was she looked much better and fitter now than in her later teen years. Making the apartment work financially proved a challenge at first—especially with the addition of a car—but she managed it. C.T. being generous with raises and holiday bonuses helped, too.

T.J. finished on the treadmill and moved to the weights. She remained standing while moving through curls and shoulder presses. The cute guy she saw in here sometimes walked in. They exchanged quick smiles, and T.J. felt herself blush as he stepped onto the elliptical. One of these days, she would talk to him. Or maybe he would make things easier and initiate the conversation.

After a few sets of squats, T.J. got flat and did three sets of bench presses. Having worked up a good sweat, she finished morning exercises with ten minutes on the heavy bag. T.J. reminded herself she needed to attend kickboxing classes more often, but at least she got to practice without leaving home.

T.J. guzzled water as she headed for the door. She caught the cute guy looking at her in the mirror, smiled, and gave him a little wave before she left. Back in her apartment, she took out her earbuds and stopped her music. While she drank another bottle of water, her phone buzzed. It was a text from Lexi.

Let's get this son of a bitch today.

T.J. smiled. She admired her newest friend's spirit and persistence.

> Yeah. I'm ready to deal with something else.

WYD?

> Just left the gym in my building. I'll be at the office in about 45 minutes.

I might come in early. Screw intern hours. Let's catch a killer before anyone else dies.

> It's good to see you get so invested in your first big case!

I'm all in now. This is fun. I can see myself working as an investigator after college.

> I hope you'll still pop by and say hi while you're rounding up suspects.

Count on it, girl. BFFs.

> BFFs!

Over the years, T.J. had made friends with other young women but this often came out of necessity. They shared information about johns who liked to get rough or ways to pull one over on their pimp and his muscle. Her only genuine friend from the old life was Amy, AKA Velvet, and she managed to get herself out, too. Both got help from former lady of the evening—and the mayor's daughter—Melinda Davenport, whose Nightlight Foundation sought to rescue girls and young women trapped in lives they needed to abandon. T.J. and Amy were two graduates of the school of Baltimore's hardest knocks.

Her job meant she spent most of her time with C.T., and while she liked him and knew she could count on the man, T.J. wouldn't consider him a friend. When Lexi called looking for internships, it made sense. The agency could use the help after the serial killer investigation in the winter led to a surge of interest and new clients, and convincing the boss had been easy.

Lexi was two years younger than T.J., and some of their interests overlapped. The resumption of college in the fall would mean fewer interning hours, but T.J. knew the pair would still be close. It felt nice having a real friend her own age for a change.

Maybe they could even celebrate the arrest of Fabian soon.

———

It was already a humid morning in Baltimore.

The heat and mugginess seemed to encroach a little more on spring every year. This year, the mercury went north of 90 before Memorial Day and showed an unwilling-ness to retreat. T.J. checked her bag and walked out of her apartment.

The hot, soupy air hit her as she opened the door. She was still a little heated from her morning workout and shower. Coffee didn't exactly help keep the body cool. When she bought her Mustang to replace the battered Civic she used to drive, T.J. knew it didn't come with many frills. She couldn't afford the ones that did. Her goal was to add better components over time as the budget allowed.

A more modern stereo and head unit was her first upgrade. The remote starter had been the second. It was made for mornings like this. So long as she left the air condi-tioning running—or the heat in cold weather—the night before, the engine would fire up and make the inside of the car more tolerable. It worked out to about seventy-five feet, and so long as T.J. slowed her usual walking pace, it was enough time to cool things off.

Her building featured an outdoor parking lot. There were no trees or shade other than the structure itself inter-fering with the early morning sun. By the time she came out most days, even this small relief was gone. By now, enough people had left for work or summer classes to leave the lot about half full.

As she passed a light pole, T.J. hit the button on her key fob.

The yellow Mustang started up, and then a bright fireball consumed it.

The force of the explosion shook the ground and knocked T.J. backwards. Alarm systems on nearby vehicles rang and chirped. T.J. stared at the burning wreckage of her car for a few seconds before taking out her phone and dialing 9-1-1.

———

"I loved that fucking car," T.J said as two officers stood with her.

The fire department extinguished the blaze quickly. One of the firefighters approached T.J. He was tall and broad, and even in his heavy gear, he might have stepped off the cover of the romance novels her mother used to read. "No way anyone could survive the explosion," he said. "Your remote starter saved your life today."

T.J. didn't know what to say. She understood his point, of course. Reconciling it with the smoldering husk of her beloved Mustang proved to be a challenge. A few other people milled about the area. Hers was not the only vehicle damaged in the blast, and the others would need body work, paint, new windows and windshields, and probably other stuff she didn't know about.

Whatever car she got next, the insurance would be higher. Would her building's management company try to evict her? Would the owners of the other damaged cars and SUVs sue her into oblivion? Even if they went after her insurance company, it would make getting an affordable policy—or being able to obtain one at all—much more challenging. "Miss?" one of the officers said, snapping T.J. back to the here and now.

"Sorry. Just thinking about how shitty this could all get over something that wasn't even my fault."

"Do you know who might have done this?" the same officer asked. He only looked to be a few years older than T.J., though his complete lack of facial hair might have accentuated his babyface.

"Yes," T.J. said. "The same prick who's been blowing up cars and killing people across the city. Fabian Charles."

"I . . . don't know the name." He wrote it down on his small notepad. "You're saying he's the Vox Populi killer?"

Before T.J. could answer, the other cop broke in. He was older, probably in his forties, and the constant smirk he displayed around T.J. gave him a very punchable face. "Sure he wasn't a disgruntled john?"

"Go to hell," she snapped. "I've been out of the life for years. I work for the Ferguson Detective Agency. We're investigating the bombings. My boss is a private investigator, and his cousin is a lieutenant in homicide."

The older cop shrugged. "I don't work homicide. Do you need to take a drug test?"

"Do *you*?"

"You're a mouthy one." He pointed at her, and it took a significant amount of T.J.'s willpower not to bite this asshole's finger. "In my experience, once you're a whore, you're always a whore."

"I told you . . . I work for a detective agency."

"And I'm telling you—"

"Hey!" another voice called. T.J. turned to see Sergeant Paul King striding toward the trio. "What the hell are you doing?"

"I'm . . . uh . . . trying to establish this young woman's story."

"Bullshit," King said. "You're harassing her. Did she tell you she works for a PI?"

"Yeah."

"She does. I've worked with them." The older cop glanced at T.J. and then quickly averted his eyes. "We've spent years rebuilding trust in the community, and you're pissing it away after her car gets blown up?"

"I don't know who you are, but I—"

"My name is King." He pulled back his suit jacket to show the badge clipped to his belt. "Sergeant King. Now, unless you want to be scrubbing toilets in Central Booking until the Fourth of July, you'll fuck off and canvass the area."

"But I—"

"Now," King said, stepping closer and getting in the other man's face. The older officer put his head down and walked away. King turned to the younger one. "And you . . . when your partner is going rogue and hassling a woman over nothing, you need to step in."

"Yes, sir," he had the good sense to say.

King jerked his head to the side. "Go. I got this." The younger uniform walked away, as well. "You good?" King asked T.J.

"I'm pissed about my car and worried about a hundred things that might happen next," she said. "That prick didn't make anything better."

"Sorry about him. I'm sure you didn't need my help, but I'm not going to let some jackass do stupid shit." A tow truck entered the lot. T.J. figured it was for what remained of her car, but she also wondered if any others damaged in the blast would need to be hauled to dealerships and repair shops. "You need a lift to the office?"

"Let me see." T.J. pulled out her phone and texted Lexi. *VP blew up my car. I'm all right. Double and triple check your own ride. Maybe have your dad look at it.*

A minute later, the reply came. *OMG!! You sure you're OK? My dad checked out the cars this morning. All good. I haven't left yet. You need me to come get you?*

No, I'm getting a lift. Just wanted you to be careful. "All right," she told King. "Let me make a phone call, and then I'd love a ride to work."

CHAPTER 23

I WAS UP EARLIER than usual to get started on the day.

We were close to finding Fabian and his uncle. Something big would happen today. Years ago, before I even worked as a private eye, Rich told me investigations were about many things, but momentum was at the top. I felt we had it now, and something big would break in our favor today. Gloria remained asleep while I went out for a run, showered, and got dressed.

I brewed coffee in the kitchen and drank some while I scrambled eggs and cooked turkey sausage in separate pans. Along with two slices of sourdough toast, I had a nice breakfast, and I ate it faster than I normally would while packing my bag. I left some egg and sausage in the refrigerator for Gloria and headed out back.

Her Mercedes coupe sat next to my S4 on the parking pad. As I'd done the past few days, I walked around the outside of each car, looking for anything like a loose wire or a suspicious stain on the concrete. Nothing. I got down and looked under both as best I could. I was no mechanic, but I felt pretty confident I could differentiate a bomb from the bottom of an engine. After popping the hoods, I confirmed nothing appeared out of the ordinary. To be sure, I used Gloria's remote starter from a safe distance. The engine purred like a tiger.

I relocked Gloria's car and hopped in mine. The supercharged V6 turned over. It had a nice sound to it, but it couldn't match the tone Gloria's coupe produced. I reversed into the alley, put the car in first, and headed out. Toward the end, I steered around a white box truck. Two guys stood by it with the back open. Their shirts advertised the junk hauling service they worked for. There wasn't an abundance of room on the far side of their vehicle, but I made the turn and then joined Riverside Avenue.

As I headed toward Fells Point, I wondered if T.J. would also make it in early. I thought about texting her, but I also didn't want to wake her. She needed her rest, too, and I was a big boy who could make coffee all by myself. I left my phone on the passenger's seat and drove to the office.

———

I got up the metal stairs earlier than normal, so I wasn't surprised T.J. hadn't made it in yet.

Because caffeine makes everything better, I set a pot of coffee to brew and hit the button. While the aroma filled the office, I logged into my laptop and checked the BPD's case notes. While several new entries appeared since I looked yesterday, none were consequential. Fabian and his uncle were still in the wind. The BPD brought in the state police to help look in locations outside the city limits. Considering the empty houses they checked, all the cops might as well have been on a real estate tour. Usual haunts, known associates, and the like turned up nothing.

I was halfway through a cup of coffee when Rich called. A glance at the time on my phone when I answered told me T.J. should make her way in soon. "We got into the flash drive," my cousin said.

"Wow. Props to your technical folks."

"I reminded them of something you told me. People tend to pick memorable things for passwords."

"I presume whatever they found will make it into the case file?" I pressed.

"Should be uploading as we speak. If you somehow had a connection to official BPD resources despite not being a part of the department, I would tell you to check in a few minutes. Obviously, an outsider having such a way in would be absurd."

"Obviously."

"I'm sure you'll figure something out," Rich said, and then he ended the call. I waited a few minutes, poured my third mug of the morning, and refreshed the case notes. A new folder titled *Flash Drive Recovery* had appeared, so I opened it. A directory of documents and pictures filled my monitor. Fabian and his uncle—maybe with some help— compiled an impressive trove of information.

No document explained how to make the bombs or rig them into cars. Still, even without such an obvious smoking gun, there was ample research here to tie our criminals to the fatal explosions. A few documents delved into the finer points of convictions in Maryland as well as the most common legal technicalities upon which someone might challenge their conviction. The research included direct citations from state law as well as cases which could have served as precedent. Considering he clerked at the circuit court, this would have been easy for Fabian to compile. His notes were dispassionate, neither agreeing or disagreeing with the ways someone might go before a judge and walk out free.

Other documents covered potential targets in depth—including all four victims of the Vox Populi blasts. In addition to field reports and observations, the files included photos of the victims outside their homes and out in their communities. I wondered how Fabian and his uncle pulled this off. Frederick worked for the state's bomb squad but nothing in his history suggested any stealth expertise or advanced training. Lexi's father—a retired Green Beret—could have pulled something like this off. The Charles men probably needed to get lucky or resort to some sort of subterfuge.

I kept digging. More recent entries included notes on the investigation into the bombings. Sure enough, the late Duncan Graves appeared, though there was nothing to suggest Fabian or Frederick ran the man down. Toward the bottom, I spotted a folder with the ominous title of *Ferguson Targets*. The documentation was a little thin. However, the pair had taken copious pictures. Many showed T.J. and me getting into or out of cars in the parking lot. Some drone-aided photos depicted T.J. in the lot of her apartment.

As I scrolled, a few of me entering my car behind my house appeared. The angle came from down the alley and on the opposite side. A recent image showed Gloria getting into her coupe. A cold pit formed in my stomach. When I left the house this morning, a box truck sat at the correct end of the alley to be the source of the photos. Two men in some random uniform loitered near the vehicle. I never saw their faces, but now, I wondered if Fabian and his uncle were waiting for me to leave.

I grabbed my keys off the desk and bolted for the door.

———

I called Gloria as I ran down the stairs as fast as I could before falling.

After five rings, it kicked over to voicemail. I muttered a curse, got into the S4, and peeled out of the parking lot on four screeching tires. I tried her again, and it went to voicemail for the second time. I left a message. "It's me. I hope I'm catching you in time. Don't go to your car. I checked it this morning, but someone might have messed with it after I left. I'm going to call the cops and have it cleared. Just stay in the house." I hit the red button to end the call and drummed my fingers on the wheel as I waited at a light.

Times like these made me wish for a more direct driving route between Fells Point and Federal Hill. The closest way was across the harbor, but I lacked a jet ski, and the water taxi schedule was too unreliable. The neighborhoods weren't far apart, but having to drive around a large body of water made a relatively short trip take longer than it needed to. Right now, every second counted.

The light turned green, and I put the supercharged engine in the S4 to good use. Before I could call Rich, my phone vibrated, and the screen between my gauges showed Gloria's name and number. I answered right away. "Hey, have you left yet?"

"I just heard your message," she said. A tremble in her

voice came through over the Bluetooth. I hoped it was only the reality of the situation hitting home for her.

"Are you still in the house?"

"No." She let out a cry, and my heart sank.

"In the car?"

"Yes."

"What happened?"

"I was packing up when you called." Gloria paused to stifle a sob. "I opened the car and got in. When I sat down, I heard a click. I held my phone near the floor and saw a blinking red light in the reflection." She became hard to understand as she cried, but I was sure she said, "I don't want to die."

"You're not going to die," I told her, hoping I sounded confident enough to reassure both of us. "Don't get up. It might be some kind of pressure plate. Try not to move very much. I'm going to call Rich, and he's going to send the experts. I'm on my way back to the house."

"All right," she choked out after a few seconds.

"Be brave. You'll be fine. I'll see you soon." I broke the connection and dialed Rich, cutting off his initial question with, "I think there's a bomb in Gloria's car."

"What?"

"She said she heard a click when she sat down and then saw a red dot reflected in her phone."

"Is she at your house?" Rich asked.

"Yes."

"I'll tell the squad to hurry. Meet you there." He hung up. I kept my foot on the gas as I zoomed through an intersection as the yellow signal flipped to red. I replayed my conversations with Fabian in my head. He was a prick who had already murdered four people, but was Rich right? Did I poke the bear? I'd like to think Fabian would have lashed out at me—and those close to me—because he figured we were softer targets than cops, the mayor, or a judge. But what if I taunted him into this course of action? No time to worry about it now. I needed to get back home.

I was about two minutes away, and they would be the longest two minutes of my life.

CHAPTER 24

I SKIDDED to a stop on my neighbor's parking pad.

He always left for work early, so the space was available. I rushed out of the car to Gloria's coupe. Makeup streaks covered her face. My heart thudded in my chest as I crouched at her open door and held her hand. "You're all right," I said, making sure to keep my weight back on my heels and not risk messing with whatever pressure plate she sat on.

Gloria shook her head. I wanted to wipe her tears away, but I also couldn't take the chance of the movement setting off the explosive. "I don't want to die," she said in a small voice.

"You won't. The bomb squad is coming. You'll be all right." My mind flashed to Fabian Charles. I pictured him as the frazzled clerk at the circuit court. It would take all my restraint not to pistol whip hard enough to kill him and the next three generations of his family.

"There are so many things I haven't done," she said, her chestnut hair waving as her head wagged. "You're busy. I have a company. We never had kids." She wiped a tear streaming down her cheek. "It was always the wrong time. What if I never get the chance?"

"You'll get the chance." I patted her hand.

"What if I don't?"

"You will."

"I want to have kids," Gloria said. "Screw the timing."

I wanted to make a joke about enjoying the practice, but this wasn't the moment. Gloria was beyond the point where such a crack would have made her smile or laugh. "All right," I said. "We'll have a lot of years left for it." Sirens approached. Gloria's hazel eyes flicked toward the sound. "See? The good guys are on the way."

A cruiser stopped on the other side of my house. Rich climbed out and rushed over. "Our demolition team is two minutes out," my cousin said. "They'll be able to disarm this."

"They'd better," Gloria said. "I just got a commitment from my husband that he's okay with having kids." She sniffled and slowly wiped her nose on her shirt sleeve. It was something she'd never do under normal circumstances—just like mentioning our stress-induced chat about offspring.

"Now, I feel like I'm sitting on a bomb, too," I said.

Rich chuckled, and Gloria followed suit. It served a nice moment of levity as another set of sirens drew closer.

———

Two massive white vans marked *Baltimore Police Bomb Squad* blocked the alley.

As armored officers walked toward the car, I kissed

Gloria's hand and backed away to give them room to work. "I'll be right here," I told her.

Two cops—one man and one woman—stopped just shy of the coupe and leaned closer. "What happened?" the man asked.

"I got in this morning and heard a click when I sat down," Gloria said. "My husband has been working on those bombings. He's been checking my car every morning."

"I did this morning, too," I said. "It was clean. There was a box truck at the far end of the alley." I pointed to my right. "No name or anything on it. Two guys stood around in junk hauler shirts. My guess is they waited for me to leave and then got to work."

"You think this is connected to the Vox Populi murders?" the female officer said.

"Yes."

"Different MO. The others were rigged to the starters. I don't want to presume much about this one, but it seems like a pressure plate switch."

I shrugged. "It's not easy to see much of the engine from the bottom. The car has a factory alarm. I'm sure there are ways to trick the system into turning off, but if the starter is hard to wire something into quickly, maybe our booby trappers took the path of least resistance."

"Maybe," she allowed.

"Hooray for buying a completely over-engineered German car," I said to Gloria. "It's fun to drive and hard to wire bombs into. Maybe Mercedes can build a new advertising campaign around this."

She smiled again, which was what I wanted. The waterworks had stopped, but I knew Gloria was panicking on the inside. It was all I could do not to join her. My heart raced like it did when I ran around Federal Hill Park, and the most strenuous thing I'd done in the last thirty minutes was stand up. The male technician ran back to the van as fast as his bulky body armor would allow. I wondered how much protection it offered in the event of a blast, and I hoped like hell we wouldn't find out today.

My phone buzzed, but I reached into my pocket and hit the side button to ignore the call. The guy returned without most of his plate mail a couple minutes later. He carried a large canvas bag which would have made him the envy of every doctor I've known. He crouched by Gloria's seat, took a small flashlight off his belt, and shone it under the chair.

"Definitely a plate," he said a moment later. "Looks like a standard setup. Goes active when someone sits on it, and it goes boom when the weight comes off. No visible timer."

"Can you disarm it?" I said.

"Sure."

He reached into the bag for a few tools I couldn't identify. Gloria's car featured memory seats, and our driving positions were different. In addition to mine being farther back, I also situated the chair lower to be closer to the road and have a couple more inches of headroom. Rockets are not always designed for comfort. Her position was a little higher, so the technician had room to get his hands in there and work.

All I could do was wait, and it was torture. The female tech approached me while her colleague attempted to disarm the detonator. "Sir? You might want to move behind the vans."

I didn't need her to draw a map to know what she meant. Even a standard explosive device might not be so normal after all, and a chance of failure always remained. I shook my head. "I'm where I need to be."

"Sir, there's a chance—"

"I know," I broke in. "My wife needs me to be here and be strong, not hiding behind an armored van. It's my risk to take."

She spread her hands. "All right."

As the male officer kept working, Gloria sweated in the increasing heat. Several minutes later, she remarked, "I'm glad I didn't wear a skirt today." I smiled. Instead, she'd opted for khaki capris.

Rich moved around the Mercedes and stood near me. "You might want to get behind the van," I warned him.

"I'll wait with you," my cousin said. "You all right?"

"For large values of 'all right,' sure."

"What the hell happened?"

"I reviewed the stuff you pulled from the flash drive. Toward the end, there were some pics of my parking pad, including one of Gloria getting into her car. This morning, I drove past some random van which would have been in the right spot. I hurried back. It was already gone, of course."

"We'll have uniforms canvass the area," Rich said. "Maybe somebody saw them."

"We know who it was. The problem is finding the bastards."

"Leave it to us."

"Like hell," I said. "When we find these sons of bitches, you two will need to pull me off of them."

"One step at a time," Rich said in his homicide lieutenant tone.

I nodded. "Right now, the step is getting my wife out of her car alive." I joined her in sweating as the male technician continued to work under her seat.

———

"I think we're good to go."

The technician's words were music to my ears, even though I would have preferred something more definitive. As I approached, I raised this objection. "You *think?*"

"The pressure plate is disconnected from the explosive," he explained. "As far as I can tell, there's no secondary way to trigger it. We're going to get your wife a heavy blanket to put on. Whoever helps pull her out will need one, too."

"I'll do it," I said right away.

A minute later, I was wrapped in the heaviest garment I'd ever held. While nothing could really be bomb-proof, the blanket would at least offer some protection in the event of an unexpected explosion. I knew a few people who slept under weighted blankets. This trumped them all. It must have exceeded forty pounds. Gloria draped one around herself as best she could. "I don't want to move too much just in case," she said. "My legs are starting to get numb." She frowned at the heft of the covering. "Good grief."

"I'm going to keep mine," I said. "If I wear it while I run, I'll be built like peak Schwarzenegger in a month."

My wife chuckled even with the lingering tension of the moment. I moved next to the open door and held my hands out. She placed hers inside them. "I know I have to do it, but I'm scared," she admitted.

The BPD set up a crash pad behind us. "We'll be all right. They disarmed everything. We'll do one, two, three, and then go. Okay?"

She nodded and took a deep breath. I counted slowly. Gloria's grip pressure on my hands increased with each number. Her leg muscles tensed as I hit three, and when I shouted, "Go!" she surged out of the seat as I pulled her up. Her head cleared the frame by less than an inch. I twisted after yanking her free, exposing my back to any potential blast, and I landed atop her as we splashed down onto the crash pad. We remained still, neither of us breathing as seconds rolled past without a fireball going off behind us.

Gloria wrapped her arms around my neck. "Thank you," she said in a barely audible whisper.

"I'm sorry you got dragged into this," I said in a similar low voice. "I feel like it's my fault."

"You didn't plant the bomb."

"I know."

"Then it's not your fault," my wife reassured me. In the moment, I needed it. I still didn't know if my barbs at Fabian pushed him into something unplanned, or if he always wanted to go after me as the second private investigator looking into things. The C.T. of six years ago—confidently working his first case and oblivious to what lay ahead—would find my current mood abhorrent. Today, I looked back on who I was then and realized I had so much to learn and simply didn't know about any of it back then. I wondered how much I remained ignorant to even today.

Maturity sucked in many ways.

We rose to our knees, backed our feet onto the solid concrete, and stood together. "I'll take the day off and stay with you," I offered.

"No." Gloria shook her head hard enough to unscrew it. "Absolutely not. You need to catch whoever did this. I'm a big girl. I'll go to my house, have a cry, drink a little wine, and then I'll be all right. Whoever's doing shit like this can't keep getting away with it. Go get him."

I bobbed my head. "Want me to stay a little while at least?"

"You need to get to work. Once my car is ready, I'll go home. Don't worry about me."

"I always do."

Gloria smiled. "Then don't exceed your normal levels of concern." We shared a long embrace. "I love you, and I know you'll catch whoever's responsible."

"Count on it," I said. As the bomb squad packed up, I bid farewell to Rich. "Thanks for coming . . . and for calling the experts."

"Let's get these bastards," my cousin said.

"We will." I headed to my car, and my phone buzzed again. T.J. called. I fired up the engine and answered when the Bluetooth picked up. "Hell of a morning so far."

"How do you know?"

"What do you mean?" It took a few instances of reversing and pulling forward, but after completing what felt like a forty-point turn, I got the S4 pointed in the right direction.

"My car blew up this morning," she said.

I hit the brakes and stalled the engine because I never pressed in the clutch. "What?"

"Fabian and his dickhead uncle blew up my car."

"You all right?" I asked.

"More or less. I used the remote starter, and it exploded. Good thing it was muggy this morning, I guess."

"Sorry. Fucking hell. I know you really liked your car."

"Maybe I'll even get another one. What happened with you?"

"Fabian and his uncle were busy. They put a bomb in

Gloria's car. Pressure plate this time. It went active when she sat on it. Thankfully, she heard the click."

"Jesus. He went after both of us."

"And we're going to nail him to the goddamn wall for it," I said. "Where are you now?"

"King is going to drive me to the office."

"See you there," I said.

CHAPTER 25

I GOT BACK to the office before T.J. made it in. Lexi was actually the next person to arrive. "T.J.'s not here yet?" she asked.

"Have some coffee," I said. "It's story time."

It turned out Lexi already knew about the Mustang, so I added details of the Mercedes near-explosion. "Holy shit." She got to her feet and hugged T.J. as the door was swinging shut behind her. "This is getting serious."

"Still want to intern for a small detective agency?" I said.

Lexi nodded as she sat again. "Bring it on. I want to get these bastards more than ever. Where are we going to look?"

"We have to come up with something," I said. "Cops will cover the obvious spots. If we're going to get these pricks, we'll need to think farther outside the box."

Rich called, and I answered on speaker. "Everybody make it in?" he said.

"We're here. Thirsty for coffee and hungry for justice served with a side of ass-kicking."

"We're actively looking for Fabian and his uncle." I

figured this was the case especially after the events of the morning. "If we turn up anything useful, we'll let you know."

"You'd better."

He affirmed they would and hung up. "We're going to brainstorm unusual places these two might be, then?" Lexi wanted to know.

"Right. No chance they're home. They had to go somewhere they assume we're not going to come up with." A thought hit me. I couldn't give much of a description of the vehicle I saw in the alley, but maybe I didn't need to. Fabian and his uncle were there. Considering what happened to T.J.'s car, they also stopped at her apartment. They probably went there first to work under cover of darkness.

T.J. took note of my pause. "What are you thinking?"

"Their truck." I called Rich back. "Can you check traffic cameras?"

"Sure, but I'm surprised you're not doing it yourself."

"I'm trying to be collaborative here. If you'd rather I not . . ."

"Glad you are. I can't do it from my desk. Give me a couple minutes, and I'll call you back." He hung up again.

"You mentioned it was a white box truck, right?" Lexi asked.

I nodded. "I don't recall much else about it. Didn't even get a plate. There are probably a hundred of the damn things driving around now. If traffic cameras can follow it on the streets, though, we—"

"We'll find where they went," T.J. finished for me, accentuating her thought with a loud clap of her hands.

"I'm hoping. Fabian worked in the legal system, so he must know cops have this capability. There's no guarantee it works."

"We have to try," Lexi said. Rich called back, and I answered on speaker again.

"I'm downstairs," he told us. "We can only do this from certain machines."

"I don't come to you with my problems," I pointed out.

Rich didn't take the bait. He asked when I saw the truck in the alley, and while I didn't have an exact time, I gave him my best guess. We knew the two people I'd spotted would have been wiring a bomb into Gloria's car after I left. While I didn't have a clue how long such an endeavor would take, the delicate nature of the operation prevented blitzing through it. "All right, we'll start about an hour later. I have the four closest cameras to your house up. We don't know which route they'd take."

"Sounds good." We couldn't hear much of what Rich said. He must have been giving instructions to another officer. I couldn't imagine lieutenants often logged in to whatever systems allowed access to the traffic system. The BPD probably had officers who specialized in this aspect of investigations.

"I see the truck," Rich said a minute later. "We have it leaving your neighborhood and heading into the downtown area."

I envisioned the route Fabian and his uncle might take. Getting out of Federal Hill and into the city proper was easy. The challenge was they could go any of about a thousand different ways from Pratt Street and beyond, and not all of them would be visible to one of the city's traffic cameras. Considering our two targets both worked somewhere in the justice system, they could have known where the dead zones were. I waited. Rich didn't need my stream of consciousness thoughts. I was still amped up after the incident this morning.

"Dammit," he grumbled. "We lost it."

"Dead zone?" I said.

"I don't know."

"They could have zipped into a parking garage."

"Believe it or not," Rich said, "I can think of these things, too." He went silent for a moment. "Looks like three garages are a reasonable distance from where we lost them."

"Which was . . . what, an hour ago? Two? They're in the wind by now."

"It's still worth checking out."

He had a point. "Fine," I said. "Text me the location, and I'll meet you there."

———

I met Paul King and a few uniforms at the first garage.

"Rich is coordinating things at the precinct," the sergeant explained. "You're stuck with me."

"Let's make the best of a bad situation, then," I said.

King flipped me the bird, and we began searching the garage. One of the officers went to the office to review security footage while the rest of us started on the lowest level. Many of the spaces down here were reserved for businesses nearby. A lot of pricey cars sat between clean yellow lines on fresh concrete. I doubted any of these conditions would hold true as we ascended the structure.

"What about the other ones nearby?" I asked King.

"We have teams in them, too."

"Wow. I really *am* stuck with you."

He again showed a gesture telling me I was number one,

and we continued walking. Up a ramp, not much changed. It took reaching the second level to see different conditions. The lines were a little more faded. The concrete bore cracks and stains. Cars average people could afford occupied most of the spots. Unfortunately, we didn't see a white box truck mixed with the sea of SUVs and sedans. We did see one on the fourth level, but it bore the name and logo of a delivery company. I confirmed for King the plainness of the one I saw in the alley. Driving past it felt like eighteen hours ago even though it was really only a small fraction of the larger number.

At the top level, vehicles parked under the sun and in the open air. Again, no trucks fit the description of the one from this morning. King used the radio for a couple minutes, walking away so I couldn't hear him. When he returned, his sour expression told me we'd struck out. "No sign of the vehicle," he confirmed.

"Garages are the most logical spots," I said. "Doesn't mean they're the only ones."

"We're going to check any hotels nearby."

"What about repair shops? Most of them do body work and painting."

"Not quickly enough to drive away with a new color in thirty minutes."

"Sure," I said, "but they could stash the damn truck out of sight. Fabian or Frederick would tell the owner not to let anyone look around without a warrant."

King threw up his hands. "This is bullshit. We can't lose them just because they drove into an area where we don't have eyes."

"We'll find them." I heard the lack of enthusiasm in my own tone, so I was sure King picked up on it, too.

I left the garage and drove back to the office. Lexi and T.J. were disappointed in the lack of success but not really surprised. We all thought it was something of a long shot, but those sometimes hit and pay off. Without much recourse, I explored the life of the man we hadn't yet done a deep drive on—Fabian's dear old uncle Frederick. I skimmed his service record and personal details. The cops would know it all better than I could because he was one of them for years. They'd uncover anything obvious. People hired agencies like mine because we can find answers beyond what's apparent.

I found his social media information and ran a scraping script against the sites, dumping the results into an XML file I could view in a browser. Frederick had as many connections as I'd expect of someone of his age and history. He shared some ridiculous memes and naive posts about what went on in the city, state, and country. One missive caught my eye—nine days ago, he posted an RIP to a longtime friend, Lou McGovern.

McGovern was in his fifties, single, and lived alone in a house in East Baltimore. A few minutes after I obtained the address, I also made my way into the local power company to see electricity service remained on. Additionally, McGovern's cable internet account was still active, and it was both transmitting and receiving data as of earlier today.

It was as good a place as any to look, but I couldn't conduct the search on my own. Bringing Lexi or T.J. was out of the question. With more than a week to prepare, Frederick could have the place covered in hidden bombs and other booby traps. I didn't see the point in risking everyone's neck checking it out. I would need someone who knew how to look for and disarm the kinds of shenanigans we might expect to encounter. "I have something," I told the young women, and I elaborated when they pressed me for details.

"It's thin," T.J. said with a frown.

"This entire case is slender enough to almost be two-dimensional," I said. "Thin is what we have. I'm going to run with it."

"You're calling Rich?"

"No. I'd rather take a more . . . off-the-books approach."

"Rich won't approve," my secretary said.

"True. It's why he doesn't need to hear about it. He's too concerned with following the police manual. These assholes went after Gloria and you. I need someone whose moral compass doesn't always point due north."

"And you have someone in mind?" Lexi said. I wondered if she thought I meant her dad. The description fit, and he was certainly capable, though he lacked the experience I needed.

"I do," I said.

"To what do I owe the pleasure of lunch?" Sergeant Paul King inquired from across the table at Chiaparelli's.

It was probably my favorite place in Little Italy. With nice weather today, I walked from the office. It was a little more than a mile. My return trip would be encumbered by takeout orders for Lexi and T.J., both of whom sulked to varying degrees when I told them where I'd be going and emphasized making the jaunt alone. If I needed to return with food every time I went somewhere, then our heavier caseload the last six months gave me the budget room to do it.

"Can't I just bask in your company?"

King snorted. "Even the women I date can't 'bask in my company' for too long. What's going on? And why's this so hush-hush?"

"I didn't want your boy scout lieutenant to know," I said.

"You want to keep your cousin in the dark?"

"We found a bunch of D and D books at Fabian's place. You ever play?"

"A little in college. Why?"

"Rich is a paladin." I moved my hands to frame my face. "I'm the handsome and lovable rogue who generally does the right things but not always for the right reasons. The paladin and the rogue sometimes don't get along."

"Can I be a ranger?" King said. I shrugged and nodded. "All right. I guess this means you have something on the case and don't want to share it."

"Nor do I want you sharing it . . . at least not yet."

"Why not just have a bunch of city and state cops kick the door in?"

"These bastards went after Gloria and T.J. I'm not going to sit here and weep about due process."

King held up his hand. Before he could talk, the waiter dropped off our Caesar salads. I obviously said yes to the question of fresh parmesan and ground black pepper. Like a philistine, King declined both. After munching a few bites, he said, "So what are you gonna do? Barge in and shoot Fabian in the face?"

"Tempting as it may be, no. Not unless he forces me to. He might fall downstairs, though, and hit his head and face a few times on each step. Some people are just clumsy. His uncle might be, too." I tried my salad. The fresh cheese and extra pepper helped. A little more dressing would have been nice, but it wasn't bad for an appetizer.

"You must have a line on where they are." I bobbed my head while I chewed. "Want to share?"

"Eventually," I said. "My concern is the uncle. He's had enough time to rig the place to blow a hole in the world by now. The last thing I do can't be kicking a door in."

"Makes sense. You need a more specialized skill set."

"Yes . . . and I'm hoping you know someone who can provide it. Doesn't have to be a person who's active on your bomb squad, but whoever helps needs the experience and the tools."

"Plus, might want to get paid," King said.

"I have a twenty and a book of McDonald's coupons."

He chuckled. "You've been doing all right since the asshole serial killer in the winter."

"We have," I said. "Maybe after this case, I'll take a vacation. In the meantime, I can pay someone a fair rate to help out."

Our waiter returned to clear our salad plates and set the larger entrée versions in their places. I opted for chicken parmesan with linguini and extra sauce. King picked ravioli. We ate in silence for a couple minutes before the sergeant spoke again. "I get it," he said. "You can't come to Rich with this because he'll make it a whole thing."

"Right. I don't want this to blow back on you. I can live with Rich being mad at me. Christ knows he's done it often enough."

"It'll be fine."

"You know anyone who might fit the bill?" I pressed.

King took a bite of his pasta and smiled. "As a matter of fact, I do."

KING CHECKED in later to say his contact wouldn't be available until tomorrow. It was something of a disappointment, but it also gave us time to try and figure a few more things out. The Charles men were in the wind, and we needed some good location possibilities. There was little point carting an explosives expert around to check for tripwires and other traps if we didn't know where we were going.

"We have a few possibilities," T.J. said. "Lexi and I did a bunch of stuff while you were out having lunch."

"I brought you back some," I pointed out.

"Still."

"You didn't miss the field trip because you had detention. What did you find?"

With all our computers able to cast their screens to the TV, we now had a large display to make sharing information like this easy. She showed a short list of addresses. "We don't know how many of these the BPD already has," Lexi said. "None are in their case notes, but that doesn't mean the cops are unaware of them." While I looked at the list and nodded my agreement about her assessment of the cops, T.J. opened another window.

"New post from our friend," she said, the last word dripping in enough venom to poison a snake. Again, the local papers helped platform a psychopath—or a pair of them, in this case.

"So You Think You Know Me? Don't Be So Sure"

To the police, to C.T. Ferguson, and to everyone who thinks they've got it all figured out—you don't know me half as well as you think you do. Yes, you've made progress. You've managed to piece together a few things, and maybe you even have a name in mind. Bravo. But there's still so much you don't know, so many things you haven't even begun to understand. You may be close, but close doesn't mean anything unless you can stop me—and you won't. I'm far from finished.

I've seen the threats, the smears, the wild accusations. They think they can make an example out of me, that all this effort will somehow scare others off from carrying on my work. Maybe it makes the investigators feel powerful, but it's a waste of time. Even now, they're scrambling to find me and my uncle, to track us down as if we're hiding in plain sight. Well, we aren't. We're out of reach, just beyond your grasp, and you can feel that frustration building. You're right to feel that way because I'm not going anywhere.

Now, let's address C.T. Ferguson. You've inserted yourself into my mission, which was a mistake. You're just one more agent of a broken system. You've tried to stop me, to slow me down, and now you think you've finally caught up. But let's be clear: if you keep pushing, if you keep bringing those close to you into this, don't be surprised when there are consequences. The warnings were there, plain and simple, and you can't skate by forever. Ask yourself if you're prepared to risk everything.

And to those who think my work stops here, think again. The movement I've started isn't about one person, one face, or one name. It's about real justice, about a city abandoned by its leaders and courts, finally reclaiming safety from the criminals they protect. There are others who see what I see. There are others willing to take a stand, to do what it takes, to step in where the courts fail. I may be at the center now, but if I fall, there will be someone else to pick up the torch. Justice doesn't die with me.

Baltimore's leaders and law enforcement might think they're closing in and the case they've built is almost over. I'm telling you right now it's not. I won't make it easy. I've always been one step ahead, and that's not about to change just because a few detectives are feeling clever. You think you've got me cornered? Try again.

—Vox Populi

"Do you think I could shove a grenade in his mouth?" I wondered.

"Probably not," Lexi said, answering my rhetorical question. "They're about the size of a potato, so unless our guy has a really big . . ." She trailed off when she saw my expression. "You weren't looking for an answer there. Got it."

"Your dad have any tiny grenades lying around?"

"Not exactly the kind of thing he keeps in the coffee table drawers."

"Pity." I scanned the op-ed again. Fabian or his uncle or whoever wrote the damn thing was careful not to make explicit mention of any incident from earlier today, but the dots were there waiting to be connected. "We do need to take this seriously. Judge Black got blown up in his own garage while county cops watched his house. Someone rigged two cars this morning when neither could have been easy. We're up against capable people here, and mistakes could be deadly."

"What are you saying?" T.J. wanted to know.

"I think we should work remotely," I said. "This is a good central location, but it's also a single point of failure. One well-hidden bomb takes out all three of us. If we scatter, we're harder to get."

"I don't have a car at the moment."

"You can come with me to my dad's house," Lexi offered. "There's a good security system, and we have enough guns to hold off a battalion." T.J. raised her brows at me, and I nodded after a couple seconds of consideration. I would have preferred the pair to work from different spots, but John Tyler's house had to be among the hardest targets in the state.

"I'm waiting for King to come up with an expert," I said. "By now, it's likely we'll be going out tomorrow. We'll stay in touch. Keep plugging away. It might be tough, but we'll get these assholes."

"I might need to look for tiny grenades," T.J. said. "Bastards blew up my car."

"I hope you find some."

———

After Lexi and T.J. left, I remained in the office.

The security upgrade would help. We had cameras now, and Manny's system covered the entire building. However, Fabian and Frederick Charles managed to get into a locked garage, ply their trade in T.J.'s parking lot, and bypass the system on Gloria's coupe enough to open the door and rig a pressure plate.

I kept my .45 on my desk while I worked.

Paul King called while I beat my head into a virtual wall. "I got someone," he told me. "She'll be good to go tomorrow."

"She? Very progressive of you."

He snorted. "She's damn good. More qualified than most men."

"She active?" I asked.

"No. Retired early last year."

I frowned. Even with pensions, cops didn't beg off the job early unless a compelling reason forced them to the sideline. "What happened?"

"She saw too much," King said. "Bomb squad is a rough detail. A couple incidents went pear-shaped, and she got sent for a psych eval. Retired a month later."

"Sounds like the assessment didn't go well," I said.

King sighed. "Look. I've done a few things in my time. You know I worked in Vice before I moved to Homicide." I nodded out of habit even though King couldn't see me. "I've always wanted to learn as much as I could. I met Trudy a few years ago when I did about a week's worth of ride-alongs with her bomb squad team."

"What did you think?"

"Not for me. It's a whole level of cowboy I just don't have in me." He let out a dry chuckle. "I know my job is dangerous. I'm the guy who runs *toward* the lunatic brandishing a machine gun at the mall. What she and her team did is something else. If someone shoots me, I had a chance. I could see it coming. Bomb detail? Shit. You might step on the wrong part of the floor, the whole house blows up, and they can bury what's left of you in a toy bucket. No fucking thanks. Maybe show a little grace when someone gets put up for a psych eval under these circumstances."

"Fair enough," I said. "I will. Thanks for finding her."

"Sure. She expects to get paid."

"Not a problem."

"All right," King said. "Unless we arrange something different, we'll meet you at your office at nine."

As much as I didn't want to use the place, it would be convenient, especially if King and Trudy arrived separately. She may not want to go to a precinct, and parking in my neighborhood could be dicey. "See you then."

King ended the call, and I wondered what the hell I'd be getting into tomorrow.

———

When I walked into her living room, Gloria sat on the couch, her laptop closed beside her.

We'd decided to stay at her house until this mess was over. In addition to a garage for her car, Gloria had a security system. Considering recent events, I figured she needed an upgrade. There was enough room to expand the garage to a two-car model, but this required time, money, and the approval of an ever-watchful homeowners' association. If my wife accrued too many demerits for the size and shape of the foliage in her yard, her proposal might get quashed.

I dropped beside her, and she leaned into me. "How are you?" I said.

She waffled her hand. "Getting better. I'm alive, so I'm focusing on that. Any progress?"

I shrugged. "A little. We're going to try again tomorrow. T.J. and Lexi put a couple places together." I didn't mention going rogue with Paul King and Trudy the bomb tech who retired after a dodgy psych eval. Gloria had enough stress at the moment.

"You up for cooking dinner?"

"Sure." I kissed her on the forehead and ventured into the kitchen. My rowhouse featured a first-floor office and an addition to help manage the extra space. The result was a kitchen which came in a little below average in size. Gloria's more than made up for it. A family of eight could comfortably sleep around the large island while I prepared food and used the stove and oven. If I ever needed to get more steps to hit a fitness goal, a few laps around the perimeter would put me over the top.

I opened the stainless steel refrigerator and evaluated my options. Turkey cutlets called to me. I breaded and fried them while baking a package of cubed sweet potato and whipping up a quick salad. Gloria's pantry could have supported an actual restaurant, so I took the smallest jar of sauce she had—for pizza according to the label, but it was really marinara with more basil—and heated it for dipping the cutlets. I ate them like this as a kid and never stopped even though grown adults shouldn't dip their entrées.

We ate at the dining room table. "Wow," Gloria said when she saw the plate and salad bowl set in front of her.

"I'm here all week. Tip your waiter."

Everything went great until I fumbled my knife a few minutes into the meal. It clattered off the floor, and Gloria nearly leapt from her seat. She'd never shown such a reaction before, but she'd also never sat on a pressure plate bomb before this morning. "Sorry," I said, picking up the knife and wiping a dot of sauce off the wood.

"It's all right. I'm just . . . on edge."

"I get it."

"Yet you're still going after that maniac."

"He nearly killed you," I said, "and he blew up T.J.'s car. If she didn't use her remote starter, she would've died."

Gloria shook her head. "This isn't reassuring me."

"Nothing will except me catching the maniacs responsible."

"I wish you didn't have . . . whatever code you live by sometimes," she said, setting her utensils down and crossing her arms.

"Then I wouldn't be me, and we wouldn't be married." I didn't mention the topic of kids which came up this morning while Gloria stared down her own mortality.

"I know," she muttered. "I'll be happy when this is over."

"You and me both," I said.

CHAPTER 27

FRIDAY MORNING SAW a deviation from the plan.

I arrived at the office to meet King and Trudy. Rather than go inside, I sat in the S4 in the lot. A blue Honda Accord coupe stopped next to my car. Lexi and I exchanged a glance. She got out of her car and knocked on the passenger's side window of mine. I unlocked the doors, and she dropped onto the seat. Today, she wore a black T-shirt for a singer I'd never heard of and black athletic shorts with a pink stripe up the outer seam. Her hair waved when she sat, and it smelled of fresh floral shampoo. If I were a dozen years younger and single, I might have been excited at a pretty girl getting in my car. Instead, I asked, "What are you doing here? You don't normally work Fridays."

"I thought you might need some backup." She unslung her bag and set it on the floorboard in front of her seat. The *thud* was louder than I expected.

"Where's T.J.?"

"She's working at my dad's shop," Lexi said. "One of his guys is off today, so there's an extra desk. They get along."

I remembered my secretary regarding John Tyler more

favorably than I did. "I guess it's a safe place for her to be," I said in the interests of keeping my reply diplomatic.

"I know this is an extra day," the intern said. "I can just take off a day next week to keep the schedule the same."

She knew payroll processed every two weeks, so the math would work out. Considering Lexi was already in my car, buckled up, and with her bag on the floor, I figured the window for me to protest anything had long since slammed shut. "Fine. I presume you brought a laptop and pistol?"

She smiled and patted the backpack. A minivan pulled into the lot. Paul King climbed down from the passenger's seat and ambled to my car. I couldn't get a good look at the driver but presumed it to be the mysterious Trudy. I already had my window down, so he bent at the waist and leaned closer. "I didn't realize it was Bring Your Intern to Work Day."

"Neither did he," Lexi said before I could confess ignorance on my own.

King and I both shrugged at the same time. "You have at least one address in mind, right?"

"I'll text it to you," I said. I found the location in T.J.'s email of the prior evening, sent it to King, and we were off a moment later. The minivan led the way along Eastern Avenue into Highlandtown. The address corresponded to a nondescript rowhouse at the end of a group. In addition to the ones connected to it, more homes stood on the opposite side of the alley and street. I could have thrown rocks to a restaurant and two pubs nearby.

If Fabian and Frederick packed the house with a lot of explosives, they could level most of the block.

It was about nine-thirty on a Friday morning, so I presumed many of the homes and businesses were unoccupied. The ease of parking near—but not too near—our target confirmed this. However, a big blast would inevitably kill a bunch of people. As I shut the engine off, I said to Lexi, "I want you to stay here and keep an eye on the operation."

"What? Why?"

"In case things turn to shit."

"You think they will?" she wanted to know.

"I think we have to presume there's a chance. If the house blows up, get out of here and get T.J."

"And if it doesn't?"

"Shoot anyone suspicious looking who takes an interest in what we're doing," I said.

"Roger that." I got out, as did King and Trudy. She was of average height and build with short black hair. She carried both an enormous bag on her shoulders and a massive duffel in her hand.

"Nice to meet you," I said and held out my hand. "Chivalry isn't dead, so I'll take the bag."

"I got it," Trudy insisted. "I don't like letting other people carry my stuff." Her brown eyes focused on me while she talked but immediately flicked away when she finished. I wondered if she'd been near one too many explosions and now looked for possible threats wherever she went. It sounded like the kind of trauma which could make someone fail a psychological evaluation.

We approached the front door. A narrow walkway and two steps led to a small porch. After getting on all fours to inspect the area, Trudy stood near the door, with King and me remaining a couple paces back. "You really think the Vox Populi guy is here?" she asked.

"It's two guys," I said. "This is a likely place. I don't

know if they're here now or have ever been, but we flagged it as a good possibility."

"You're a PI?"

"Yes."

"Been at it long?" She set her ginormous backpack down on the porch as well. If it contained a pressure plate rigged to blow at a certain weight, we all would have been road pizza by now.

"About six years," I said.

"What did you do before?"

"Answered a lot of questions. Still do sometimes."

She smirked and got to work. A bunch of tools and doodads I'd never seen came out of the canvas enclosure. Trudy looked through what I would have pegged as a rifle scope before poking and prodding at the door jamb with stuff she might have stolen from her dentist. The small mirror seemed very useful, at least, and she used it longer than the other tools. "We have a tripwire just inside the entrance," she said a minute later. "Very fine. I can't tell what it's connected to, but I'm sure we don't want to find out."

"We definitely don't," I said, confident I was answering for King as well.

"I can check the back door, too, but it's likely we'll find something similar. Who the hell knows what's inside?"

"I can get us past the lock," I said.

Trudy waved a hand. "I have tools for that, too. One-stop shopping."

"Told you she was good," King said, and I figured he offered it as much for his friend's benefit as mine.

As she said she could, Trudy popped the main lock and deadbolt. "I have to be careful swinging the door in," she said. "There's not a lot of room before the tripwire." She looped a slender rope around the knob, knotted it tight, and guided the door open inch by inch. Once she reached the limit, Trudy held the rope and placed it under her knee to pin it down. She shone a slender beam of light inside. "I think I can cut it safely."

"Go ahead," King said. He seemed confident for something Trudy only said she thought she could do. I moved off the bottom step. It probably didn't make a difference against a strong enough blast.

Trudy's next tool looked like a small pair of scissors with a cartoonishly long handle. She moved it inside, nodded to herself, and cut a wire we couldn't see. I winced.

Nothing happened.

"Let's check it out," King said. He and I both drew our pistols. I gave Lexi a quick thumbs-up and pointed to my eyes. She nodded. We went into the house.

———

Most Baltimore rowhouses are fairly similar inside.

Some are a little bigger than others, but layouts are pretty static once you adjust for size. We went through the front door and took a single step up into a living room. The place was somewhere between neat and a mess. Considering no one had used it for a while, I didn't know what I expected to find. Fabian or his uncle clearly thought we would come here because they rigged the door. What else was in this house? It made me wonder if the tripwire was to get us to think we'd find something of value in here and just waste our time.

"Not a very powerful bomb," Trudy said as she checked

out what the wire connected to. "Maybe not even enough to kill whoever opened the door."

"I wonder if we'll find anything here," I said.

"What do you mean?" King asked.

"Think about Fabian's house. He'd set up some hidden closet to blow, and it damaged the structure and almost killed the woman who opened it. He'd stashed important stuff behind the door and wanted to make getting it as hard as possible. This was a simple tripwire connected to what sounds like a weaker bomb."

"So you think this is a wild goose chase?"

"I think our suspect has worked at the courthouse for a while. He's read police reports and the relevant laws. It means he knows what constraints are on you and how you tend to operate within them."

"Or a little outside them sometimes," King offered.

I shrugged. "Either way, I'm not optimistic."

We cleared the living room. A small dining area was next, and it led to the kitchen and rear entrance. Beams on the ceiling probably replaced load-bearing walls in a renovation designed to transform the first level into an open-concept layout. I again cursed the number of home renovation shows I ended up watching with Gloria. Over the years, I'd learned a bunch of new terms, and I hoped they didn't push any actual useful knowledge from my brain.

The dining room held a table for six, buffet, and china cabinet. It was the neatest area on the main floor, but we found nothing of interest. Trudy inspected every doorway we moved through, and she carefully opened the fridge, oven, and every cabinet and drawer in the kitchen. We only uncovered the things one might expect to find. I learned

Fabian's friend kept an impressive stock of organic bread flour in the pantry but nothing we could use in the case.

The rowhouse was three stories, which meant two more above us as well as a basement below. We went down first. Once Trudy evaluated the door and pronounced it safe, we headed into the musty sublevel. Like my basement, this one's ceiling stopped just shy of six feet tall. The space was unfinished and mostly held HVAC systems, duct work, and old water stains.

We proceeded to the second level and then the third. Trudy led the way each time. The top two stories held three bathrooms and two bedrooms, with the third devoted to the primary suite and a bathroom lifted from a spa. I felt a little jealous.

I also felt unsatisfied because we didn't find anything.

"Seems like a bust," King said as we regrouped on the front stoop.

"I'll see if my intrepid assistant has come up with another option," I said.

"She needs a raise."

"Thanks, but I'm not accepting any applications for HR right now."

King put up his hands. "Just saying. Her fucking car blew up."

I took a breath before answering in a very uncharitable way. Only the remote starter she recently added saved T.J. from blowing up. I knew it, and I felt terrible about it. I even wondered if taunting Fabian made him lash out at the two women I spent most of my time with. Whether he meant his comment as a guilt trip or not, I didn't need one from King. I also didn't need to bite his head off as he was out on a limb here already.

"I'll take care of her," I said.

King bobbed his head, and I called T.J. "It's going fine," she said when I asked. "If I'm not busy, I might learn how to change brake pads."

"Great. We can offer it as an add-on. Maybe Manny will let you use a service bay."

"Ha ha."

"We struck out here," I said. "A small bomb on the front door but nothing of interest inside. You have any other potential addresses?"

"Lucky for you I didn't get pulled into an oil change," T.J. said. "The guy whose house you're in was an investor in some apartment building. They were trying to renovate it, rent out all the units, and all that."

"You think Fabian knew about it?"

"According to the socials, Fabian advised him to buy into it."

"Worth a drive, then. Can you text me the address?" As soon as I finished the question, my phone buzzed once in my hand.

"Just did," T.J. said. "I'll keep plugging away here in case you whiff again."

"Thanks for the vote of confidence."

"Anytime, boss."

"Don't you have a head gasket to replace?" I asked before ending the call. I texted the location to King. "Got another possibility."

He looked at it and frowned.

―――――

"I can go off the books for a single house," King said. "A whole building?" He shook his head. "It's a lot. Too much for Trudy to clear on her own for starters, and too many units and rooms for you and me to search."

"You're right," I grumbled. "Can you spin it as something we've uncovered and leave out the events of the morning?"

"I didn't make sergeant for no reason." He got on his radio and walked away to call it in.

Trudy spread her hands. "Sounds like I'm done for the day."

"I guess so," I said. "In the event we need your expertise again, I'll let King know. Give me your Venmo or whatever, and I'll pay you for your time."

"I'll have him send it to you," she said.

A couple minutes later, King walked my way again. "I brought Rich into it. He bought what I told him about this being new intel you happened to pass on to me."

"For now at least."

King shrugged. "All's well that ends well. If we wrap it up, he won't ask anything else. We're going to have a bomb squad van and three cruisers meet us there. A team of four should be able to clear things a lot faster. We'll have six uniforms helping us inspect the place." He paused for a breath. "You feel good about this?"

"I don't know yet," I said. "So far, Fabian and his uncle haven't been anywhere we thought we'd find them. I hope they're at this random apartment, but it feels like a reach."

"Your secretary came up with it," he pointed out.

"I'm aware. You guys sometimes listen to psychics because you have to investigate leads even if they come from crackpots." I shrugged. "I'd like to think T.J. and I are a few steps above."

"One or two."

"Fuck off," I said, and we both chuckled as we headed to the car.

"I guess I'm riding with you," King said. "Trudy took her van."

"Lexi has shotgun, but you'll have more legroom behind her." King climbed into the back, and Lexi moved her seat up a little to accommodate him. With the intern waiting in the S4, it was already running with the air on, so we headed off. The apartment was in northeast Baltimore off Moravia Road. I made a left just past a McDonald's. Moravia Park Drive became Bowleys Lane around a bend, and the building in question sat on the right. The area bridged the gap between commercial and industrial on Moravia Road and the nearby Route 40 and the residential neighborhoods ahead. Armistead Gardens lay to the south, and the lush greenery of Lower Herring Run Park stared at us from across the street. Other than a walking trail, all I could see were trees.

The structure was long, squat, and narrow. Unless it featured a level below ground, there were two stories for apartments. A few green doors poked out from the dingy red brick exterior. Several windows were boarded up. Despite these imperfections, the place didn't look to be in bad shape. I lacked enough knowledge of the area to opine on the investment quality, but a decent rehab investment should have yielded a slew of tenants.

Two white vans and three cop cars pulled into the lot. King coordinated with a few people while Lexi and I waited near my car. The conversation went longer than I expected and included multiple people pointing in our direction. "Am I sitting this one out, too?" she asked.

"I think we both are," I said. "This is a much more official operation now. My guess is King is getting pressure not to let us civilians inside."

"Why?"

"It's a liability issue for the department." She sighed, and I sympathized. "It's important for interns to learn on the job, so here's a free lesson . . . lawyers ruin everything."

"My dad would agree with you."

"Do I need to reconsider my position?"

She smirked. "You two probably have more in common than you think."

She had good odds of being right, but I didn't respond. Instead, the two of us watched as the armored contingent checked all ground floor windows—even the ones whose glass had been replaced by plywood—and entrances. As far as I could tell, no one discovered any issues. Someone used a snap gun to pop the main door, and the four members of the explosives team filed in ahead of the six uniforms. The door remained open, but we lost visual as they went up the steps.

"I hate waiting," Lexi said.

"Me, too. Sometimes, it's the right thing to do. It can save your life."

"Another thing you and my dad agree on."

"You're fired," I said.

Lexi chuckled. "T.J. told me you 'fired' her at least once a week for a while."

"I still do on occasion. It never seems to stick."

Before Lexi could answer, a blast rocked the building, and the windows at either end blew out.

CHAPTER 28

ANOTHER FLEET of police cars arrived immediately ahead of trucks from the fire department.

Other than the windows blowing out, the explosion didn't seem too bad from outside the building. Once it became clear there was no risk of collapse, Lexi and I moved toward the main door to help everyone out. In a stroke of luck, none of the officers were seriously hurt. Besides a few getting knocked flat and a bunch of ringing ears, the BPD contingent got off with nary a scratch.

"What the fuck?" King fumed as he stalked near the cars.

"I don't think they're here," I said.

"No shit."

"Everybody all right?"

"I think so. Seemed like a couple of weak bombs. One of the techs thinks there was a plate under the floor. It's kind of a mess inside. Easy to hide something."

"I'm glad no one got hurt."

"Any other bright ideas for where these assholes might be hiding?" King wanted to know.

"None at the moment." I pointed back toward the main road. "I don't know about coverage right around here, but there are some major streets a couple blocks away. You might get something from cameras."

"Already thought of it."

"You'll make sergeant if you keep coming up with all these good ideas," I said. King flipped me off and walked toward a gaggle of uniforms. One produced a laptop from her cruiser. They set it on the hood and looked at the screen. I guessed the two were accessing camera footage from the area. Bowleys Lane and Moravia Park Drive would see some natural traffic connecting to Moravia Road. There could be a lot of noise and not much signal.

"You think they'll find anything?" Lexi asked me.

"No idea. The last time the cops thought they had a lead on a car, it turned out to be nothing."

"So we're not interested if they come back with something?"

"Depends," I said. "I'm leaning no unless they tell us concrete details. We'll figure something out. Fabian and Frederick are getting desperate."

"They might not even be in Maryland anymore."

"True. Whatever they rigged here could have been done quickly. It's a short drive to Ninety-Five south, and Virginia is about an hour away." The aforementioned Moravia Road would also lead to I-95 North, though places like Delaware and Pennsylvania took longer to reach.

"You think they're on the run?" Lexi wondered.

"I don't know. Part of me thinks Fabian is pissed at how things went. His Vox Populi persona has peaked in popularity. We've seen more negative editorials lately. T.J. and

Gloria both survived the attempts on their lives. I don't think he's finished yet."

"What about the uncle?"

"He brings the expertise," I said, "and I think a lot of the vendetta was his initially. Once they got rolling, though, Fabian's vitriol has been the guiding factor."

"We have an SUV leaving the area," King called out. "It's not on cameras farther along the neighborhood, so it must have come from here. Looks like it was sometime last night. I'm not sure what we'll find, but we're seeing where it ended up. Let's go." The fire department continued working on the fire, which seemed well in hand. King jogged to where Lexi and I stood. "You coming?"

"Not this time," I said. "You don't lack for people to ride with, either. Thanks for sticking your neck out for us today."

"Don't expect it on the regular." We bumped fists, and he trotted back toward the phalanx of BPD cruisers.

When they left, Lexi and I climbed back into the S4. "What now?" she asked.

"We'll go back to the office."

"I thought we weren't using it."

"Me, too," I said, "and then you showed up there this morning. If you'd rather go work at your dad's, I'm fine with it."

"We're finding this prick today."

"Damn right we are."

———

I dropped Lexi at the office. We both inspected her Accord, found nothing out of the ordinary, and she drove off for her dad's shop. I asked Manny if he had a service bay he and the crew wouldn't be using today. He said he did, and after a promise of pizza, I parked my car in there. Once I got upstairs, I locked the door, ordered lunch for delivery to uphold my end of the bargain, and got to work.

T.J. called a few minutes later. "You didn't go with King?"

"No," I said. "The last time the BPD thought they had a line on the car, it ended up being nothing. I'd rather try and be productive when we're this close."

"What are you looking at?"

"Fabian and Frederick. I have two suspects and two screens. The ratio works out well."

"I'm glad your need for symmetry is satisfied," my secretary said.

"Me, too."

"Any ideas on where to look? I can take one. Lexi can help when she gets here."

"All right. You work on the uncle. I'll handle the clerk."

"On it, boss," she said. "I'll let you know if I uncover something."

We ended the call, and I focused on Fabian. We'd just returned from checking out a couple properties belonging to his friends, so I went down this rabbit hole. At the risk of sounding like my parents, social media has broadened the usage of "friend" over the years. Fabian had collected more than a thousand actual friends, acquaintances, and hangers-on over time. It was a lot to sort through, but with the aid of my scraping tools and some common sense, I knew I'd find something.

First, I dumped the list of names and scrolled through it. I stopped when I got to Karl Koenig. KK. One of the goons who made a highly unsuccessful visit to the office wore a

Movado watch with those initials. *KK, graduation day.* I wondered if he'd gotten it fixed after I tossed the damned thing down to street level. If Fabian knew Karl Koenig well enough to send him after us, then Karl might be able to make an educated guess as to his friend's whereabouts.

Getting Koenig's address was easy. Now, I needed to see if he'd be home. A dark web search found several compromised credentials in his name including a popular webmail platform. If he were smart and turned on two-factor authentication, I would need to take some extra steps to get in. He hadn't. An email popped up about a new login from an unexpected location, but I deleted it and then removed it from the trash. Koenig's emails were banal, and nothing of note was on his calendar. Digging into him a little more, his LinkedIn profile suggested he worked from home and fancied himself as some sort of high-end consultant.

I decided to drop in without an appointment.

CHAPTER 29

KOENIG LIVED in a nice townhouse community over the county line. I knew the area as Carney, but residents called it Cub Hill because it sounded fancier and probably let them charge a little more in HOA fees. The homes were wider than traditional models to accommodate the two-car garage built into the front of each. Koenig's place was an interior unit in the second group. I parked in a visitor's spot farther along and checked out the area.

One man walked a dog on the other side of the street, so I pretended to busy myself on my phone. A couple minutes later, the German shepherd took care of business, and the pair reversed course and headed inside their house. I texted T.J. and Lexi to tell them where I was and what I hoped to find. The latter was unclear. This venture represented something of a shot in the dark, but it was the best option we had for now.

I got out of the car and walked toward Koenig's property, keeping an eye out for lookie-loos or anyone heading outside. The coast was clear, so I walked up the five steps to his porch and knocked on the door. He didn't have a video doorbell—

the houses on either side of him did—but I still turned away. I wished I'd worn a hat. I heard footsteps approach, and the dark green door swung in a few inches. "Can I help you?" a familiar voice asked.

I turned and surged forward, hitting the door with my shoulder. It opened all the way, and Koenig staggered inside. I followed him and kicked the door with my heel, closing it behind us. "Hi, Karl." We stood in a small foyer. He wore a short-sleeve white button-down and black cargo shorts. A powder room and closet were on the right. Behind Koenig, six more steps led to the main level. "I just wanted to see if you got your watch fixed. I like to follow up personally."

His eyes widened in apparent recognition and then narrowed. "Fuck you."

"Eloquent as ever. We need to have a chat about your buddy Fabian." I stood loosely ready for him to attack without telegraphing my intentions by taking a combat stance.

Instead of coming at me, Koenig retreated to stand on the third step. He smirked and spread his hands. "Do your best. I have the high ground."

"This isn't *Revenge of the Sith*," I told him.

"Prove it."

I shrugged and approached. When I got within range, he predictably threw a kick at my face. Standing above me meant he didn't need to raise his leg much past his waist. I shifted to the side a half-step, nudged his foot higher with my forearm, and drove my fist into his groin. Koenig doubled over and almost fell. Before he could, I grabbed his hair and rammed his face into the wall. It left a nice dent as he sagged to the stairs. I moved past him, wrapped my hand in his collar, and dragged him to the living room. Koenig choked and cursed the whole way.

I let him go and positioned myself out of range for a wild punch. Koenig rubbed his throat and raised himself to his knees. "What the hell, man?"

"Shit has gotten serious, Karl. Your buddy tried to kill two people close to me."

"So?"

I glared at him. "So I think you know where he might be."

"You gonna kill him?"

"If he forces me to," I said. Koenig scowled and lunged at me. I shoved his ineffectual attack aside and moved ninety degrees. "This isn't going to end well for you, Karl. You didn't do a very good job when you tried to menace me in my office. Home-field advantage might matter in football but not here."

Koenig stood and bolted for the kitchen. I followed. He picked a knife from the block and waved it between us. I hated fighting people with blades. The untrained ones were even more dangerous because they were unpredictable. One wrong slash or cut, and things would go downhill quickly. I kept my eyes on the sharpened metal and my adversary's midsection. Shakira wasn't kidding when she sang about the veracity of the hips.

Koenig's movements clued me in to the feint. I didn't fall for it, instead backing up when he made his real move—a sweeping swing near my neck. As the knife passed, I rocked forward, grabbing his arm at the elbow and wrist. His swing left Koenig a little unbalanced, so I moved him toward the closest counter. "Nice granite tops," I said as I rammed his hand down onto one. He grunted, and the weapon slipped from his hand. I spun him toward the open part of the kitchen near his back door and kicked him in the chest.

It didn't put Koenig down, but I didn't need it to. The attack allowed me to insert myself between him and the knife block. If he went for another—or tried to grab the one he'd just used—I could intercept him. If he broke for the doorway back toward the living room, I could at least run into him and knock him off course. Koenig's options narrowed, and the glower on his face told me he realized this fact. "I ain't telling you shit," he said in his best defiant tone.

Koenig threw a punch. I blocked it, hit him with a jab in the stomach, and then used my momentum to drive an elbow into his face. The blow knocked him backwards where the wall saved him from a tumble. "Listen, Karl. I don't have time to dance with you. Your buddy Fabian tried to blow up my wife and my assistant. I'm going to make him pay for it, and you're going to tell me where he went."

"Fuck you."

I jerked my thumb over my shoulder. "You have a nice kitchen here. Looks like a professional grade oven."

"Yeah," he said. "So what?"

"It's pretty big. If you don't tell me what I want to know, I'll find a way to stuff your dumb ass inside. Once I do, I'll lock the door, set the whole thing to broil, and walk away."

"Bullshit."

I charged forward. Koenig bought my feint with a left, so he was wide open for a hard right cross. His head turned hard enough for his face to hit the wall. I followed with a series of fast body blows, finishing the sequence with another elbow to the face. Koenig's eyes lacked focus and he started to slump down the wall. I grabbed him by his collar, dragged him across the tiled floor, and kicked him in the back of the leg. It put him on his knees, and I rammed his face into the oven door. His head missed the handle by less than an inch. A crack appeared in the glass, and blood ran down Koenig's forehead onto his cheek. "Still think I'm bullshitting you?" I demanded. "Tell me where he is, or your neighbors are going to be smelling barbecued asshole later."

Koenig shook his head and turned enough to sit on the floor facing me in full. He blinked a few times as his eyes focused on my face. "All right." He paused for a breath, and I gave him the time to do it. "All right. Fine. I don't know where he is." Koenig put up his hands as I advanced again. I stopped as he cowered, hitting his head on the oven again. "I don't! I swear."

"You'd better tell me something useful in the next five seconds."

"He's been in the wind for a few days. His uncle, too. I think they're traveling together."

I moved around him and set the oven mode to broil. "Try again. I'm running out of patience."

"He's got it in for you," Koenig said. "Bad. He didn't like how you wouldn't back off. Something about the cops should come after him, but other people should know their places. I know your wife not blowing up really pissed Fabian off. He told me he'd find a way to get back at you for it in a big way."

"The only bigger way would be to blow up . . ." *My house*, I finished in my head. "Shit." I'd been gone for hours, so if Fabian and Frederick set up shop somewhere nearby, they'd know I was out, and my travels left them plenty of time to make the place go boom.

I ran out the door, got into the S4, and sped off toward Federal Hill.

As I greatly exceeded suggested speed limits en route to Federal Hill, I called Paul King.

"You were right not to come along," he said. "It's been a dud so far."

"I have a line on Fabian and the uncle."

"Where? How?"

"Apparently, I massively pissed him off by not dropping my investigation." And probably by taunting him when he called the office twice, but King didn't need to know all my secrets. "I talked to a friend of his who confirmed this."

"The friend tell you willingly?"

"More or less. I'm pretty sure he's ramped up his vendetta against me. I'm headed home where I hope to find my house still standing."

"I'll make sure some units meet you there," King said. "I'll get going your way, too."

"See you there."

Before I could hang up, King added, "Hey . . . these two are dangerous. Don't go blundering in without us."

"Sure," I said and ended the call. A moment later, I turned into Riverside Avenue and drove by the front of my house. I didn't see any unusual vehicles and picked up no activity inside. I swung a hard right into the alley. A box truck similar to the one I'd seen the prior morning sat on the concrete past my parking pad. It would be a tight fit, but most cars and SUVs could still get past it. I left the S4 near the truck and hopped out, drawing my .45 as my feet touched down.

The interior remained dark. The most logical place for Fabian and Frederick to work was the basement. They could wire a bomb into the HVAC system designed to detonate the next time the AC switched on. Taking out the foundation ensured the rest of the structure would topple. If Fabian detested me as much as his friend suggested, he would want to atomize me and leave my house a smoldering ruin.

I approached from the rear. Like most, my backyard was a small rectangle of concrete. A simple chain link fence and gate separated it from the alley. I checked both, found nothing amiss, and continued my advance. The only things I kept in the "yard" were a hose and grill. The latter was charcoal and thus probably not of interest to the bombers. Propane provided inferior flavor and made it easier for maniacs to cause explosions if they decided to target you. Score another one for briquets.

I stayed low as I neared the rear entry. The storm door stood ajar by about an inch, and scratches marred the wood near the locks of the main door. They must have been inside. King told me to wait. It was sound advice. I would have backup plus the expertise of the bomb squad. Then again, it also meant standing here for an unknown length of time while a pair of vengeful lunatics wired explosives inside my house.

Despite their obvious signs of tampering and forced entry, I didn't notice anything else unusual about the doors. I pushed the interior one in a few inches. No tripwires lurked at the bottom or just across the threshold. Two killers, however, waited for me at the bottom of the basement stairs.

"The hell with it," I muttered as I slipped into the kitchen.

CHAPTER 30

I WAS glad Gloria remained at her house.

Now, I wondered if I could ever get her back here. Between two maniacs wiring a bomb to her car, and the same pair of jackals later trying to blow up the place, I figured she would prefer to remain in Brooklandville indefinitely. It was a concern for another time. If I didn't stop Fabian and Frederick, the notion of Gloria being able to spend time at a home in Federal Hill—or even having a living husband—would be moot.

My kitchen wasn't huge, but the floor didn't make any noise. The previous resident was some sort of doctor and added an extension, moving the kitchen to the new part to make space for a ground-floor office. Whoever laid the tile did a damn good job, and I silently thanked them for their handiwork. With the .45 in my right hand, I held my phone in my left, using its flashlight feature to look for things like tripwires or irregularities in the floor which could indicate some sort of pressure plate.

All appeared on the up and up. The door to the basement bisected the wall between the dining and living rooms.

Like the rear entrance, it remained ajar an inch or two. I always kept it closed. The Charles men were getting careless. I nudged the door farther open, leaving it just wide enough for me to pass through. The stairs led down into a basement where the lights were on. To the right—the front of the house—was nothing but storage. Everything important lay to the left. The HVAC equipment and breaker box were both at my seven-o'clock.

Depending on what Fabian and his uncle did, I may or may not have been able to get the drop on them. Waiting for the cops flittered to mind, and I dismissed it as quickly as it came. I didn't hear any sirens. I edged as far to the starboard as I could and moved slowly down the steps. When I set up some exercise equipment down here a few years ago, I also paid a contractor to handle insulation and repairs to the stairs. They didn't rattle or squeak as I descended. I bent at the waist and faced left, leading with the muzzle of my gun.

As I neared the bottom, I spotted two men. One was definitely Fabian, and I presumed the other to be his uncle. Sure enough, they worked on my HVAC system. Fabian faced away from me, but Frederick stood with his head in my direction. He happened to look up, and when he did, he saw me.

———

"Heat and air work fine, guys," I said.

My heart pounded in my chest. Since I would never be confused for an explosives expert, I had no way of knowing how much progress they'd made. The mess of random components and wires looked incomplete to my eyes—I couldn't even see a clock or timer—but my guess as to the bomb's completion would indeed be an uneducated estimate.

"How'd you figure it out?" Fabian wanted to know. He turned enough to look at me in profile. Frederick stopped working. A large bag of parts and tools stood atop a small table they'd brought and set up. I didn't know what a lot of the things in there were, but the butt of a revolver caught my eye. As far as I could tell, Fabian was unarmed. He wore shorts and a thin T-shirt, and didn't have a gun concealed in any of the obvious places.

"Your buddy Koenig's a talker," I said.

"Son of a bitch."

"Not his fault. I went to his house, and he wasn't capable of defending himself. Using your friends is a bad idea."

"We have a mission," Frederick said.

"Bullshit. You have half the city frothing at the mouth because they're idiots. They think vigilantes are all like Batman instead of a batshit duo like you."

"I mean my brother."

"What happened to him was a shame," I said. "None of it excuses what you two have done since then. Do you think you're going to make a difference? Change laws?" I scoffed. "Once you're in jail, the press will stop covering you, the people will forget about you, and nothing will change at City Hall. The machine moved forward. In the end, you murdered a bunch of people for nothing."

"It wasn't nothing," Fabian said. He moved his hand back toward the mechanical unit.

"Stand still, you prick," I ordered him. "Keep your hands where I can see them. Both of you."

"You arresting us?"

"Considering what you nearly did to my wife, I should shoot you both and pistol whip your bodies into pulp."

"You'll go to jail."

"I can afford a good lawyer. Besides, you two have made vigilantes popular. Maybe I'll just give myself a cool nickname after the fact." Frederick lowered one of his hands toward his bag. "Keep them up."

"You're not going to shoot," the older man said.

"Try me."

"You don't have it in you."

"Stop, Unc," Fabian whispered harshly.

"Yeah, Unc," I said. "Stop. In case you can't tell, this is a forty-five. If I put you down, you're not getting back up. I'm a very good shot inside of twenty-five yards . . . never mind at fifteen feet."

Frederick quit moving. I didn't trust either of them, however. The whole thing could have been part of a ruse to lull me into a false sense of security. I couldn't see Fabian's tool bag very well. He could have brought his own pistol. Neither of them had any compunction against murder. We all stood without saying a word. My eyes shifted between the pair looking for any covert signals or sudden motion. I took in a breath and let it go, keeping my lungs empty in case I needed to fire.

After a moment, Frederick thrust his hand toward the revolver in his bag. I fired twice, hitting him in the right side of the chest both times. He grunted, and the force turned his body away from me as he collapsed to the concrete. "Uncle Fred!" Fabian shouted. His mouth hung open for a few seconds before he turned to me with malice in his eyes. "You bastard."

"I have six more rounds ready for you," I told him. "You

almost killed my wife and assistant. All I need is the barest hint of a reason. Maybe your family will get lucky and find a two-for-one sale at the funeral home."

"Fuck you. You shoulda dropped this when you had the chance."

"Instead, I waited it out and dropped your uncle." Fabian's hands clenched into fists. Maybe I'd taunted him too much before. I certainly did now, but the circumstances had changed. We weren't trying to puzzle out the identity of the mad bomber. They stood in my basement—technically, one of them lay on the floor—and with their work incomplete, neither was a threat.

"Maybe we have a working bomb here," Fabian said.

"I don't think you do. Even if you somehow got it finished before I interrupted you, I'll shoot you before you get a chance to activate anything." A siren rang out from the distance. I hoped it was the cops headed here. Fabian's eyes flicked in the direction of the noise. He heard it, too. "Your fate awaits. I'm happy to send you away in the back of a police car. If you force my hand, though, you can join your uncle in the back of a meat wagon."

Fabian glanced toward Frederick's body before putting his hands up again. His glare didn't soften. Multiple sirens approached. A minute later, footsteps sounded through the main level from the rear. "Police!" someone shouted. "Anyone in the basement?"

"We're here," I called back without looking away from Fabian. "Two suspects, one down. I'm armed."

A crash of cops came downstairs. Four uniforms arrived, and then Paul King ducked his head enough to move around. "You good?" he asked me.

"Fine. The uncle's down on the other side. Two to the

chest. He's probably dead. There's a gun in his bag, and he reached for it."

"Bullshit!" Fabian hollered. "He shot my uncle down like a dog. He was gonna kill me, too, until you all showed up."

"Eat shit, you lying prick," King said. He pointed to the loudmouth and instructed a couple cops to slap the cuffs on him. Fabian possessed the good sense not to resist, and King read him his Miranda rights as the restraints clicked into place. A uniform walked to where Frederick lay and confirmed the man was dead.

My job hadn't required me to shoot someone in a while. When I first started working as a PI, I figured I could do almost everything from the comfort of my desk. My very first case taught me how wrong I was, and each one since reinforced the lesson. The first time I needed to open fire—a gunman who was about to get the drop on Rich—I made it count. Rich was there to offer perspective and advice as I vomited on the side of the road a short while later.

Since then, I've stopped puking, but I didn't get into this line of work to shoot people. Frederick Charles made his choice, however. He worked with his nephew to murder a bunch of people in a horrible fashion, and the pair almost succeeded in adding Gloria and T.J. to their body count. He reached for a pistol and paid for it. I wouldn't shed any tears, lose my breakfast, or even send flowers to his funeral.

"You good?" King asked.

"Yeah."

"I get the feeling you'll want to be nearby when we question this son of a bitch."

"You bet," I said.

"We'll have to leave some folks here to process the scene

. . . and get the experts to dismantle whatever the hell these two were working on."

"I think it was designed to blow up if I turned the AC on," I said. "Considering the temperature, they might not have made it out before everything kicked on." Bomb squad technicians arrived. The basement grew crowded until uniforms led Fabian back to the main level.

"Might as well get going downtown," King said.

"Might as well," I concurred.

I CALLED Gloria as I drove to Central Booking. "Thank God," she said when I told her the good news.

"Along with me and the police."

"Of course. Is your house going to be all right?"

"They didn't get to finish their work," I said. "It'll still be standing another hundred-odd years."

"I'm going to stay up here for the time being." Gloria blew out a breath. "You understand, right?"

"I do. I'll join you once we've put all this to bed." We said our adieus. As I pulled into a parking spot, I texted T.J. with an update.

Fabian's headed to Central Booking, Frederick to the morgue.

OMG. Are you all right?

Fine. They were at my house. I talked to KK, and he said Fabian really took it personally when I wouldn't leave things alone.

Where are you now?

Just pulled up at Central Booking. I'm going to sit in on the interview.

Try not to make a scene. :)

Moi?

If there were an emoji to indicate mock offense, I would have selected it. Alas. I headed inside. It would take a few minutes to process Fabian, and I knew he would lawyer up. Someone who understands the system won't let it get used against him. I sat in a waiting area, checked messages, and then started a vigorous round of word games as things dragged on. A well-dressed man in a sharp gray suit arrived after I switched to sudoku. He must have been Fabian's lawyer. The other criminals I saw get hauled in didn't strike me as the types to afford a fancy attorney. The man's cologne nearly choked me as he passed..

A few minutes later, King emerged and waved for me to follow him. Central Booking didn't make the ideal venue for an interrogation, but it had a couple rooms reserved for the occasion. King led me into one. Fabian and his lawyer sat on the far side of the table. Rich waited on the other. I noted a third chair on our half. It was nice to see. They usually made me stand. "What the hell is he doing here?" Fabian demanded.

"He was instrumental in your arrest," Rich said.

"He's not even a cop."

"Yet he still managed to corral you," I said, "shoot your uncle, and seamlessly talk about himself in the third person."

"My client objects to his presence."

"Save it for the courtroom, counselor," Rich said. "He stays."

The lawyer shrugged. "Fine. William Mathers representing Mister Charles." I figured he made this introduction for my benefit. "We'll be happy to mention this irregularity in court."

Rich snickered. "Your client murdered a judge. I don't think you're going to have too many things go your way."

Mathers crossed his arms. "I didn't expect such unconventional procedure from a lieutenant."

"And I didn't expect to share a room with someone who bathed in his cologne," I said. "Looks like the day is full of surprises. Roll with the punches, Billy."

"It's William."

"Let's get started," Rich broke in. "Your client is charged with some very serious offenses. I can't imagine the state's attorney is going to be in a charitable mood."

"My client has nothing to say."

"His uncle is dead. There's no one else to pin anything on. Still, understanding why Fabian did what he did could make a difference."

"My client has nothing to say," Mathers repeated.

"We don't really need him to say shit," King said. "We have a reliable witness putting him in a house with his uncle wiring a bomb." I smiled and waved at the pair across the table in case they harbored any doubts as to this witness's identity. "Our experts have confirmed the similarity between it and the pieces of devices we and the county police recovered at the various crime scenes. I'm pretty sure our tech people will be able to pin those editorials on your boy, too." King spread his hands. "Talk or don't. Your choice. We got him either way."

Neither Fabian nor Mathers said a word. "We still want to know about motive," Rich went on. "There's always the chance it might help your client at sentencing."

"Why?" Mathers asked. "Maryland hasn't had the death penalty in years. At best, we're talking about life without parole versus a chance at parole . . . and I'm sure it would be a very slim chance."

"Better than nothing, Willy," I said.

"William," he responded past clenched teeth.

"You might pooh-pooh the offer," Rich said, "but I think you're required to present it to your client."

"No deal," Fabian piped up.

Mathers made a quieting gesture with his hands. "I hate to keep repeating myself, but my client has nothing to say."

"He's been awfully chatty in the past," I pointed out. "Always had a lot to say to the press. Full of shit every time, of course, but then again, rabble rousers tend to be." I looked at Fabian. "You're a boring carnival barker who built some bombs and found a megaphone. I don't even know why the cops are sitting here with you. You're not special in any way. There are thousands of assholes like you in prison already."

"Fuck you," Fabian said. "I started a movement."

"You incited people who like to watch car accidents and train wrecks. Not exactly a high bar."

"Vox Populi will survive me."

"Probably," I allowed. "Any idiot can figure out how to make a bomb. The only thing you brought to the table was a list of targets. Someone else on the outside could get the same thing with a little more work." I'd taunted Fabian in the past, and while I'd never know for sure, it probably pushed him to target me and those close to me. Here, however, he didn't pose a threat to anyone. I could push his buttons with glee, and I intended to.

"I'm the most popular man in the city." Fabian pointed to his chest again and again. "Me. A white guy beloved in a majority black city."

"For now. When they learn you're just another average white guy with family issues, they'll forget about you."

Fabian scoffed. His lawyer tried to defuse the situation. "My client isn't interested in talking to you."

"I think you're wrong again, Bill."

He slapped the metal tabletop three times. "It's William." The attorney's face reddened, and a little spittle flew out with his words. "William! William."

"I'm not sure you have the temperament to take this to court, Billy," I said. "You going to foam at the mouth when the judge overrules an objection?"

"Listen here, you prick—"

"Let's get back to motive," Rich said. Mathers turned away so he could hyperventilate in private. I offered no reaction but smiled internally. Pushing his buttons was just as enjoyable as taunting Fabian.

"The city and state sold my uncle down the river," Fabian said. "His entire career flushed for nothing. Some asshole who never should have been out of jail plowed him down."

"And explosives were the way to get back at the people you thought wronged him?" King pressed.

"People don't know how to deal with bombs. You can duck and avoid a gunshot. If we rig something, and you don't know it's there?" Fabian smiled and spread his hands. "Boom, bitch."

"And Judge Black?"

"Judge Black." Fabian snorted. "I made sure I got to clerk for him. He didn't know who I was, and I made sure he never found out. I was a good clerk. Did what he asked. Never let on."

"If he'd stopped letting criminals go on technicalities," Rich said, "would you have spared him?"

"Doubt it. All this shit was his fault from the start." Fabian jutted his chin and looked impressed with himself. Mathers sat with his head in his hands. He'd lost control of his client and the situation a while ago. "I didn't necessarily plan on killing him when we did, but things change. Vox Populi got popular, and people were realizing Judge Black was part of the problem. Might as well show them a solution."

"A carnival barker," I reiterated.

"What would you have done if I blew up your wife?" Fabian asked.

"Made sure you could get buried in the family plot . . . after a closed-casket funeral, of course."

"It was all revenge?" Rich wanted to know. His pen was poised over the small notebook he wrote things in. I wondered when concessions to age would force him to use larger paper or a more technologically appropriate way to record information. "The guy who runs down your uncle gets off on a technicality, so his brother and you murder a bunch of people."

Fabian shrugged. "It's the world's oldest motivation."

"And another reason you're not special," I added. Fabian snorted, shook his head, and began staring at the metal tabletop. "There you go, Willy. Your client finally has nothing to say."

Mathers did not seem impressed by this recent development.

———

After finishing up with the cops at Central Booking and the precinct, I drove to Gloria's house.

It was Friday afternoon, and a lot of people getting an early start on the weekend made the trip take a little longer than normal. I pulled into the driveway, opened the garage door, and shut it behind me before entering the house. My wife was nowhere to be found on the main level, so I headed upstairs. She wasn't in the office, either. I found her in bed, sitting against a stack of pillows with a laptop across her shapely legs. Today, they were covered in athletic shorts which rode up her thighs thanks to the presence of the computer. She smiled at me, but it wasn't the full-wattage version I usually got. "Hey, handsome. Got your man?"

"Got them both," I said. "One alive."

"You all right?"

I nodded and sat beside her on the bed, kicking my shoes off before swinging my legs up. "Yeah. I never imagined shooting anyone when I got into this, but I gave him a chance. He reached for a gun."

"You're not getting in trouble for it, are you?" Gloria wanted to know.

"I'm sure the police don't like PIs being involved in fatal shootings," I said, "but it's a clear case of self-defense. He'd still be alive if he'd just kept his hands up and waited for the cops."

Gloria closed her laptop, set it on the carpeted floor, and snuggled up to me. "I'm glad this is over."

"Me, too."

"I can't interest you in a fundraising job, can I?"

I chuckled. "No. My parents tried to push me toward something safer after I got shot. I can't sit behind a desk and sell computers to people. It's just not me. I'm good at what I do, and I think it has value."

Gloria's head bobbed against my chest. "I figured."

"I'm sure you want to stay here for a few days."

"Yes. I actually submitted plans to the association to expand my garage. Considering what happened . . . and the fact that my husband has become something of a famous private investigator . . . I think they'll approve it."

"Good," I said. "My house is a crime scene, anyway. I also need to have someone replace the back door."

"I guess you're stuck living here for a while, then."

I wondered how long—and potentially permanent—a while would be. This wasn't the time to bring it up, however. Gloria felt safer here, and I would support her. "I guess so."

———

Monday morning, I rolled into the office to find both Lexi and T.J. already there.

"Happy Monday, boss," my secretary said as I shut the door behind me.

"You sure you don't have a brake job to do?"

She snickered. "If I'd spent a few more days there, they probably could've given me some easy jobs. It's good to be back here, though."

I logged on to my laptop and saw our general inbox balloon with new messages. "We seem popular in light of everything."

"A few articles and op-eds over the weekend basically killed the mystique of Vox Populi," Lexi said. "Once people learned he was a court clerk who originally set out for revenge, he became a lot less interesting."

"To most," I said. "The worst people will always find some followers."

"Pretty cynical outlook."

"Why do you think I never vote?"

"What's in the bag?" T.J. asked, pointing to my backpack which was stuffed fuller than usual.

"Might as well show you now." I took out a bottle of champagne—Veuve Clicquot yellow label. I set it on the desk where it announced its presence with a resounding *thunk*.

"Oooh." T.J. wheeled her chair closer. "Actually from France, too."

"Anything else is just sparkling wine," Lexi said before I could. "Do we have three glasses?"

"I don't think we have any actual glasses," I said, "and aren't you still twenty?"

Her face colored a little. "Yeah."

"I think we only need two cups, then."

"Really?" The intern crossed her arms. "This was my first case, and I think I turned in some good work. If you don't—"

"Relax." I put up a hand. "I'm messing with you. Just don't dime me out for giving alcohol to a minor, and I'll be happy to pour you some."

"I hate you," she said with a chuckle.

"It's only hate if it comes from a certain region in France. Otherwise, it's just sparkling enmity."

T.J. found three disposable coffee cups, and we had the

world's most basic champagne toast in history. I took a sip before looking at my inbox again. "We're getting swamped with new case requests. We'll need to be choosy."

T.J. set her cup down. "Or . . . wild thought here . . . we could hire an extra investigator. Even part-time, someone else would make a difference."

"Can't I just keep underpaying the two of you?" I asked.

"No," the two women said in unison.

"I'll think about it." I pointed at my assistant. "You're responsible for drafting all policies."

"I'll download some good ones."

I raised my cup. "Work smart, not hard."

"Are we going to look at any of these emails?" Lexi asked.

I checked my watch. "It's ten-thirty. I'm a little hungry, so I'm thinking about lunch. I don't want to deal with anything while I've got food on the brain. I think we should enjoy our bubbly, venture out for a nice lunch, and then come back."

"At which point, you might be too full to consider a new client," T.J. said. "That will push us to later this afternoon or even tomorrow."

"No plan is foolproof," I said.

END of Novel #17

When a true-crime podcaster approaches C.T. to review a murder case, he accepts. However, C.T.'s cousin Rich was the investigating officer . . . and the review leads C.T. to conclude Rich got the case wrong. *Digging in the Dark* will release in the summer of 2025!

. . .

THE END

AFTERWORD

Thanks for checking out this novel! I hope you enjoyed reading the book as much as I enjoyed writing it.

I write mysteries and thrillers with action, snark, and flawed heroes. If this sounds like something you like, you can check out my catalog below.

The C.T. Ferguson Crime Novels

1. The Reluctant Detective
2. The Unknown Devil
3. The Workers of Iniquity
4. Already Guilty
5. Daughters and Sons
6. A March from Innocence
7. Inside Cut
8. The Next Girl
9. In the Blood
10. Right as Rain
11. Dead Cat Bounce

12. Don't Say Her Name
13. Night Comes Down
14. Concrete Angels
15. Conduct Unbecoming
16. Bleeding into Winter
17. Unreasonable Doubt
18. Digging in the Dark (Summer 2025)

The John Tyler Action Thrillers

1. The Mechanic
2. White Lines
3. Lost Highway
4. Four on the Floor
5. Forced Induction
6. The Low Road
7. Backfire
8. Redline
9. Collision Course (March 2025)

I release 3-4 new novels per year. For the most current list of books, please visit:

- https://tomfowlerbooks.com - Direct sales
- www.tomfowlerwrites.com
- https://books2read.com/tomfowler

(**Note**: C.T. Ferguson appears in *White Lines*. John Tyler appears in *Don't Say Her Name*.)

While the suggested reading sequences appear above, each

novel is a standalone mystery or thriller, and the books can be enjoyed in whatever order you happen upon them.

Connect with me:

For the many ways of finding and reaching me online, please visit https://tomfowlerwrites.com/contact. I'm always happy to talk to readers.

This is a work of fiction. Characters and places are either fictitious or used in a fictitious manner.

"Self-publishing" is something of a misnomer. This book would not have been possible without the contributions of many people.

- The great cover design team at 100 Covers.
- My editor extraordinaire, Chase Nottingham.
- My wonderful advance reader team, the Fell Street Irregulars.

www.ingramcontent.com/pod-product-compliance
Lightning Source LLC
Chambersburg PA
CBHW061657190726
48289CB00006B/1912